# CARELESS TALK

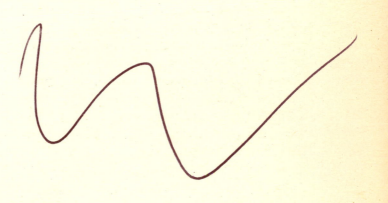

# Careless Talk

## Michael Richardson

**Tindal
Street
Press**

First published in October 2007
by Tindal Street Press Ltd
217 The Custard Factory, Gibb Street, Birmingham, B9 4AA
www.tindalstreet.co.uk

A CIP catalogue reference for this book is available
from the British Library

ISBN: 978 0 9551 384 6 1

Typeset by Country Setting, Kingsdown, Kent
Printed and bound in Great Britain by Clays Ltd, St Ives PLC

*For Arthur*

*and in memory of*
*John Narbett*

# CARELESS TALK

# I

It was quite cold for early September but Morley Charles had left his mac wide open to display the brand new bottle-green blazer and striped tie of Balsley School of Art. Strictly speaking it wasn't *quite* the regulation blazer: it lacked the gold edging that had adorned the genuine pre-war garment and it was also without a badge. Mind, the latter could soon be remedied; the school outfitters in Corporation Street had assured its customers that they would definitely be having the art school badges by next week. The impressive badge on Morley's cap, however – pre-war and acquired for him by his friend Micky Plant – clearly proclaimed his exalted rank. It bore the outline of an artist's palette enclosing the interlaced letters BSA; peeping from behind the palette were three brushes and in a flowing cartouche below was the school motto: '*Plus Est en Vous*'.

Contrary to his usual custom, Morley had chosen to sit on the lower deck of the tram, on the smaller of the pair of fixed seats that faced each other next to the rear platform. This was so that he had an audience of three on the seat opposite to admire his smart new uniform and he was able to admire himself – when a building was near enough and dark enough to transform the tram window into a mirror. From this point, as well, his splendour was fully exposed to the gaze of new passengers as they climbed aboard.

Sitting directly opposite was a very attractive young woman who had looked in his direction quite a few times. She had a university scarf wrapped two or three times round her neck. She was looking at him again with the suspicion of a smile, perhaps that of a kindred spirit, as of one selected person to another. (The headmaster at Balsley School of Art made much of the school's selective status: 'All right, I grant you, it's *not* a grammar school, but it's a highly selective school: only about one out of forty children has the necessary skills to get into this school.') A particularly fetching thing about the young woman was that her coat and skirt ended just above her knees, which were a little apart. Her unstockinged, somewhat plump legs were slightly blue-mottled with cold, but Morley forgave her this while wondering how best to contrive a position where he would be able to see well beyond her knees without arousing her suspicion. He planned it in detail. He'd let his eyelids drop as if feeling tired – first day of term, after all – pretend to resist it, yawn, fold his arms, let his lids drop again, this time unresistingly, slide down into his seat, let his head loll to one side and, through almost closed eyes, view what lay at the end of the gap between her knees.

He pulled himself together. Was this suitable behaviour for a selected lad on his way to his first day at the art school? A day when he particularly needed to be at his best; a credit to his soldier father.

His plan was thwarted anyway by the arrival on the tram platform of three boys wearing King Edward's School uniforms. One of them looked closely at Morley, then nudged his companions, who stared at him intently for a second, before all three broke into great peals of mocking laughter which continued as they climbed the stairs to the top deck. Even five minutes later Morley fancied he could still hear occasional snatches of laughter between excited conversation. Had he been wearing a peculiar expression, he wondered: mouth open showing his slightly protruding teeth and his brace? His mother was constantly telling him to put his face straight.

The panic that had afflicted him from time to time since he had woken up returned. What perils lay in store for him at his new school when even the journey to it was proving such a trial?

After Selly Oak, the King Edward's boys were back on the platform waiting to alight. They gave Morley more curious looks and resumed their laughter. As if unaware that anything was amiss, he studied the tram's destination box opposite: it read 'Redhill 71' – backwards. But he could feel his face flushing fiercely. He stole furtive glances at the passengers facing him to see if they were witnessing his discomfiture. The attractive young woman had left; an airman with very fair hair was reading his *Lilliput*; a thin middle-aged lady was repairing her make-up. He looked to his right. On a nearby forward-facing seat a man sat half skewed into the aisle. His mouth was so caved in that you couldn't actually see it. He wore a boot on one foot and a carpet slipper on the other and below his too-short trousers an inch or so of pyjama bottoms was visible. The man caught Morley's gaze and winked. Morley did his best to wink back but he had never really learned the knack. He gave a vague smile. The man went on winking as if he couldn't stop.

A loony! He'd probably got on at the same stop as Morley, the terminus stop outside Redhill Asylum. Enormous relief washed over him. It was the loony the King Edward's boys had been laughing at! He felt the return of the rather precarious optimism he had enjoyed between the feelings of panic. He hoped for the umpteenth time that perhaps he would get on much better at Balsley School of Art than at Redhill Council School, that his stammer and brace would arouse less comment and amusement and that his backwards-sounding name, Morley Charles, might go down rather well for a change.

But his anxiety grew again as he waited for the Outer Circle bus for the last short stage of his journey; in about ten or fifteen minutes he'd be there. 'There'll be dozens of others just as anxious as you are, duck,' his mother had said just before he left the house. Morley denied that he was anxious but knew it must be obvious. He wished that Micky Plant, his friend from Redhill Council School who had also passed for the art school, were with him. They had arranged to meet at the terminus stop at twenty to eight and Morley had waited till eight minutes to. Though it could hardly be said that Micky was the most loyal or reliable of friends.

Morley's stomach tightened at the arrival of the bus. Fearful that he might miss his stop, he sat downstairs next to the exit. 'First day, then?' asked the conductor, laughing what seemed a quite unnecessary laugh. Morley looked round for other art school pupils but there were none. He had come this way just once before with his mother a few weeks after he'd heard that he had passed the entrance exam. Successful candidates were required to visit the school for a brief interview, bringing with them a selection of their best art work.

He had wondered at the time whether there was still the possibility of being turned down if the paintings and drawings he'd brought didn't measure up.

The deputy headmaster, Mr Boldmere, had looked through his work. 'And *all* these drawings are your own unaided work?'

Morley managed a 'Y-Yes, sir.'

'They are all original?'

'Yes, s-sir.'

'Then *you* are the originator of these characters, eh? And I suppose, er, Mr Disney came along and copied them.'

He held up a sheet of Mickey Mouses, Donald Ducks, a Pluto and a Dopey and Doc from *Snow White and the Seven Dwarfs*. However, he had looked at the wrong side of the paper, where against each drawing was a little cross to show that it didn't count (Morley had been loath to cancel them by scribbling all over them). The other side was the proper side, a watercolour of the Clent Hills with wooded slopes and a glimpse of a white house. He tried to explain all this but it became complicated . . .

He leapt up; here was the crossroads, the railway bridge beyond. He had difficulty in swallowing. He took a deep breath and tried to generate some confidence.

Two girls in art school hats came downstairs to the platform talking animatedly, seeming oblivious to his presence. Obviously not newcomers. They made Morley feel curiously inadequate because they'd chosen to sit upstairs while he, a boy, had sat downstairs.

The school was about four hundred yards away. The road looked as if it had seen better times. It was lined with grimy trees and large Victorian villas, most of which had become offices or workshops.

He paused at the bus stop, searching his pockets as if for something important, to allow the girls to get well in front of him. Over the road just ahead was a bike shop with two lads looking through the window. They were wearing navy macs and no caps but Morley was sure that they were art school pupils. They looked about fifteen: two years older than Morley. He fixed his gaze directly ahead and walked with what he hoped were brisk, purposeful steps. Then he fancied that he was being watched. He stole a glance towards the bike admirers. He wasn't wrong: they were looking at him and grinning broadly. But then, being laughed at was an all too familiar experience. He continued on his way, careful to keep his distance from the pupils in front. He tried to banish an image of his soldier father watching with dismay his son's embarrassing progress.

The school looked a bit smaller than he remembered from his interview but then it was a *selective* school, not huge and modern like Redhill Council School, which was also known as the Shredded Wheat Factory because it resembled the picture of the factory on the cereal packet. He bore in mind the rule that boys had to use the Linden Grove entrance; the main entrance was for staff and girls.

Something else to be borne very much in mind on the first day was to say very confidently that you *had* seen a blue goldfish should a senior boy ask you. A no might lead you to having your head shoved into a washbasin of cold water in the senior boys' lavatories, or worse, a WC pan. At least, this is what had been rumoured on the day of the entrance exam.

He was practically there. A short-trousered boy with a shiny new satchel coming from the opposite direction was determinedly ignoring his mother's urgent whisperings and cap straightening. He had no cap badge Morley was pleased to note – he had the advantage there. And fancy coming with his mother! His mood fractionally lightened. Suddenly the lad tore himself away and hurried down Linden Grove, the quiet road flanking the school.

On one side of Linden Grove was a bombed-out pub; on the other, the side wall of the school with lights dimly gleaming from obscured-glass windows set behind iron railings and half below pavement level. What mysterious activities went on down there? Morley wondered nervously.

Shouts and the thump of a ball came from beyond the green-painted double gates, one of which was wide open. Morley's lips had gone dry and he realized he was barely breathing. Just for a moment he almost wished he was going back to the familiarity of Redhill Council School – forgetting the stomach churning he had endured there too at the beginning of every new term. He straightened up, licked his lips, forced a smile, breathed deeply, rubbed his cheeks to induce a healthy-looking glow, pushed his cap to the side a trifle and walked into the yard. He was fleetingly aware of girls standing at the school's back entrance, lads kicking a ball about, others chatting in small groups, the noise of machinery from the factory next door, before realizing that he was attracting the amused attention of four senior-looking lads. They were standing by a small building with SENIOR BOYS' LAVATORIES painted on the door, which struck Morley, at that moment, with the same chill as if it had read GESTAPO HEADQUARTERS. The boys didn't have to move very far to form a ragged line, blocking his path.

# 2

Yeh, I've seen loads of blue goldfish, he was rehearsing. In spite of the painful thumping in his chest, he was trying to smile confidently to show he was up to their little trick, even approved of it, a neat tradition; but *he* wasn't the victim type – perhaps somebody else. Where was the boy in the short trousers? he wondered, looking round uneasily. Why hadn't they stopped *him*?

One of the four seniors, a boy with dark, curly hair and a tanned complexion, drawled, 'My, oh my, what have we got here? Aren't we the smart young fag, then.'

'No, I think he's overdone it just a little teeny bit,' said a boy with carefully combed blond hair, head on one side, one eye closed, chin cupped in hand. 'Looks a bit top-heavy.'

'When did this new fashion come in, then?' asked the first lad.

One of the other two started quietly singing the old music hall song, his mate joining in:

> '*Where did you get that hat?*
> *Where did you get that hat?*'

Morley gaped uncomprehendingly, his hand stealing towards his cap. Some other trick, he thought, one he was unprepared for. From the corner of his eye he saw other pupils moving nearer to see what the fuss was all about. As they got closer he saw that two of them, perhaps second or third years, were wearing caps. Each bore a small, neat green shield edged in gold no bigger than a half a crown, with the interlaced letters BSA – and that was it: no palette or brushes, no flowing motto underneath.

Morley closed his eyes in horror, snatched the cap from his head and, not daring to look at it, stuffed it in his pocket and backed out of the boys' entrance into Linden Grove to the guffaws of the seniors; silently cursing himself, his mother and Micky Plant; and trying to get rid of the image of his father that had insisted on popping up again to witness his son's latest misadventure.

'But d'you really think th-they'll remem-mber me?' asked Morley.

'Who?' asked Micky irritably, engrossed in 'Rockfist Rogan' in his *Champion*.

'The kids at school – about m-my cap. The wrong badge on it and that.'

'God, you still going on about that? You in't stopped since we left school. Naw, course they won't, they've got much better things to think about.' He turned back to his reading.

They were sitting upstairs at the back of their homeward-bound tram.

'Yeh, I s'pose you're right,' said Morley. He should have left it there. Micky had been reassuring, untypically so, but Morley wanted certainties. 'But you kn-know that kid at our old school, that evacuee kid who had to wear those w-women's shoes that time, when it was snowing?'

'Naw, can't say I do,' Micky said distantly, still reading.

'Course you do,' insisted Morley, 'they were yellow.'

'What were?' asked Micky, looking up frowning.

'His shoes, well, not a proper yellow, m-more a bright yellow ochre.' He was pleased with the precision of his description, but it did nothing to cheer him. 'They were wom-men's. It was obvious. They were fancy shoes with wh-whatsits . . .' He hesitated: it wouldn't do, he thought, to show too much familiarity with women's shoes. 'You know, those big thick w-wedge bottoms – wedge soles. He said his own shoes had worn through and were at the m-menders, and they'd made him wear these women's –'

'In't got a clue what you're going on about.' Micky's eyes returned to his story.

'You have, you knew him, that ev-vacuee kid who lived at the fish shop in Redhill. He used to serve there sometimes at nights, wore specs. What was his name? Graham, Gordon . . . anyway, Shaw, someb-body Shaw, used to be in 2B.'

'Ah, him,' said Micky. Then, lowering his voice, 'You mean old Shitshoes?'

'See!' said Morley, with hollow triumph. 'He only wore these yellow women's shoes *once* just after he came there and the name st-stuck ever since. Everybody called him that, even if they didn't know wh-where it came from.'

'Mm,' said Micky, reflectively, 'I thought *your* name was a nickname in bottom juniors; you know, *Morle*. As if you went around *mauling* things, like tomatoes and that.' He put his mouth near Morley's ear: 'Or perhaps you went round mauling tarts' tits.' He turned back to his *Champion*. 'Yeh, but don't worry too much, Morle, they're sure to think up something just as good for you.'

'W-What you talking about?' Morley pulled an anxious face, which fully exposed his brace and slightly protruding teeth.

'Nickname for you.'

'I don't want a b-blasted nickname, you, you . . . That's the whole point. Anyway, you just said they'd f-forget.'

'Only kidding, Morle. But I'm not God; I can't *guarantee* they'll forget. Still, if you're scared of anybody recognizing you, you can always stick a paper bag on your head. No, joke –' as Morley's mouth dropped wider. 'Naw, in this evacuee kid's case, I don't think it was *just* cause he wore yellow shoes that kids took it out of him. I reckon people would've taken it out of him anyway cause he was, you know, a weed and wore goggles.'

Morley shrank within himself. He often saw himself as a weed, a weed who, if not goggles, wore something worse – a brace.

Micky stuck his left hand into his trouser pocket, pulling back his unbuttoned mac to exhibit his blazer badge, neatly sewn on in the correct place. With the folded *Champion* in his other hand he flicked lightly at the badge as if removing dust.

Morley fell silent, defeated. Anything else he said would invite further ridicule: Micky was in that sort of mood.

The tram was approaching the luxury flats called Viceroy Close. Morley knew this route well. Facing the entrance to the flats was a large, cream-painted villa, number 144. On the ground floor, his bed close to and facing the window, lay a pale, bedridden old man. If you waved to him from the top deck of a tram (the only part he'd be able to see because of a high wall), he might wave back. He had been lying there as long as Morley could remember. With Micky again absorbed in his *Champion*, Morley turned and waved hesitantly, already feeling foolish in case the man didn't respond. He didn't.

He wondered, not for the first time that day, what had led him to think that his blazer badge *was* a cap badge. How was it that he of all people could make such a ridiculous mistake? He who could accurately draw dozens of German and British army uniforms with their insignias. And, as he had assumed it *was* a cap badge, why hadn't he wondered about the blazer badge? After all, he'd seen two senior boys with art school uniforms assisting at the entrance examination six months ago. He had no answers.

He remembered his mother complaining as she sewed it on. 'How am I expected to sew a great big flat badge onto a round cap? It doesn't look *right*. I'll have to put a bit of a tuck in it,' she'd said.

They were at Selly Oak, Micky still lost in 'Rockfist Rogan'. Morley envied his ability to lose himself so easily in this other world while he himself was tied fast to the trials of this one. It was Micky Plant, he suddenly decided, who was responsible for his problem.

Calling for Micky at the beginning of the summer holidays, Morley had been unexpectedly invited into his house – the front and back doorsteps were usually the closest Morley got. After removing his shoes, he was allowed upstairs and into Micky's bedroom to see his newly bought uniform – Morley had yet to buy his.

Micky slipped on his blazer and cap and carefully tied his tie. Morley could smell their unmistakable newness. 'Neat, ay?' said Micky. He strutted up and down a bit self-consciously then wandered into his parents' bedroom to look at himself in the wardrobe mirror. Morley followed, making noises of approval.

Back in his bedroom Micky said, 'Now then, have a dekko at this, then.' He opened the top drawer of his tallboy and took out an art school badge. 'Y'know, Morle, I might be the only first-year kid to have one of these.'

Morley inclined his head questioningly.

'See, you just can't get 'em for love nor money. They've got all the grammar school badges and that but they haven't got the art school ones, haven't had any since last year. Probably won't have any for weeks, the bloke in the shop said.'

'So, wh-where did you get this one from then?'

'Ah, that'd be telling,' Micky said mysteriously.

'Oh,' said Morley, remembering to sound neutral; pressing Micky further would achieve nothing.

'No, our dad got it. From a bloke at church he knows. His kid went to the art school before the war. It was a wonder he'd hung on to any of his stuff, he said.'

Micky took off his uniform, sat on the bed and arranged the badge on the front of his cap. 'Looks real neat, doesn't it, Morley? I think I'm going to get our gran to sew it on: her sewing's better than our mom's.'

Morley looked on not a little enviously.

Micky went back to the drawer in the tallboy, took out a similar badge and threw it negligently onto the bed. 'That's yours, Morley. His kid had two.'

The badge was only slightly inferior to Micky's: a small bluish stain on the gold A in BSA. Morley was enormously grateful.

But he had been naive: Micky had deliberately misled him into thinking it was a cap badge. His apparent generosity was really a plot to make a fool of him. Morley's mistrust was reinforced by Micky not turning up at the tram terminus this morning.

He was tempted to confront him outright although he knew it wasn't a very good idea: Micky could easily deny it, then give him a miserable time. Best just to accept things. But suddenly, he heard himself blurting, 'You didn't turn up at the terminus this morning, M-Micky, on purpose cause you *kn-knew* that I'd got my bl-blazer b-badge on my cap and you knew that if you t-turned up you'd have to say something and you *knew* I'd see your badge on your blazer and not on your cap and . . . and . . .' He ran out of steam.

Micky looked up happily, as if enjoying the prospect of battle. 'Hang on, hang on, *Morle*' – to Morley's ears it sounded exactly like Maul – 'I wish I *had* turned up while you were still there: you'd've given me a good laugh. God, I bet you looked a right twerp parading around with a ruddy great blazer badge stuck on your cap. But I'm not a mind-reader, Morle. *I* didn't know you'd gone and sewn it on your cap. But that wasn't why I didn't see you at the terminus stop. I've already told you, I had to go back for our key. There was lots to remember on the first day. I clean forgot our key and they'll both be at work when I get back.' Micky's parents – his father the superintendent, his mother the matron of Redhill Asylum – worked shifts. 'I was at the terminus at five and twenty to eight – before *you* were to start with. I told you before.'

'Anybody could say that,' Morley protested.

'You calling me a liar?'

'N-No, but you could've easily –'

'I wish I hadn't given you the ruddy thing in the first place, if this is all the thanks I get.'

'Well, I *did* thank you and I was very pleased but you only gave it to me so you could m-make a fool of me –'

'Nobody could make a fool out of you, Morle. You're that already.'

The exchanges continued through Upfield and past the Motor Works, with Morley getting the worst of it, increasingly regretting his accusation and inclining to think that perhaps, after all, he had been wrong.

Instead of staying with Morley all the way to the terminus, which made for a much pleasanter walk, his usual habit when they came this way from town or Upfield, Micky pointedly got off at the Marshfield Drive stop, which was barely any nearer to his house. His parting shot was, 'Let's hope you get out of bed the right side tomorrow, Morle.'

Morley felt battered. He wondered what he was going to say to his mother about his badgeless cap. He had taken the badge off under the cover of his desk in the boys' drawing room while the headmaster addressed the assembled new boys. He had pulled viciously at the badge as if it was something malevolent until a master standing in the aisle, noticing his odd hand movements, had leaned towards him and mouthed, 'What on *earth* do you think you're doing, lad?' He'd finished off the job in the privacy of a cubicle in the first year lavatories at break.

# 3

Morley's bedroom was the boxroom. A compensation was the hot-water cistern in the airing cupboard at the head of his bed that was even now giving out a gentle heat. Tacked across the boarded wall of the airing cupboard was a large Nazi flag given to him by Russell Hartmann, an American soldier who was courting their neighbour Percy Pinder's daughter, Beryl.

The woodwork in the room was painted olive green, the walls eau-de-nil with textured vertical stripes in reddish-brown. Morley had done these with permanganate of potash dabbed on with a sponge. The method was from 'Home Front Hints' in the *Evening Despatch*. The article promised an effect comparable with difficult-to-get wallpaper if the home decorator took great care and measured and marked the position of the stripes beforehand with a soft pencil and a length of straight-edged timber.

The gift of the olive-green oil paint from Percy Pinder (similar to the olive-green paint used to camouflage the Motor Works where Percy worked) and the discovery of the large rusty tin of eau-de-nil distemper in the shed had fired Morley with a passion for interior decoration that had excluded all else. His mother had allowed him to paint the pantry as well as his room, before the craze had ended as suddenly as it had begun.

Another gift from Percy, an enthusiastic decorator himself, was a paint-spattered, black leatherette-covered loud-speaker, which sat on a shelf in the corner and was connected with the wireless downstairs. Percy had installed it, threading the wire through an over-large, clumsily made hole in the corner of the living-room ceiling and another in the corner of Morley's bedroom floor. These holes, Morley discovered later, enabled him to hear conversations downstairs if he put his ear close to the floor.

Oblivious now to the décor and the slightly crackly dance music from the loudspeaker, Morley lay in bed reviewing his day, one of the worst he could remember, poisoned from the beginning by the badge incident. He was sure that he was going to be as permanently labelled at his new school as Shitshoes Shaw, the evacuee from 2B, had been at Redhill Council School. Today should have marked the end of the reign of the weedy, awkward, stammering lad, the undersized, underweight butt of jokes who had, he believed, been his former self at his previous school. Today was to have been the beginning of a New Life, with New People who would view him afresh; a day where he would begin to earn respect and popularity and make close friends.

He'd prepared for it ever since the good news of his passing the art school entrance exam in early June. He had followed the instructions for self-improvement in the medical section of *Monroe's Universal Reference Book* – a big red book about almost everything on earth that Morley frequently consulted. The article promised increased vigour, robustness and self-confidence if the reader would only follow a daily regime of rational exercise. Morley had performed the daily routine of arm flinging, press- and pull-ups, running on the spot, deep breathing and cold bath followed with brisk rubbing down with a rough towel for a whole week with enormous zest. Then his enthusiasm had gradually waned till he was exercising only about once a week. But in his occasional hopeful moods he had believed he was making progress.

From the dictionary section of *Monroe's Universal Reference Book* he had started to learn three new words a day. This he had more or less adhered to ever since.

When finances permitted he had eaten lots of fattening foods, even the rock cakes and scones made by Big Gwen, Percy Pinder's wife, which usually had a hint of white spirit or Steradent about them and which in the past he'd just nibbled at, transferring the remainder to his pocket, or politely declined. If the weighing machine outside the chemist's was to be believed, he had put on four and a half pounds in three months.

And he was coming to grips with his stammer. One of his latest techniques was to *try* and stammer, to reverse the impulse to stop stammering that usually failed. This was just one piece of advice in the booklet from the Guy Olivier Institute in Dean Street, London, for which Morley had recently sent off a three-shilling postal order. Another tip was to think of something funny before you spoke: the 'Smile Technique'. He certainly stammered a good deal less now than about a year ago, according to his mother and Big Gwen.

His protruding teeth were getting ever closer to where they properly belonged. Nine months to a year and he could dispense with his brace, they predicted at the Dental Hospital.

He had been as well prepared as he could be. Yet throughout the first day at his new school he had felt awkward, conspicuous and edgy, afraid to open his mouth for fear of stammering; convinced that every glance in his direction, every snatch of not-quite-caught conversation, every smile and laugh, however remote, was about him and the ridiculous badge on his cap. He had made no new friends and fallen out with Micky Plant.

If only . . . Eyes tightening and prickling with threatening tears, he went back mentally to the afternoon. A senior boy had ushered all the new boys into the boys' drawing room on the first floor for an introductory talk from the headmaster and the filling in of timetables. He directed them to their seats in the vast room which, as Morley could see from the arrangement of the windows, stretched the entire width of the building. An enamelled badge in his lapel read 'Head Boy'. He was good-looking and self-assured. Relying on stylish hand and arm movements and only a few words, he settled the boys down efficiently, without the aid of a teacher. When he had everybody seated, he said in a deep, carrying voice, 'Now keep quiet and sit up straight; if there's one thing the headmaster can't stand it's slovenliness.'

The boy was a leader, somebody who commanded respect. Yet he was not a lot taller than Morley and had a port wine stain on his cheek. And if everything hadn't been spoiled at the very beginning, if he hadn't made himself a lasting target for mockery, then nagging doubts about his own physical shortcomings would have disappeared like magic on seeing this impressive lad who seemed oblivious to *his* imperfections; and he would have been well on the way to becoming the sort of lad he wanted to be on his dad's return from the army. If only . . .

You're being punished, my son, a voice not unlike Canon Reilly's said in his head. If you won't go to confession, what do you expect?

Morley hadn't been to confession now for over four months, mainly because it had become too much trouble – not made any easier by the awkwardness he'd feel in having to confess to self-abuse again. For all that time, every other Saturday morning he had set out giving every impression to his mother (who confessed on the Saturdays in between) that he was off to SS Peter and Paul at Upfield for confession. Sometimes he actually went to Upfield and wandered around the shops and went to the library, but the closeness of the church and chance meetings with other parishioners increased his feelings of guilt. More frequently now he tramped the Lickey or Waseley Hills and occasionally, when he had enough money, went to town.

Missing confession meant that Morley dare not go to communion. Morley's mother was equally ignorant of this as she went to High Mass at eleven o'clock while he went to Low Mass at eight.

He should have learned his lesson. Once before he had missed confession for a lengthy period and believed that he had been punished for it by the news of the death of his father on active service. Then, less than a week later, he learned that his father was alive in a field hospital, merely wounded and not seriously at that. A warning! Morley's gratitude was enormous and he'd gone to confession shortly afterwards.

But only once. After that he put it off again and again. And nothing unpleasant happened. In fact, looking back now, it seemed a particularly happy and exciting period. VE Day with a bonfire and party; the letter informing him of his art school success; VJ Day with an even bigger street party with lots of pre-war food; pleasant days in the summer holidays at his aunt May's at Droitwich, walking and drawing in the countryside; losing himself in May's *Pictorial Book of Knowledge*; the gift of the loudspeaker; the German army field cap, *Luftwaffe* badges and other bits and pieces brought to him by a newly demobbed mate of his father's; and the Jerry flag from Russell Hartmann.

His fortnightly Saturday morning wanderings became routine. Eternal Damnation seemed increasingly remote, hardly more real than Father Christmas. Then Adriaan Verhoeven hadn't helped. Morley had read about the heroic Dutchman in *Time*. Verhoeven, a staunch member of the

Dutch Resistance, had saved scores of Jews from the Nazis. Many British and American airmen also owed their lives to him. Two nations had already awarded posthumous honours; he had been tortured and executed by the Nazis in late 1944. He'd been an artist. And a Catholic. In his teens Verhoeven had abandoned his Catholicism and later talked and wrote fiercely about its tyranny and absurdity. Morley had found himself nodding. But now . . .

Yes, everything had been going quite well recently – for a change. Too well. He should have seen it! He really had to hand it to God for His choice of punishment. His first day at art school, a day when it was so important that nothing went wrong, then bang, wallop: He strikes.

Perhaps if he was really good and promised *definitely* to go to confession this coming Saturday – fortunately the correct Saturday – maybe tomorrow *would* be okay. Perhaps Micky's reassurance would come true and everybody would have forgotten him.

'There's always them that's worse off than you,' his gran was fond of saying. He climbed out of bed and went to the shelf where, next to the loudspeaker, he kept his boys' papers and magazines. He took out *Time* and found the article on Adriaan Verhoeven. He held his breath and forced himself to read again about how the Nazis had cut off the hero's thumbs in an effort to get him to give away Resistance secrets. He sweated with horror as he read, imagining it happening to himself. He said his prayers, making his pleas and promises to God and stressing that he would be in confession on Saturday morning.

# 4

Morley's torment continued into the night with a chilling dream of an *Obersturmführer*, his iron cross pinned to his cap, cutting off Morley's thumbs. He awoke sweating, the terror persisting, the prospect of school alarming. He considered looking for an excuse to stay at home, until an image of his heroic father looking disappointed shamed him into changing his mind. He travelled to school alone, feeling drained and miserable, his cap in his pocket to disassociate himself from the foolish cap-wearing boy of yesterday. He was too preoccupied to remember to wave to the bedridden man.

Approaching the school gates, he ruffled his hair and thrust his hands into his pockets before forcing himself to amble slowly into the yard, his expression of casual unconcern at odds with the fierce hammering in his chest. But there were no senior boys hanging around the gates; and no one else in the yard paying him the slightest attention. He breathed a bit more easily.

But his anxiety came back at the end of assembly when the headmaster, ignoring the girls, frowningly scrutinized the rows of new boys one by one. Was he looking for someone in particular? Had someone said something?

The headmaster had a marked Birmingham accent. 'Always make sure you're standing up straight, lads,' he commanded, 'your weight equal on both of your feet. We don't put up with or tolerate slovenliness at Balsley School of Art.' Morley obediently stood up straight. 'A straight, upright body is telling the world it's alert or paying attention. Absorbing things . . . Like a sponge,' he added a bit uncertainly. He then explained, as he had already done yesterday, that the school motto, *Plus Est en Vous*, meant More is in you. He expanded on this. And that was it: assembly was over. Morley released his breath.

The English lesson that followed was equally uneventful; no one sniggered or gave him searching looks. At break, Micky made no reference to their skirmish on the tram last night. Towards the end of break Morley dared hope that his prayer had been answered and his punishment would go no further, that it was just another warning. He sent up his thanks and reminded God of his promise to confess on Saturday. An interesting thought struck him: perhaps if Adriaan Verhoeven hadn't lost his faith, he'd still be alive and whole.

To raise his spirits further, he counted his blessings. He had thumbs; he savoured their presence, wrapping his fingers protectively around them. He thought of the return of his father – that he *had* a father. He'd be home in about six weeks. Giving Morley just enough time, if he really worked hard, to be closer to the sort of boy he wanted to become. Filing into the classroom for history he felt almost happy.

Mr Griffiths – history, geography and architecture – was well built though not very tall, with rather longish black, curly hair. He spoke with a public-school accent with a touch of Welsh about it and wore a gown. He had a perpetual, slightly condescending smile. He gave the impression of enormous energy denied an appropriate outlet. He strode up and down the aisles frequently, doing a sort of heel and toe step dance, flexing his feet, sometimes taking a kick at an imaginary ball. He stretched and contracted his shoulders, also his hands when they weren't in his trouser pockets. Cock of the walk, Morley's grandmother would have said. He might have come straight from St Cuthbert's, the public school of Nigel and Dick, the boy sleuths from Morley's favourite books. Because of this, Morley approved of him.

Mr Griffiths wrote 'History' on a very battered blackboard mounted on an easel, one hand in his pocket. 'What do we mean by history?' he asked, turning to the class. 'Just call out.'

'The study of past events, sir,' said a fair-haired girl on the other side of the room. She pronounced it 'parst'. Again Morley approved: touches of the magic middle-class world of his books and *Children's Hour* were falling thick and fast.

'I can't disagree with that. Anything else?'

'Is it the olden days, sir?' said a very tall boy who was too big for his desk, with ears so flat against his head that he looked earless from the front.

'Which olden days?' asked Mr Griffiths.

'Just the ordinary olden days, sir.'

'Oh, you mean when everything was old-fashioned,' Mr Griffiths asked, 'and everybody lived in old-style houses?'

'Yes, sir,' said the boy brightly. The class tittered.

'Mm,' said Mr Griffiths. 'Okay, tell me, anybody, what period of history were you last doing at your previous school?'

'Ancient Greeks,' a girl with glasses called out.

'Egyptians.'

'Middle Ages.'

Morley remembered to try to stammer. 'Saxons,' he said quite fluently.

'Does history *have* to go a long way back?' asked Mr Griffiths.

There were uncertain murmurs of 'No, sir.'

'Well, for me history is just as much about this moment as any other time, so let's start *here* with *you, now*. In your rough book write your name at the bottom of the page like this.' He wrote 'Tommy Atkins' on the board. 'That's me.' He then proceeded to explain the principle of a family tree and added a lot more comic names. 'All right, are you getting the idea? Do it in pencil first so you can easily correct things if you make a mistake.'

'Morley Charles', Morley wrote, the only name on that level, no sisters or brothers. A vertical line; on the left his mother, Esther Morley, her brothers Walter Morley, and John Morley, who had died at about three. Then her sister May.

He thought of May as he worked. Glamorous May who looked like a film star, with flawless teeth and skin and fair hair cut in a pageboy style. Her nose perhaps just a little bit long, but Morley liked it. She had an alluring figure and was very stylish. Although she closely resembled his mother, May was strikingly attractive and his mother wasn't. He pondered this strange phenomenon as he often did: similar ingredients but different results. 'b. 1915' he wrote against May's name, 'b. 1908' against his mother's. He wasn't sure of Walter and John's dates of birth. Another vertical line and then Grandma Morley: 'Emily b. 1886 m. to John Morley 1906'. Morley didn't know John's date of birth, only his death. He wrote 'd. 1918' and added '(In Great War)'.

Mr Griffiths was adding to his own diagram. 'Put in dates as near as you can, but check them at home. That's your homework, a well-researched, neatly presented family tree going back as far as you can.' He threw his chalk at a boy near the front, who caught it expertly. It was the short-trousered boy who had yesterday come to school with his mother. 'You're my chalk monitor for today,' Mr Griffiths said. He dusted his hands and went to the door at the back of the room that opened into the neighbouring classroom, making bowling actions as he went. 'A word with the fair Miss Swealter.'

Morley, nervous at the prospect of one day being the chalk monitor, in case he failed to catch the chalk, started on his father's side of the family. His father: 'Albert William Charles b. 1907'. There were some brothers – two or was it more? A sister. He knew neither their names nor anything about them. He lightly pencilled in three rectangles in readiness; above, two more for his unknown paternal grandparents.

His only connection with what might have been some of his dad's family was before the war. He had a dim memory of a wedding – or was it a funeral? A big room above . . . a big shop. A Co-op? Very hot. Open windows, blue curtains blowing gently in a breeze. An old lady with a fur round her neck who smelled of something funny (camphor, he realized much later) stared at him. He felt scared. Was she his grandmother? A younger woman gave him a chocolate éclair and patted his head. A man gave him sixpence.

His interest in his father's family had started only about a year ago, but all his attempts to elicit information about it from his mother had been met with frowning refusals and he had got out of the habit of trying. Now he had an excuse. He set the scene. Interesting, Mom, we've got this homework in history: family trees, our personal history. I'll be the only one in the class not to do it. The teacher said we've got to do it by next week.

He looked at all the blanks on his diagram and considered making up the missing names and dates. He would later, he decided, if his mother continued to refuse to tell him. Not being able to proceed further, he sat back and looked around him. Most pupils had their heads down writing. There was little talking but these were early days:

Mr Griffiths had yet to be tried and tested. And, unlike Redhill Council School's double desks, the ones here were single; there was no close neighbour to whisper to.

He caught occasional snatches of Mr Griffiths' conversation with Miss Swealter in the next room, but couldn't quite catch all she said.

'No, actually, it doesn't have liquid ink, just a sort of paste.'

'No, no nib, either, just this small ball, like a tiny ball bearing. Glides pretty effortlessly across the paper.'

There was a murmur from Miss Swealter.

'No, not an American, surprisingly, some Hungarian chap. Damned expensive as well, at least if you buy it from a shop. I, er, came by this one courtesy of the government.'

A long interested murmur from Miss Swealter.

Morley looked at his name on the bottom line of his family tree. Morley, the only Christian name among all those he had written that sounded like a surname. He had never known why on earth his mother had decided to call him by her own maiden name, a name that had long been a source of ridicule and confusion to him. But that was history. From now on, at this school, he decided, he would bear it with pride. He thought of other surname-sounding Christian names. Famous ones.

He took out his notebook and jotted them down. Sherlock, Mycroft, Conan, Rudyard, Clark, Sexton. He was in very grand company. If he became a famous artist, he already had the name, something to boast about. No, it's my real name. Not a . . . a pseudonym. He added his own: Morley. He sat back and thought of fame.

He felt a hand on his shoulder. He had the impulse to leap up but the hand was strong and kept him down.

'Sorry, didn't mean to startle you,' said Mr Griffiths, sounding as if he did. 'Now, it's my custom with a new class to decide blindly in advance on my first victim. To show no fear nor favour, see?' He addressed the class: 'Can anybody *honestly* accuse me of making a beeline for the prettiest girl in the class?'

A ripple of polite laughter went round the room – Micky's louder than the rest.

'So I decided, with my eyes closed: third row from left, third from front and here you are. So how far have you got?'

'A few gaps, sir, still a b-bit uncertain about my father's side of the family,' Morley said, again remembering to try to stammer.

But Mr Griffiths seemed to have his mind more on the class's response. 'Well, you are a half-lucky lad, equipped, at least, with one set of grandparents. And you know their years of birth. Good. Ah, and you've included died on active service. Well done.'

Morley felt his ears burning with pleasure.

'But wait a minute, haven't you made a mistake? Your Christian name is Morley, correct? And yet your mother's maiden name is *also* Morley. Is that right?'

'Yes, sir. It's a s-sort of er, family tradition, sir.'

Mr Griffiths seemed satisfied. Then, about to move on, he looked at Morley's open notebook and his list of surname-sounding Christian names. 'Good habit keeping a notebook. Mm, what have we got here? Sherlock, Mycroft, Conan . . . Ah, yes. Sherlock: Sherlock Holmes; Mycroft: Sherlock's brother; Conan: Conan Doyle, their author. Yes, yes, Rud-yard Kipling, Clark . . . mmm, not sure. Sexton, er, Blake. Emphasis on crime fiction. How am I doing?'

Morley mumbled approval.

'And Morley? Ah, that's you. Are you thinking of becom-ing a detective yourself, then, should you fail as an artist?'

Morley made sounds that might have been respectful laughter. The situation was unpleasantly familiar: trying to explain something that even if he could get it out with-out stammering would still make no sense to most people.

The class was very quiet. 'No, sir,' he mumbled feeling extremely conspicuous and ridiculous. He was forced to resort to invention. 'It was just that I'd finished the f-family tree, sir, and to fill up the time I was working out some ideas for this quiz, a sort of brains trust, and this round about, well, mainly crime f-fiction. For church, sir, youth club.'

'Ah, which church is that?' asked Mr Griffiths, not sounding particularly interested.

'The Catholic church at Upfield, sir.'

'Ah, a papist!'

Morley sighed inwardly. Admitting you were a Catholic wasn't always very bright.

But Mr Griffiths was finished with him. He looked round the room. 'Just out of interest, historical interest, how many Catholics have we here?'

The fair-haired girl, another girl and a boy with a face covered in pimples put their hands up.

Mr Griffiths said, 'Let's see, how many in this group?'

'Thirty-seven, sir,' said the fair-haired girl.

'Mm, four out of thirty-seven, that's more or less what I would have expected. Interestingly, though, excluding chapels, if you explore this and some other inner-city areas you might well find nearly as many Catholic churches as Protestant. Do you know why? No, don't tell me now; see if you can find out. I'll swoop on someone some day for an answer.' He looked at his watch, yawned, stood on one leg and rotated the foot of the other, reversed the procedure, did some knee-bending, then returned to the back of the room.

Morley went over what had just happened, wondering how he had fared in the eyes of the rest of the class. Perhaps not too badly. He had been a bit of a butt but he'd also been complimented.

What had Mr Griffiths said about Catholic churches? Why were there so many in this area? He supposed because of Irish immigration. A pleasant thought struck him. He didn't have to go to Upfield for confession. He could avoid both the fearsome Canon Reilly, who might recognize him and have something very serious to say about his continuing sin of self-abuse, and gentle Father Smythe, who, Morley was sure, would be terribly embarrassed and hurt to hear what he got up to at night. No, he could go to one of these local churches. He'd find one without delay. Perhaps pop in first to get familiar with it. He was enormously pleased with his idea.

'Yes,' came Mr Griffiths' voice from the back, 'any decent pen shop, I imagine. Ask to see some Biro pens.'

# 5

Morley was looking forward to doing his history home-work. He carefully cut a sheet of precious quarter imperial cartridge paper in half with a ruler and razor blade. Taking one of the half sheets and allowing generous margins, he ruled faint lines and roughly pencilled in what he knew of his family tree – leaving plenty of space for the unknown members of his father's family. Then with Indian ink and a broad pen he began to ink in the lettering. As a guide for style, he used an old calendar which had the names of the months printed in old English script.

He was anxious to impress on Mr Griffiths that even a first-year lad doing his first homework had skill and origi-nality. Towards the end of the lesson Mr Griffiths had shown them half a dozen or so history exercise books from third-year pupils. They were full of highly detailed illustrations, novel page arrangements, titles that looked as if they'd been printed, elaborate borders and highly decorated initial letters which wouldn't have disgraced a medieval illumin-ated manuscript. There were even designs that popped up as you opened the page. At Balsley School of Art pupils were encouraged to embellish all academic work as much as they liked except maths.

Morley worked contentedly, a play on the Home Service keeping him company. He could almost hear the gasps of admiration from the history class as his book was held up for its inspection, Mr Griffiths shaking his head in silent disbelief.

He had had little chance of even broaching the subject of his unknown relations with his mother as he had seen very little of her on her own so far this evening. She worked part time in the kitchen of Redhill Asylum and hadn't got in until nearly half past six. After tea she had gone down to Big Gwen's.

The Indian ink dry, Morley took the paper to the kitchen, turned on a front burner of the gas stove and adjusted it to low. His object was to char the edges of the paper to create the impression of an ancient document. The inspiration was from a very impressive poster he had seen under the glass of the notice board at Redhill Parish Church advertising an Olde Tyme Dance.

He gingerly passed the top edge of the paper through the gas jets. It immediately caught fire, flames rapidly advancing towards his precious text. He blew them out. But here and there remained glowing edges that moved more slowly. He found he had some control over these, extinguishing them with his fingers when they had made their contribution to the effect he was after. He repeated the process, showering stove and floor with white ash, till the top edge of the paper resembled a ragged piece of coastline. He did the bottom of the document with even greater success. He laid it on the kitchen table and gazed at it admiringly.

To his intense irritation, Frank, the lodger, wandered in just then and looked over his shoulder. 'Ah, but that's a great shame, nipper,' he said. 'But then a clever feller like you – could you not cut them burned bits off?'

Morley explained that he was trying to achieve the effect of an ancient document.

'Ah, right you are, I can see what you're after now: like them old treasure maps. I remember seeing something like that in that picture – you know the one, with that feller with the thin moustache, not Clark Gable, the other one.' An inch of ash fell from Frank's cigarette and mingled with Morley's ash on the red-tiled floor. Frank seldom took out his cigarette to talk: it lived in the left side of his mouth, causing his left eye to stay permanently closed to avoid the smoke.

Morley found it difficult to concentrate with Frank hanging around but he was anxious to see the finished effect. He passed the left-hand edge of the paper through the gas. This time he held the paper there a bit too long. Fierce flames leapt up and his attempts to blow them out fanned them further. He rushed to the sink, set his document on the edge and doused the flame with the side of his hand. But a large bite was taken out of John Henry Morley, his uncle who had died at the age of three. He was not too dismayed: he had already decided that this was only a practice run.

Frank was watching Morley's every move. 'Maybe, nipper, that stove there wouldn't be the best thing to use, after all. How about using me lighter, now? Then you'd be able to manage things a bit better.'

'What do you know about anything, anyway, Frank?' Morley said under his breath. But it seemed a good idea. He thanked Frank.

He laid his document with its untreated side overhanging the edge of the kitchen table. Then anchored it securely in place with the tea caddy and a bottle of milk. This time the process was indeed more manageable with the lighter: the right-hand side turned out to be the best of all.

'You see what I told you?' said Frank proudly. 'But I'll have to leave you to it, nipper. I must be away now to me devotions.'

This meant he was off to the Hen and Chickens. He always called it his devotions when Morley's mother wasn't around.

'And you can hang on to the lighter if you like, nipper. I can easily get meself a light down the pub.' He smiled lop-sidedly because of his fag, and Morley heard him going up the stairs whistling.

This raised his opinion of Frank. Not too much, though, because Frank, as his mother would claim, was probably trying to curry favour. Just lately he had started bringing in the coal, taking his cup and plate to the sink, changing his socks more frequently and being more careful with his cigarette ash. It was because he didn't want to leave his lodgings. Morley's mother had at last plucked up the courage to tell him that it would be best for everybody if he found new digs before her husband was demobbed.

Morley frowned at his document. It looked too white. The extreme edges were okay; they were burnt black. But he wanted a gradated effect. It needed scorching. He passed the lighter to and fro underneath the paper but the flame was too small in area, so it was back to the gas and a much wider source of heat.

He turned the gas on again and passed his document over the flames with a circular movement. He had to keep turning it face up to see how it was going. Progress was slow. He turned the gas up. Whoosh! The flame broke through near the middle and made a rapidly enlarging hole. He chucked it into the sink. A failure, but now he knew what to do. With his next attempt he would scorch the paper *before* doing the lettering. He would do the final document tomorrow.

He cleaned up the top of the stove and the sink, then sat on the settee and tried listening to *The Michael Howard Show*, but his mind kept drifting.

As an artist he was one in forty or more, he reflected. That was something to be proud of. As a Catholic he was one in about nine or ten – according to Mr Griffiths. On the whole he felt pleased with that as well: it made him more interesting, different. As a stammerer? About one in sixty it said in *Monroe's Universal Reference Book*. As a brace-wearer, one in – he didn't know; perhaps one in three or four hundred. Although according to Russell the Yank, who courted Beryl Pinder, half the kids in his neighbourhood back home wore them. He was certainly different, he acknowledged, in some ways positive, in others . . . negative.

What was the proportion of people with both thumbs missing? he wondered. He went through all the motions of making a charred family tree without thumbs. Holding the pen, guiding the paper over the flame. It was very difficult to make the lighter work.

It would be a good idea, thought Morley, if disabilities could be shared. Yes, everyone in his group at school would have to have protruding teeth and a brace for one day in, he calculated, about every five weeks. Mind, he'd have to take his turn in having his face a mass of pimples and wearing glasses. He was reminded that Micky Plant had gone for an eye test after school that evening with his mother. Perhaps Micky might have to wear glasses soon, he thought happily.

Was he intelligent? he wondered. His mother often called him dense. Not least because if she sent him on an errand for even a couple of items he would almost always get it wrong if she didn't write it down. Yet he had always been in an A class, although his last teacher's assessment of him was confusing. His final report from Redhill Council School said, 'Morley has done quite well but is inclined to be rather slow.' The one before said, 'Morley has done quite well but is inclined to be rather hasty.' Frank the lodger thought him bright, had often said as much, but he was very given to flattery. Big Gwen had also once said, 'A clever lad like you . . .' But he couldn't remember about what.

# 6

'What's that funny smell?' asked Morley's mother as she entered the kitchen.

Morley held his breath, wondering if his cleaning up of charred paper and ash had been thorough enough. It presumably was: after a few moments of moving and sniffing around she came into the living room looking surprisingly cheerful. Morley suspected she'd had something to drink.

Her mood improved further when Morley told her that Frank had gone down to the pub. There would be at least a couple of hours before he got back.

'Make us a really nice cup of tea, duck. I'd be the last one to criticize but Big Gwen's tea always tastes, well, a bit funny.' She put a paint-spotted brown Virol jar onto the table. 'I'll give you some of that when you've poured the tea,' she said.

He pulled a face.

She almost smiled. 'It's all right, duck, it's American whiskey. Russ got it from his PX.'

Settled with their tea, she poured a generous dash of whiskey into his cup. 'You had a good day at school, then, duck?'

'Yeh, very interesting. Our history teacher got us to do our f-family trees this morning,' he said as neutrally as possible. 'He said history's a living thing. It's happening now and we're an important p-part of it.'

She smiled mechanically. 'That's nice, duck.' She never called him Morley.

'I was the first to finish,' he said provocatively.

'Well, you can do anything if you try.' Morley could see that she wanted to change the subject: she never liked to enquire too deeply about what he had been doing in case he told her something that would upset her.

'No, the reason was, Mom, I didn't have so much to do as the others. I mean, after I'd p-put down the names and dates of *your* family, and Dad's name, there wasn't anything else I knew.'

She was all attention now. 'I've told you before, son –'

'No, no, just saying, Mom. I wasn't going to ask you, just saying why I'd f-finished first. That's all.'

'Well, so long as that's all it is, then.' She sighed heavily.

He knew that talking about his father was rash. During the last year of the war her anxiety about his father's welfare had grown to an extent where a mere mention of him was sometimes enough to plunge her into the deepest of her dark moods.

Things should have been better with the war over, but he had recently overheard her explaining to Big Gwen that if something happened to Albert now it would be even harder to bear than if he had died during the war when you were always more or less expecting it. On top of that he was now enquiring about the forbidden subject of his dad's family.

Purse-lipped, she poured a drop more whiskey into Morley's cup.

'It's okay, Mom, it's just that our history teacher told us to always find out about things, ask questions. One of the most important things in education is curiosity, he said. Seems a very clever bloke. Heard him s-saying to another teacher he'd been to Oxford University,' he lied. His mother was in awe of schoolteachers and priests.

'Yes, that's all very well, but your teacher doesn't know the reasons –'

'No, no, it doesn't matter, Mom, really. It's only that I w-wanted to get good marks in history, well, in everything really. And I didn't want to be the only person in the whole class not to be able to f-finish.'

Morely felt quite moved by his display of ambition and self-denial.

She lit a Minor and took a sip of her whiskeyed tea. She was looking thoughtful. 'Your dad wouldn't like it if I told you anything. But even if he wanted me to tell you, there's not much I really know.'

'It's okay, Mom, I don't want to know anything about them at all, but Dad has *g-got* parents and brothers and that, hasn't he?'

She nodded resignedly. 'Yes, of course he has.'

'Well, can you j-just tell me the name of his mom and dad and when they were born, then?'

'I'll tell you everything I know then perhaps you'll stop mithering me.'

Morley nodded.

'His father's name was Thomas, his mother's Phoebe. Joyce was the oldest child – the only girl – then your dad. His brothers were Wilfred and George. I don't know when any of them were born. Two or three others died in child-birth or when they were very young. I don't know when they were born either. And that's that. Some people in families just don't get on with each other. Got different ideas, think they're always in the right. They imagine things. They tell lies. It's just life, duck. Big Gwen's got a sister she hasn't talked to for over twenty years. Now, no more questions about them again.'

His appetite was whetted; he wanted to know more, much more. *Where* was his dad's old home? What was it *like*? Was it near Nechells where his mother came from?

Or somewhere posh like Edgbaston? Perhaps it was in the country. But he didn't dare ask.

He lay in bed with the Jack Payne Orchestra crackling quietly from his loudspeaker, trying to reconcile his dad's unbending attitude about his family with the dad he remembered: easy going, always joking, clowning.

He dreamt that Mr Griffiths had a huge box of coloured chalks and appointed a chalk monitor for each colour. Every boy was involved; there was no escape. Morley was the yellow chalk monitor, which was Mr Griffiths' most-used colour. Mr Griffiths threw yellow chalk to him throughout the lesson and Morley missed every time. The class jeered and Mr Griffiths grinned so widely it seemed that his face would split in two.

The only marks awarded by Mr Griffiths were for catching chalk. Morley was bottom of the class. On his report, against Chalk Catching it said, 'Terrible, this lad's fingers are all thumbs.'

'That's funny, I thought you hadn't *got* any thumbs, duck,' said his mother.

# 7

There was a Friday afternoon feeling of suppressed excitement among the pupils in the boys' drawing room. In an hour's time the first week of the new term at Balsley School of Art would be over.

The huge room was full of boys from the school's every group: Draughtsmen, Cabinetmakers, Signwriters and Modellers. And from every year: first, second and third. The girls in their own groups were doing something else elsewhere. Morley was a Draughtsman. The subject for all first years was My House.

This had struck Morley as rather feeble for an art school until Mr Sitwell had explained this was but one component in a much wider project.

For the first ten minutes of the lesson, each pupil had to draw the front of his house with his eyes closed on a small piece of paper known as visual paper. Results weren't important: this exercise was designed to stimulate visual memory.

Now Morley was doing the final drawing – with eyes open – on eighth imperial paper. This had to be completed in watercolour. A perspective drawing of the same subject, made on the spot, had been set for homework.

Mr Sitwell, the first years' teacher, was young, shy, anxious to please, very helpful and highly talented but not very strong on discipline. Today, with nearly two hundred boys gathered together, Mr Plume's authoritative presence kept the whole room at a level of brisk activity and tolerable noise. Occasionally he would descend from the dais and stroll around like a lord of the manor to show he was in charge and deal with the second- and third-year pupils, who were doing different subjects. The rest of the time he was bent over some mysterious artwork on his desk.

Mr Sitwell was clearly a great fan of watercolour. He rhapsodized about its luminosity; how important it was to be spontaneous, how to simplify. He said luminosity quite frequently, often pronouncing it luminoshity – a lot of his esses, in fact, came out this way. Nearly every time he said it, there was a very faint echo of 'shitty' from the back of the room where the seniors sat, but only when Mr Sitwell was out of hearing.

His fifth day at Balsley School of Art, Morley marvelled, and things hadn't gone too badly after all – apart from his disastrous-seeming start. Nobody had referred to his badge at all. Now he berated himself for his hysterical reaction. He examined his immediate future.

Confession he had sorted out. He had spotted a Catholic church at dinner time the other day. Micky, he and a boy called Dawkins had wandered the neighbourhood on what Dawkins called a familiarization exercise. And there it was: the Catholic Church of St James. Confessions, Saturdays 10.00 a.m. to 12.00 noon. He took it all in as they passed by. He returned alone after school to make doubly sure and write the times down in his notebook.

'Laid 1879' it said on the foundation stone. He went inside. Rows of votive candles flickered as he opened the inner door. It was much older than his own church, SS Peter and Paul in Upfield, which had been built in 1937. Its gloom was deep, the scent of incense and candle wax strong, the stained-glass windows very rich. He had a strange feeling of nostalgia: a brief but deep desire to be living in an earlier age when the church was built. He liked the atmosphere; it was almost cosy. He felt pleasantly anonymous in the near dark, far away from Upfield and familiar churchgoers. 'Fr. Denis Phelan' it said on the first of the confessionals, 'Fr. M. Michalowski' on the other.

Who would be the more easy going? he wondered. He would wait until Saturday, then perhaps toss a coin, or see which priest had the bigger queue. He felt less nervous than he had supposed; perhaps he was growing up. He knelt down and said a prayer, hoping that one of the priests would appear so he might get an idea of what he was up against. But none had.

Morley gave the drawing of his house an arched entrance, beyond which he drew a front door with flanking windows, all with leaded lights. This was a big departure from the concrete canopy above the plain door of his real house, common to all the municipal houses in Woods Park Road. Actually, his house hadn't got a front door at all: the main door was at the side. He wondered how many other lads lived in municipal houses. He decided to take a look when he went out to get some water. Although, of course, other boys from municipal houses might be altering their houses as well. Micky Plant was faithfully reproducing his own house in Marshfield Drive that really did have leaded lights in the front door and windows. Morley could just about see it if he craned his neck. If Micky accused him of cheating he would say, sounding quite honest and unapologetic, Well, our house is so lousy, so plain, that there'd be hardly any point in painting it.

Anyway, Micky might not bother to come and have a look. He remembered that Micky's eyes were okay.

'Naw. It's just a bit of a stigma,' Micky had said the morning after his eye test. 'This bloke at Scrivens' said it's hardly worth bothering about, but come back next year. It's just a bit in my left eye.'

'Nobody would ever know,' said Morley sympathetically, peering closely, not knowing what he was looking for. 'Looks completely normal to me.'

'Course it does, you twat. It's not something you *can* see: it's *inside* the eye. It's like – Anyroad, he said *everybody's* got a touch of it.'

On reflection, Morley was pleased. It occurred to him that a boy with a brace going around with a boy who wore glasses would draw even more attention.

Any other problems? he wondered, as he started to draw a tree to the left of the composition. In geography and architecture, he had managed to sit near the back, out of range of Mr Griffiths' chalk flinging, and this he would continue to do . . .

He became aware of Mr Sitwell by his desk. Mr Sitwell was such a pleasant, amiable man that Morley would have felt completely at ease with him had it not been for the fear that he might unwittingly offend him.

'Is thish all *your* house?' he asked.

'N-No, sir, I started a bit too small, and too far over to the right, so I put in most of next door as well.'

'Ah, Flemish tilesh, I shee,' pointing to Morley's roof, which showed their right-angled arrangement.

'Yes, sir,' said Morley managing only by a hairsbreadth to avoid saying Yesh, shir. Morley knew his tiles; there was a coloured double-spread of roof types entitled 'How Britons Keep Dry' in May's *Pictorial Book of Knowledge*.

'Intereshting,' said Mr Sitwell rubbing his chin. 'Not so thick on the ground in the Midlandsh, Flemish tiles. More south easht and Easht Anglia, and of course the Low Countriesh. Although I think the council imported shome from the Continent before the war. For munishipal houshing. Intereshting, mosht intereshting,' he said, nodding and moving on.

Morley coloured, convinced that Mr Sitwell knew that

he lived in a municipal house and knew he was trying to disguise it.

He put his work under the desk and made his way to the sink at the front. He passed a drawing of a flat, then Micky's semi-detached – Micky was furtively reading his *Champion*. Next was a very large, impressive house of three storeys with a coach house. Morley paused. The artist was Dawkins. He looked up and grinned. Further on there were two Victorian terrace houses, but most of the rest of the drawings were semi-detached houses like Micky Plant's.

He filled his jar with water. Turning to return to his desk, he met the enquiring gaze of the boy with dark, curly hair who had barred his path near the senior lavatories on Monday. Another much smaller senior boy drew up alongside with the sort of ears that had Morley automatically saying to himself, Ay, mate, you've left your cab doors open.

'Are you the fag who had his blazer badge sewn on his cap?' asked the first boy, smiling.

'No,' Morley lied, looking puzzled.

'You sure?'

Morley tried to cover his brace with his upper lip. 'I-I thought you couldn't *get* badges. Anyway, I haven't even got a cap – yet.'

'Ooh, you'll cop it,' said sticking-out ears, thrusting his jaw forward.

Morley had an intense desire to put him in his place with a withering look and a heroic explanation about only just returning from France where he'd spent the war working with his parents in the Resistance, and caps were far too trivial for his kind to think about. Instead he said, without stammering, by keeping himself amused with thoughts about the boy's ears, 'I never got around to it, I was laid up in hospital.' If you go out in the wind like that, mate, you'll take off, he added mentally.

'You look all right to me.'

'Broken collarbone,' Morley added recklessly. 'I was in this car accident. I was only discharged Monday night.'

'You weren't here Monday then?'

'Couldn't have been, could I?'

'Are you trying to be funny, fag?'

'N-No,' said Morley innocently.

The first boy gently steered his protruding-eared mate away.

Morley was very pleased with himself although he knew that if the exchange had been any longer his brief spell of confidence would have fizzled out and his stammer would have got the better of him. A small victory. His heart pounded wildly.

Towards the end of the afternoon Mr Sitwell collected the holiday work and the competition entries.

Instructions for holiday work and for the Wrighton Prize Competition for Landscape had been set out with the school rules issued to Morley at his interview. His entry for the competition was a watercolour of Cofton Hackett Church with a large grave surrounded with an iron railing in the foreground. He and Micky Plant had walked there and done preliminary drawings at the beginning of the summer holiday. Morley had been very pleased with his final version and thought it slightly better than Micky's. But now, catching glimpses of other boys' work being handed in, it struck him as pale and timid.

# 8

Boots clunked up the aisle of the Catholic Church of St James, Balsley. Confident, precise. Army, Morley guessed. He was right. The soldier genuflected and knelt in a front pew. He had a maroon beret tucked under his shoulder strap. Paras, wow! A sergeant, two stripes better than his dad. Morley envied his son – if he had one. There was a flutter of nervous excitement in his chest and he felt rising pimples of duck flesh as he thought of his dad's homecoming – not long now. In a way, he would have liked it to be longer because once his father was at home, he would no longer have anything so exciting to look forward to. He closed his eyes and tried to recall his dad's face – and found it difficult. It was easier to remember the snap taken at the beginning of the war: his dad with a mate in front of a tank. Greatcoat much too long, mop of very wavy hair, too wavy, like a perm. His dad pulling a face and looking through fingers arranged to look like goggles. God, always fooling about. And small. People called him Titch. He loved him, yet everything about him was, well, not quite right. But he's alive, he told himself. And a war hero. And nearly played for Villa before the war. And . . . Rommel was small. And they said Alan Ladd had to stand on a box for some of the shots in his pictures. Consoled, he opened his eyes. Then he remembered where he was and what he was here for.

He was waiting to confess to Father Michalowski: his was the longer queue. Until now he hadn't felt too bad. During the tram journey the bedridden man had waved and there had been the prospect of going to town afterwards. But he had been waiting a very long time and there were six people in front of him. From overheard whispers it seemed that neither priest had yet turned up. Time began to hang heavily; his uneasiness grew; he wished he had gone to Upfield. Say the foreign priest's grasp of English was so bad that he wouldn't understand self-abuse – or masturbation – and Morley would have to explain. In detail. He quailed at the prospect. In case he forgot it, he repeated masturbation several times until it took on a repulsive, slowly writhing shape. He felt shaken. His stammer threatened. He remembered the smile technique from the Guy Olivier Institute. He drew a deep breath and, as he exhaled, thought of Micky wearing thick glasses and everybody calling him Goggles Plant. He felt his lips curl upwards. Another outwards breath: the senior lad from school with the right-angled ears. If you go outside like that, mate, you'll take off! And the boy in his own group who appeared to be earless from the front. He saw them sitting next to each other on the tram: flat ears and sticking-out ears: each looking enviously at the other. He shook with mirth. But he could hardly use images of the afflicted in preparation for confession. What else made him smile? The only image that insisted on coming was the university student's slightly plump but shapely naked knees, slightly apart, facing him on the tram. He grinned and felt briefly excited; then scared that he might be committing sacrilege. God, he'd have to confess to that as well.

The man waiting after him kept taking his watch out, but Morley couldn't see the face as the man always turned it away from him to catch the light coming in on his right. A boy before him in the queue was tapping the back of the pew in front of him; a girl sniffed every few seconds. A woman sitting further up the church kept turning to give them disapproving looks. To his right Morley counted eight people who had come in after him. Father Phelan's queue behind was about seven strong. He reckoned he'd been waiting twenty minutes.

What on earth was keeping the priests? he wondered yet again. Trust things to go wrong when he had finally made the effort to come and confess. There were sighs, fidgets and whispers along the row. Then someone to his left got up, genuflected and left. People shuffled along the bench to fill the gap. The joyful possibility of not having to confess at all with a reason beyond his control occurred to him. But it conflicted with the desire to get it over and done with; he didn't want to run the risk of anything bad happening before his father got back. Two recently arrived women also left, whispering loudly. The man with the watch took it out again; this time Morley stood up as if to fish a hanky from his trouser pocket to get a good view of it. It was just after a quarter past eleven. He'd been waiting for nearly half an hour! He glanced behind him: the queue for Father Phelan was reduced to five. He would count to three hundred – slowly. Three hundred seconds: five minutes. Then he would leave. As he finished his counting the tapping boy and the sniffing girl got up and left. People slid nearer to the confessional; there were only three people in front of him now. The sergeant at the front genuflected smartly and strode down the aisle. Count to three hundred once more, Morley decided, and then he would definitely go.

Counting done, he excused himself into the aisle, hoping that the priest wouldn't arrive now, now that he had lost his place.

There were quite a few people near the porch talking animatedly.

'. . . but twas a *Protestant* church they was working on,' said an old woman with startlingly vivid make-up.

'What's that got to do with anything, you daft creature?' said a young man in a smart suit. 'D'you think they'd have not fallen if it had been a Catholic church?'

'Ah, yes, they may well have fallen but not struck dead like that.'

'We don't know that yet. You shouldn't be spreading rumours.'

The man with the watch appeared. 'What's up then, Tom, are they coming or not?'

'Search me, Michael. Seems they was called to give extreme unction to some fellers demolishing a bombed church – in Ladywood I *think*. They fell from the roof. At least one was a Catholic from this parish. But that was well over an hour and a half ago. And they haven't yet got in touch. Father Mich went as well to drive the motor.'

Morley stood outside the church. If it hadn't been for the priests' absence, or the bombed church, or the *Luftwaffe* or the Germans or Hitler, confession would have been over. Now he had to face it all over again. He could, if he hurried, go to confession in Upfield – perhaps even in town. But it was getting late and he *had* made the effort. It wasn't his fault. He'd leave it till next week.

The feeling of relief after the ordeal of confession and the prospect of town as a reward had been denied him. Still, town hadn't lost all its appeal. He thought of the Central Library, the Museum and Art Gallery, the book-shops, the model-plane shop and Hobbies in the Bull Ring. All to be effortlessly enjoyed – if he was Dutch.

Morley had been masquerading as a Dutch boy for two and a half months. He became Dutch in potentially awkward situations when he felt out of his depth. The transformation worked like magic. He felt immediately confident, the fear of stammering and of making a fool of himself evaporated and he knew that even if he did slip up over something it would be seen merely as the natural behaviour of a foreigner unused to strange English ways. It was of necessity limited to people met well away from home.

Dutch was the second foreign identity he'd adopted. Originally he had been French. The transition to Dutch had been forced upon him. But for about six months, whenever occasion demanded, he had been a highly successful French boy. But French, it was gradually impressed upon him, was too widely understood for comfort. Even the most unlikely people might have some knowledge of it. He still winced when he thought of his encounter with the park keeper at Rose Hill Gardens, which had finished his French career for good.

Lost in thought and certainly without intending to, Morley had walked across a small lawn – almost the only ornamental feature of the entire gardens, as nearly everywhere else was still under wartime vegetable cultivation.

The park keeper, red-faced with a nicotine-stained grey moustache and medal ribbons on his dark blue uniform, limped furiously from his hut at that precise moment. 'Ay you, what the hell do you think you'm aplaying at, you swining ignoramus? Can't you read?' He pointed to a keep-off-the-grass sign.

Morley's paralysis lasted only a second: this was only an old parky. Confidence flowed into him as he slipped into the familiar role. 'Oh, *pardon*, *M'sieur*, *je*, I do not, eur, undeurstand English very good. In France, eur, *le jardin* . . .' He raised his shoulders, smiled and spread his palms apologetically.

'Dog bite me! We're swining French, are we? Froggy French, ay? I might have knowed it. No respect for anythink, you lot. Bet you walked on that grass apurpose. Think you'm all above us, don't you? Huh! You in't even got proper closets in your country. Swining holes in the floor to shit in, more like, that's what you got. Wipes your arses on your fingers. Oh, I know, I know, I been there in the last lot. Swining Verdun, swining Somme. *And* you eat frogs and slugs. Filthy buggers. Then you goo and walk all over my precious bit of grass, apurpose, the only bit left . . .'

Morley had seen him before though not close to. It was clear the man didn't recognize him. Morley remained cool, even amused, the man's invective hardly touching him; although in a detached sort of way he was outraged about the crude attack on his borrowed nationality. He was on the point of retaliating, of saying something really cutting. Perhaps calling the man a peasant or – what about pretending to think his uniform was military and saying, *Pardon, mon général . . .* ?

'. . . then you goo and pretend you don't understand English – only cause it suits you, mind. All right then, you goo and talk to me in French, then. Goo on. I'll understand all right. I can talk your bleeding language, I can. I was there three year. And I'll mek you understand you can't bleeding goo round doing what you like.' And he came limping threateningly after Morley.

Morley froze, retreated and broke into a run, his nerve gone. The man lumbered behind him shouting in what might have been any language, though even in his fright Morley made out *idiot, imbécile.*

He'd enjoyed being French despite all its risks; it was the only time he had felt at ease with strangers and people in authority. But now the time had come to find another nationality, one whose language not many English people knew. So he became Dutch.

He felt he had an affinity with Holland. That's where his dad had been wounded. He had done a watercolour of a canal where he imagined his father had been killed –

before learning that the report was a mistake; and, not least, there was the thumbless ex-Catholic artist Adriaan Verhoeven.

A Dutch accent was the main problem as it wasn't so commonly heard on the pictures or on the wireless as French. A few Dutch words were also necessary, but unlike French and German, there were no Dutch phrases for the traveller in *Monroe's Universal Reference Book*. Neither was there a Dutch dictionary in Redhill or Upfield libraries. Fortunately he heard that *Rendezvous Rotterdam* was on at Upfield Cinema. He watched it three times and learned *dank u, alstublieft, mijnheer* and *mevrouw, nei* and *ya*; and wrote them phonetically in his notebook. He learned that a Dutchman speaking English puts a lot of energy into it, uses esses that are slightly thickened. And that Dutch words should be spat out very emphatically with a lot of noisy throat clearing.

He consulted May's pre-war *Pictorial Book of Knowledge* and found under Netherlands: 'In the cities your typical Dutchman will look like the most healthy and alert type of Englishman, well-dressed and well-educated, well built with a clear ruddy complexion, fair hair and blue or grey eyes, who will often speak English uncommonly well.'

He had looked in the mirror above the stone fireplace in May's lounge. Pale blue eyes, light brownish hair tending, at a pinch, he thought, towards fair, clear complexion though hardly ruddy. Certainly closer to Dutch than French, though. And, he mused, he did speak English uncommonly well – for a Dutch lad.

If asked, his name was Jan van der Velde, born in Hilversum (this from the wireless dial), father shot by the SS for railway sabotage, mother missing. He had come to England to study art. The name van der Velde was from the film *Rendezvous Rotterdam* so Morley knew how to pronounce it and, from the credits, how to spell it. And

Jan he discovered – from *Topping Tales for Boys*, borrowed from Micky Plant – was pronounced Yan.

As Morley entered Balsley Road, a tram to town had just left the stop. He walked to the next one. Opposite was a second-hand bookshop. It was unlikely that there would be any Nigel and Dick the boy sleuths books, but it would be an interesting diversion to go in and have a look round.

# 9

The shop was scruffy, its exterior of mainly bare, sun-bleached timber, although blue, brown and dark green paint still clung to recesses in the mouldings. Its many-paned windows were so grimy you could barely see inside. Like most bookshops, they kept the bargains outside. Morley riffled through cheap westerns, romances, thrillers and American private eye stories. Their condition was poor.

'Plenty more and better inside, son,' said the proprietor, who had appeared on the step, snapping his braces with his fingers.

'Ah *ya, dank u,*' said Morley, immediately Dutch.

He went confidently into the dark interior that reeked of damp paper, cats and stale cooking. Had he not been foreign he would have felt trapped, speechless, obliged to buy something he didn't want, scared he'd be overcharged and afraid that he'd lack the courage to protest.

Hands in pockets, Morley took his time, savouring the search. He scanned the shelves of bookcases made largely from orange boxes. Unlike a library, nothing was classified. One shelf held three volumes from a set of ancient encyclopaedias, ancient school textbooks, a history book, novels and piles of *Picture Posts*, *John Bulls* and *Lifes*. Morley took down a stained book on art but it had no pictures.

Being foreign released a strong desire to perform. 'Will you tell me, if you please, vhere I must find, some book of van Gogh or de French Impressionists?' Not that he had any intention of buying anything of the kind.

'Ooohh,' said the man, sucking air through his teeth, 'well, we might 'ave, but this is what we call your brow-sers' shop: everything's all mixed up. On purpose, mind. You come in for your art book, let's say, and you have to 'unt for it. You might not find your art book but while you're 'unting for it you come across, let's say, a nice book on 'orses or a nice 'istorical novel or a nice book about pewter-collecting that you really like but you wouldn't 'ave come across if everything was in proper order. Gives more chice to your customer. Get what I mean?' It was as if he was taking great care to drop his aitches.

'Now this'll suit you. Put you at the top of the class.' He stood on a beer crate and brought down a book called *Flora of the Nile Delta* with pages already coming adrift. 'Two bob and all you need is a drop of paste. Just look at them,' he said, caressing with a grimy, nicotined-stained finger an engraving of a plant showing its roots. 'And all coloured by 'and. That's real art, that is: not like some of the tripe you see nowadays.'

Morley shook his head and smiled easily.

'You could regret it, you know, you being – you are from the art school, I take it?'

Morley nodded. 'I am, but no danks, *mijnheer*. But have you some boys' books by Edmund Willis Frazer? Books of de boy detectives, Nigel and Dick?'

The man shook his head and noisily sucked in air again. 'Ooh, no, son, no. No nothing like that, no. No, 'ang on, 'ang on, I tell a lie, there *might* be, there well *might* be: but it's like I said before, a question of 'unting.'

Morley hunted with little hope. He occasionally pulled out a book which, while obviously not a Nigel and Dick story, looked promising. But nothing worth parting with a shilling or sixpence for. He studied a book called *The Settler* by Ralph Connor. 'A Tale of Saskatchewan', it further explained. The red cover was stained, the inside peppered with brown spots, some pages stuck together: a gloomy thing altogether. Pasted in the inside cover, though, was a label which caught his attention. It was printed in red, green and gold. The ornate lettering read: 'Prize awarded to', then, in copperplate handwriting: 'Harry Fisk, Second Prize, 1906, Rev'd D. D. Otterley' and something too smudged to read. Opposite in, presumably, the prizewinner's own hand, was written:

Harry Oliver Lucas Fisk,
9, Sandringham Terrace,
Handsworth Wood,
Birmingham,
Warwickshire,
England,
Great Britain,
Europe,
Earth,
Universe.

'Very good, exciting tale that,' said the man. 'I'd 'ighly recommend it. I won't say no more lest it spiles it for you. But you'll like it all right. Sixpence. Good as giving it you. Let's say fivepence.'

Morley's poise was impregnable. 'No, it must be a Nigel and Dick story, for I have dem already in Dutch, you see, and now I need dem in English for dey fill be very helpful for improving my English.'

The label and the boy's address continued to hold Morley's fascinated interest. He suddenly knew why: his father also had a book with a prize label pasted inside. He hadn't looked at it for years, but wasn't it a book about scouts? And hadn't his dad also written his boyhood *address*? He fancied that he had. Excitement gripped him. He decided to give town a miss and go straight home and check.

# IO

As Morley breasted the rise in Woods Park Road and his house came into view, he was relieved to see that none of the scruffs was around. None of them had seen him in his school uniform yet and he was uncertain of how they would react and how he would respond.

'The scruffs' was his mother's term for the lads who played in the street and gathered round the pig bin to no particular purpose. Typically they were ragged-arsed, down at heel, weak on cleanliness and used foul language.

Morley hurried towards his house, his head filled with the image of the label in his father's prize book with his father's boyhood address written alongside. He wanted to find out about his father's family before he was demobbed. He couldn't see himself making secret excursions to his dad's old house once he was back, it would be . . . deceitful. Deceiving his mother didn't matter so much.

But what if he did find his father's old address and went to the house? Would any of his family still live there? And if they did, what was he going to do about it? Knock the door and say I'm Morley, Albert's son? And get kicked out because of something terrible his father had done? Hang about hoping to see his dad's mother or father come out? Then what? Follow them? He passed the Pinders' house; there was an American military Chrysler parked outside: Russ Hartmann, Beryl Pinder's boyfriend, was there. Still, it would be interesting to know where his dad had lived. He could go out one night after school or next Saturday. Just have a look.

His house was empty. Standing on tiptoe he could just reach the top of the dresser where the household's books were kept. There were some Dickens, *Modern Home Management* and others in this vein, his own books, his mother's prize books, and his father's *The Scouts of Seal Island* by Percy F. Westerman. Morley had read it years ago. He held his breath and took it slowly up to his room, deferring the moment of revelation.

He sat on the bed and opened it very slowly. Nothing. He turned over the endpaper. Again nothing. He turned to the back with the same result. He held it by its front board and shook it in case the prize label had somehow migrated inside and might flutter out. He examined the book again but there was no sign of a label ever having been there. Neither was there a boyhood address, just his dad's name neatly written in pencil: 'Albert William Charles'. He rushed downstairs, got the kitchen chair to examine the top of the dresser at closer range. He scrutinized every book, looked behind books to see if another had got hidden. He took down his mother's prizes, sat on the settee and examined them. They were *Lives of the Saints* and *The Little Flower*. Both bore prize labels, though neither in colour. Both were for Perfect Attendance and Punctuality. In each his mother had written 'Esther Morley' and her childhood address on the facing page in the familiar spidery handwriting.

Could he have *imagined* the coloured label and the address? After all, it seemed a bit unlikely that his father had won a school prize. He'd often light-heartedly boasted of the many scrapes he'd got into and how he was always getting belted. But Morley would have sworn both existed. He could *see* the label: red, green and gold with fancy lettering and, more particularly, his dad's old address. It had to be another book and his mother had hidden it . . . *because* it had his father's address in it and because he, Morley, had recently been asking questions!

He rushed up to his mother's bedroom where there was a large, built-in closet. Inside were old clothes, an old-fashioned photo enlarger, some photographic stuff in a wooden box and the pieces of a small cupboard his father was in the process of making when he was called up. The only book visible was a huge Victorian atlas too big to go on top of the dresser. Guiltily, ears alert for the return of his mother, he began to search for the hidden book.

Just checking something in the atlas for homework, he'd say if his mother suddenly appeared.

Level with his head was a broad shelf filled with mil-dewed shoes and handbags. He sorted through them. It is important to eliminate even the most unlikely of possi-bilities, Nigel the boy 'tec often advised his less astute chum Dick. Of course, if his mother had hidden the book it *would* be in an unlikely place. But there was no book there.

Idly he opened the atlas. He turned the pages to find the United States and Milwaukee, the town that Russ came from. But before he got there, he found a postcard wedged where the pages met. The address on the right said:

> Master Albert Charles,
> Rose Brae,
> Clarence Street,
> Ashted,
> Birmingham.

And the message on the left:

> *To Albert on his Fifth Birthday. With Fond Love and Many Happy Returns of the Day. From Mrs Prentice.*

His father! He turned it over. No picture but a birthday

rhyme got up to look like a medieval manuscript: an ornate initial letter, a decorative border of flowers along the top and down the left-hand side. The colours were mainly red, green and gold. *This* was what he had confused with a prize label. He had seen it before ages ago and paid little attention. But now it was full of exciting significance.

He put the card in a used brown envelope and slipped it under the lino in the corner of his room. There were sounds downstairs. His mother was talking to someone. Big Gwen. His mother sounded grave. His heart missed a beat. He hoped it was nothing to do with his father. He went downstairs and into the living room.

'I didn't know you were in, duck,' his mother said. She turned to Big Gwen, who was smiling broadly. They seemed pleased to see him. 'He'll know more about it.'

'More about what?' asked Morley. He did up his blazer, hoping Big Gwen would notice it and say something.

'About the plane crash.'

They knew more than he did. 'What plane crash?'

His mother gave him a strange look. He felt uneasy. 'You've been to confession?'

'Yeh, c-course, Mom, but –'

'And you don't know anything about the crash?'

'No, I, er, went St James. B-But what crash?'

'St James?' She frowned and mouthed something, which meant he was in for it when Big Gwen had gone.

He was. Big Gwen went without commenting on his school uniform, obviously aware that something was wrong.

'It's a church b-by our school.'

'I didn't know you were going over there to confession.'

'Well, I w-wasn't to begin with. But then I found out I'd left my maths book at school and the h-homework's got to be in by Monday, so I went over to get it. I was coming out of school, going towards the bus, then I saw this Catholic church and I thought best to go then – instead of coming back to Upfield. I mean, say I'd been too late?'

'So if there hadn't been a plane crash I wouldn't have known you'd gone there.'

'W-Well, what does it matter? What's wrong with going to another church, anyroad? It was Catholic.' He improvised wildly. 'Father Smythe said we *ought* to go to other churches sometimes, particularly to St Chad's up town. He said it was a masterpiece and it was *our* cathedral.'

'You never said anything to me.'

'Well, it's hardly anything to tell: I didn't th-think you'd be interested.'

'I'm always interested in what really matters.'

He rushed in. 'Well, I'm never sure. You only asked one little question ab-bout the art school. You never asked about what it was like, or about friends or teachers or lessons or anything.' He sensed some of his shots had gone home. 'Anyway, what about this plane crash?'

She heaved a deep sigh. 'In Upfield. They were talking about it in the Co-op. Mrs Cameron saw it when she went to confession. It crashed in Baltimore Road by the park, and I thought you'd been there, and well . . . naturally, I was a bit worried. She said it just missed the church. It was a miracle.'

# II

'Avro Anson, be buggered,' jeered Reggie Nolan. 'It was an Auster, a light plane.'

'No it weren't,' said Reggie Kelp, 'it was an Avro Anson, big plane. Our Ernie seen it crash. He was *there*.'

'Funny, your Ernie don't go nowhere, don't do nothing all day long for months and months on end, then all of a sudden he just happens to be just where this plane crashes. Funny.'

'You calling me a liar?' demanded Kelp.

'Well, I don't really know, to be truthful, do I? I mean it might be it's your Ernie what's the *liar* and you're just daft enough to believe him.'

'Naw, course I don't believe him – all the time.' Kelp's long, rubbery face looked confused.

Instead of, as usual, hanging round the pig bin, the scruffs had moved a few yards down the road and were hanging around Morley.

Morley was drawing his house in pencil. It was a perspective view: the task Mr Sitwell had set them for homework. He had left out his strangely situated main door; he would be replacing it later with a window. Later still he'd go to Eachley Lane and find a suitable front door to graft onto the front wall of his drawing where main doors properly belonged. Even the scruffs had doors at the fronts of their houses, Morley reflected a little glumly.

'Was anybody k-killed?' he asked, for something to say.

'Yeh, pilot, a whatsit, a copper and two kids,' said Kelp. 'Blood everywhere. Bloody Jerries.'

'Er, Kelpie,' said Nolan gently, 'the war's been over five month. Can't you remember them parties in the road – two of them? And the bonfires?'

'Add it was od the dews at the flicks, add od the wireless,' said the adenoidal Betts twins, chewing vigorously on their gum.

The Betts twins were very neatly dressed but still scruffs in Morley's mother's eyes as they hung round the pig bin with the Reggies.

'Naw, nobody killed,' Nolan said to Morley. 'It come down in the road, hardly any traffic. Got smashed up a bit. The pilot was okay, and the bloke what was with him. Was on our wireless.'

'Add ours,' said the Betts twins.

Humiliated by Nolan, Kelp turned on Morley. 'You're just a great big show off, you are.'

Morley had thought twice about wearing his blazer and art school tie to go out drawing in the road: perhaps it *was* showing off. 'Well, our other coat's ripped and –'

'What you going on about?' said Kelp, brow furrowed. 'I mean *you* standing in the road, doing your drawing, just so's everybody can see you. Showing off. Just cause you go to that daft drawing school.'

'He's drawing his house, you twat,' Nolan answered for him. 'In't you, Morle?'

'Yes, yeh, gorra do it for homework.' He shrugged as if he didn't think much of the idea.

'Yeh, I *know* he's drawing his house,' retorted Kelp, 'but why's he got to do it standing out in the road is what I'm going on about. Why can't he do it *inside* his house? I would, it'd be warmer and that and you could sit down and everything.'

'Cause he's got to *look* at it to see what it *looks* like, bollockbrains.'

Kelp was in a D class, second from the bottom according to his summer report, which he'd been foolish enough to show them. 'Don't he know what his bleeding house looks like yet?' he screeched. 'God strewth, Morle, how long you lived there? I bet you're always coming home and going in the wrong house.'

'Ar, good idea, you could go in that Beryl Pinder's by mistake, when she's having a bath, like,' said Nolan.

Eric Beswick joined them. 'Beryl Pinder. Whoa-er.' He spat. Eric, known as Perky, was tall, thin, dark haired and also well dressed. Like the twins, though, a scruff, according to Morley's mother. He was about a year older than Morley and had recently started work at the Motor Works.

'Warrow, Perk,' said the Reggies and the Betts.

'Warrow, Ec,' said Morley, not quite daring to call him by his nickname.

'What'd *you* do then, Perk, if you seen Beryl Pinder bare in the bath?'

'Dive in,' said Eric, his face expressionless. 'Give her a seeing to.'

The others laughed and Morley did his best to join in.

Eric looked at Morley. 'When's your dad coming home, then?'

''Bout five weeks, he's . . .'

But Eric was looking at Morley's drawing. 'Dying out, drawing. Wun't last. Teks ages. Get a camera. Snap. Finished,' he said in his strange clipped voice. 'Our uncle said. Used to be all drawings. In the papers. Not now. All photos now. What's your new school like, then?'

Morley could have said, Smashing, we started a formal design based on wild flowers and seashells and we're also designing a child's alphabet. I'm doing G for golliwog. But he didn't. He couldn't think of anything else to say that wouldn't be ridiculed. He said in an accent as tough as he could make it, 'Orright, we have a birrof a l-laugh and that.'

'Sonly pansies go to them schools,' said Kelp, 'pansies and sissies.'

Nolan said, 'But you got to have artists. Okay, not in the papers no more, like Perky said, but you still got to have them.'

'What for?' asked Perky.

'Ooh, for loads a things.'

'Yeh. But what?'

'Well, er, whatsits, comics for one thing,' said Nolan.

'Ar, comics. But nothing else.'

'No, nothing else really.'

Morley found it difficult to concentrate while the need for artists was being discussed as if he weren't there. He looked at the circular landing window on the side of his house: the perspective was going to be tricky. Perhaps he could substitute a rectangular one. Anyway, weren't circular landing windows another indication of municipal houses?

'Them blokes what do the lines in the road,' said Kelp, apparently forgetting whose side he was on. 'They got to be good artists to get it straight and that.'

'Not much cop if the road goes round a corner,' observed Nolan.

Neil Gunn came round the corner. If anything, Neil was a shade more intelligent than Reg Kelp. He was small with a pink angelic face but was plainly a scruff in all other respects. 'What's Morle writing then?'

I collect house numbers, you twat, Morley said mentally. I've just got up to 218. He laughed bleakly to himself. He wasn't getting the respect he deserved. However, his mental laughter freed him enough to find a voice that wouldn't stammer too much. 'Course, you're right, Ec, there in't *very* m-many drawings in the papers no more, but like Reg Nolan said, there's comics. And there's books and b-book covers and th-that. The writing on shops and on lorries and vans: it's all art. But the really b-big thing nowadays for artists is cartoon films, like Disney, W-Walt Disney.'

'Who's she when she's at home?' asked Kelp.

Morley ignored him. 'Mickey Mouse, D-Donald Duck, Snow White, they got to be drawn by artists. *And*, *and* wallpaper's got to be designed, like, by artists and all.'

Perhaps wallpaper wasn't such a good example: the scruffs' interest, such as it was, was waning.

'And you do all this kind a stuff at this school?' asked Nolan with a yawn that showed dirty crooked teeth.

Morley nodded the lie. Then thought of something to reclaim their attention. 'Oh and there's J-Jane in the *Mirror*; that's drawn by an artist.'

'*You* don't draw her, at *your* school,' Kelp told him.

Morley decided that that was more or less what he *would* be doing. 'Yeh, in a way, cause next year, we'll be drawing tarts.' He cringed a little. His mother was several yards away over the road indoors but he had the uncomfortable feeling she could hear.

'You got tarts at your school, thed, Borley?' asked the Betts twins, chewing gum gleaming.

'Yeh, it's mixed like Redhill, but we do a lot a things separate. But we don't draw *them* tarts, the tarts who – what go to the school, we got proper models, *bare* models.'

'Models!' scoffed Kelp. 'That's no bleeding good.'

'Mind you,' said Reg Nolan, 'I wouldn't mind having a model of that Beryl Pinder, all bare, ay, Perky, with her legs wide open?' He turned to Morley, his expression mocking. 'If you *really* got these models, Morle, what they med out of, then? Whatsit, balsa? Balsa-wood tarts?'

The others laughed.

'No, not b-balsa models: real live, grown-up tarts.'

'You just said bodels, Borley,' said the Betts, 'didd't he, Perk?'

'Y-Yeh, that's what they *call* them: *m-models*, *artists'* models,' said Morley just avoiding saying bodels. He cast a wary glance towards his house and dropped his voice a little. 'Jane in the *Mirror* in't just a m-med-up tart out the artist's head, y'know. No, the artist's got a model – two, really. He uses the one tart cause she's got a bostin face but only small tits and the other one cause she's got neat tits and legs but a lousy face. They pay them l-loads of money, m-models.' He had their close if suspicious attention now.

'Get out of it,' said Nolan, 'pull the other one.'

'Liar,' accused Kelp.

'What's he draw them for?' asked Neil Gunn, screwing his face up.

'Who cares,' said Perky, almost smiling, 'if he really does.'

'Honest, Morle? You *really* draw real bare tarts? Tits and hairs and everything?' Nolan's usually narrowed sly eyes were wide.

'Second and third years do: we do it next year,' improvised Morley. 'You can't do it till you're fourteen, it's the law. Your mom or dad has gorra sign this pap-per to say you can. All artists do it; it's normal. Go up the Art Gallery up town and see, if you don't believe us. They say it's harder than anything to draw a bare tart, but if you *can* do it p-properly, then you can draw anything.'

They were silent, undoubtedly convinced and impressed. It was no more than his due. He was, after all, part of a superior world of selected people.

Then Perky Beswick and Reggie Nolan said, 'You dirty little sod, Morley.'

'Dirty little sod, Borley,' echoed the Betts twins.

'Dirty little sod, Morle,' added Neil Gunn and Reggie Kelp a little raggedly.

# 12

'Do we not all of us, now, know somebody, with lots of, shall we say, charm?' asked Canon Reilly of the congregation at eight o'clock Mass. 'Perhaps you have a friend – or a cousin – Peter we will we call him – who has this wonderful charm, who does conjuring tricks and clever impersonations, who talks in a fancy kind of way, is reckoned to be handsome, a great one with the ladies, very popular with everybody at the pub. A man with many talents who is very well read, who likes valuable antiques and pictures. Has his own motorcar! "Good old Peter," says everybody.'

Morley was taking in every word; Peter sounded close to the sort of person he wanted to be.

'But would he be at your bedside when you had the pleurisy?' went on the canon. 'Would he pay for a Mass for the repose of the soul of your poor, recently dead mother? He who has got on in life and wants for nothing. "What an important fellow I am," he says to himself strutting around Rathkeale. But the important thing to consider is, would Almighty God necessarily agree?'

Morley had less interest in these latter aspects of Peter's nature. He turned his attention towards himself – a transformed self with no brace or stammer strutting around Redhill thinking what an important fellow he was. The scruffs treating him with great respect; Sheila Godden at the bottom of the road, who until now had merely looked through him, smiling shyly . . . No, better, at school: effortlessly catching the chalk, giving in the best homework, winning competitions. The fair Catholic girl hanging around the back gate of the school at hometime: *How on earth did you think up that wonderfully original idea for your history homework at the beginning of term? And you won first prize in the Wrighton Competition as well . . .* Nearby, invisible to the fair girl, is his dad smiling with pride – not *too* small after all.

A talented and popular Morley . . . like Peter. And why not? Maybe Peter had once been like him. Had sent away for a conjuring outfit (as Morley had once considered doing as a route to fame and popularity), practised his impersonations, developed his talents. He thought of his history homework with a warm glow of satisfaction: a step in the right direction. Although much more was needed. But the Wrighton Competition? He could have done much better there. There was still time to submit another painting, Mr Sitwell had reminded them on Friday. He could start it today. He could improve his English homework as well; Miss Swealter might read the best essays out. Popularity had to be worked for. He was creating much to look forward to. He glanced around at the familiar congregation, already beginning to feel superior. Most people were getting up to go to communion. He was a fortnightly communicant and this was his week off, he tried to convey to anybody who might be wondering. Anyway, he would be going next week. Or perhaps leave it for a fortnight – yes, after all, he had made the attempt yesterday.

It was late on Sunday afternoon. Morley scrutinized the half-finished watercolour of Redhill Farm pinned to a board, lying on his bed. The farm was a half-timbered building more than three hundred years old and lay at the edge of the asylum boundary. He'd started it this morning. He'd gone with Micky. The autumn tree to the left made a nice splash of colour and he was pleased with his imaginative treatment of the sky. And yet . . . For all its age, the house lacked character, just black and white, no visible brick or stone except in the chimney. He considered painting it as if it were in strong sunlight and perhaps substituting brick for the whitewashed areas of the lower floor. Still, it was better than his other entry. He put the board onto the floor and turned it to the wall. He'd look at it afresh later.

He started packing his satchel for the following day. He picked up his history book and looked at the final version of his family tree now complete with the names of his dad's family – excluding the children who'd died – dates of birth invented. He admired again the old English lettering, the browned edges of the cartridge paper done to a turn; the pencil-crayoned wax seal and length of ribbon pasted in the bottom right-hand corner. He felt tempted to put it in his satchel and show Micky Plant tomorrow. But Micky might copy his idea; better wait till Tuesday when Micky would hear Mr Griffiths' praise as he held it up to show the class. About to put the history book back on his bedroom shelf, he was struck by a pleasant thought. He looked at the family tree again.

His father had two brothers and a sister. There must be *cousins*. Cousins were nearly as valuable as brothers – relations he had often felt the conspicuous lack of. Perhaps his cousins were good at art like him. Maybe there was *already* a cousin at Balsley School of Art, who would become a friend. His imagination leapt. Suppose he'd already *met* one of his cousins. Although there was no one else with the surname Charles in his year, there might be in the second or third year. He would listen out. Or if this cousin were the son of his father's sister then his surname wouldn't be Charles. And of course, his cousin might be a girl. Perhaps the fair girl who'd said 'parst' was his cousin!

Now keep cool, said Nigel, the boy sleuth inside his head. He put a brake on his fantasies.

He took out the precious birthday card from under the lino in the corner of the room and examined it closely, hoping it might reveal further secrets about the unknown half of his family. This was a link to a *real* mystery, so different from the ones he'd only dreamt up in the past: spies in the Lickey Hills; the caretaker at Redhill Council School shining lights up his chimney to direct German bombers to the Motor and Aero Works less than a mile down the road; Harry Braithewaite, a spy posing as a loony outside Redhill Asylum, counting the military vehicles and the unassembled bombers on their low loaders coming from the Aero Works . . . He was thrilled by the card but there was nothing further to learn from it. He returned it to its hiding place.

But suppose his dad's family were people to be ashamed of and *that* was why his father and mother would have nothing to do with them. Finding out who they were might add to his problems. Half seriously, his mind went to a future history lesson. Mr Griffiths, still on family history, asking about occupations. Let's start with your paternal grandfather. His finger pointing at random. Farmer, sir. Foundry worker. Coach driver. Shopkeeper. Blacksmith. Schoolmaster.

Then Morley: Lavatory attendant, sir. The laughter. The pale, undersized, stammering brace-wearer who wore his blazer badge on his cap with the funny dad and no front door, whose grandad was a lavatory attendant.

He packed his English book with its page on 'My Favourite Fictional Character'; just changed from Nigel the more intelligent of the boy 'tecs to Tom Sawyer – a choice befitting a more successful, newer Morley.

He heard the kitchen door open and close. His mother was back from Benediction. He mentally viewed her progress through the house to the coat hooks at the foot of the stairs, hanging up her coat, putting on her pinafore.

'Are you up there, duck?' She sounded quite cheerful, Morley was relieved to note. Of course, Frank was out of the house, at his brother's in Coventry.

'Yeh, Mom, just finishing my homework.'

'What's happened to the badge on your cap?' Her voice had suddenly switched to its more usual sour pitch.

Morley's heart sank. Anything not quite as it should be was enough to make his mother jump to all sorts of disturbing conclusions. 'Ah, still got it safe, Mom,' he said guardedly. 'Just coming down.' He obviously hadn't stuffed his cap properly into his mac pocket. He sauntered into the living room affecting a yawn to suggest unconcern, without any idea of a suitable explanation.

'So why isn't it on your cap, then?'

'It is,' he said stupidly.

She stared at him. 'I sometimes wonder if you're right in the head, son. You say the badge is safe, whatever that means, then you say it's on your cap. I've just picked your cap up off the bottom of the stairs and there's isn't a badge on it.' She took the cap out of her pinafore pocket and plonked it on the table.

It should be easy enough tell the truth; he'd committed no crime. But honesty wasn't always the best policy with his mother. To confess that the badge wasn't a cap badge after he'd insisted that it was, then not telling her that he'd pulled it off when he'd discovered his mistake would be asking for trouble. It might result in her bad mood continuing for hours. 'That isn't m-my cap,' he heard himself saying. Thank God he hadn't yet put his name in it: something he'd planned to do sooner or later with Micky Plant's marking ink.

He found the pressure of her mood enormous. 'It was in PT, Mom. I picked it up by mistake. I didn't realize till afterwards that it w-wasn't mine. I'm sure I know whose it is; he must have got mine. He was next to me in the changing room. Thin kid. Called Babbage. And d'you know what? His mom brought him to school on the first day. *And* he wears short trousers.'

She seemed determined not to smile. 'Why didn't you get it sorted out later, then?'

'Because it was Friday, right at the end of the day. After PT we went straight home. I only saw it wasn't m-my cap when I was on the bus.'

Morley felt resentful. In spite of his perfectly reasonable explanation about the badge, his mother had seemed distant and suspicious all through tea and her mood had barely lifted when she went down to Big Gwen's. It wasn't fair, always thinking the worst of him, never believing him. He'd show her he was telling the truth, all right. He went to her sewing basket and took a needle and a length of bottle-green cotton. He would sew the badge on again. She would be at Big Gwen's for at least an hour. Babbage, he would tell her on her return, had called in with his cap. Lives quite near the Motor Works, he'd say. Bumped into Micky Plant who told him his address.

Up in his room, his resolve weakened. Why on earth was he bothering? It was too much like hard work. It was a lousy story, anyway. And he'd have to take the badge off again before school tomorrow; and still sooner or later come up with an explanation. Blow her: he'd got more important things to get on with. If she asked tomorrow he'd say that Babbage was absent. He stuck the needle in a tram ticket, wound the cotton around it and shoved it in his satchel, then without too much difficulty lost himself in his painting of Redhill Farm.

# 13

It was English on the following day. Morley was trying to think amusing thoughts to reduce the risk of stammering should he be called upon to read. But images of Micky Plant wearing goggles and the boy with cab-door ears were, by repetition, becoming humourless. He tried to think of something new.

Two pupils had already read their Favourite Fictional Characters. Now a girl with plaits was coming to the end of her piece. She liked Kim, she said, because he was colourful, resourceful and had a sense of humour, and she was impressed with Kipling's prose.

Miss Swealter nodded approvingly. 'Splendid, very well expressed, er, Nancy.'

Micky Plant was chosen next. His favourite character was Rockfist Rogan, RAF. He summarized two of Rockfist Rogan's exploits without saying why he liked him or anything about him. He read in a curious low monotone that was quite at odds with his usual confident-seeming manner.

There was an awkward silence. Miss Swealter said, 'Mmm, I don't think I've come across this character. Rockfist, er . . . ?'

'Rogan, miss,' mumbled Micky.

'And the author?'

Micky didn't know.

'Perhaps you know the name of the book he appears in?'

'*The Champion*, miss,' said Micky, his voice barely audible.

'Is that one of your, er, boys' papers?'

It was clear that in Miss Swealter's book proper Favourite Fictional Characters did not come out of *The Champion* or any other boys' paper.

Morley was delighted. This was a valuable addition to a collection of things to laugh about. He spluttered almost audibly with glee. Which was probably why Miss Swealter noticed him and asked him to read next. The possibility of serious stammering when reading in public wasn't high and his amusement at Micky's poor performance increased his confidence enormously. Nevertheless, his heart beat wildly as he stood up and cleared his throat. He was particularly pleased with the last paragraph of his account even though it was largely culled from *Monroe's Universal Reference Book*.

'And now at the foot of Cardiff Hill,' he concluded, 'in Hannibal, Missouri, where Mark Twain lived for most of his youth, stands a fine bronze statue of Tom Sawyer and Huck Finn. A fitting tribute to these famous heroes of fiction.'

Miss Swealter said, 'Very well composed and expressively read, and I like the way you round things off with an interesting snippet of geography and history. It's Charles, isn't it?'

He was sure he had avoided blushing. His first homework – and his reading praised so highly in front of the class. And she knew his name! He was already on his way to being someone who stood out from the crowd. For most of the remainder of the lesson, when he wasn't congratulating himself he gazed adoringly at small, slender Miss Swealter. How could he not have seen earlier how very attractive she was? And tomorrow, he thought happily, he would be handing in his much more elaborate history homework; he could hardly wait.

He gave in his second Wrighton Competition entry at break, pleased that it had turned out quite well and certain that it was better than his first entry. He didn't think about his badgeless cap until he was at home, but his mother seemed to have forgotten all about it.

In Mr Griffiths' history lesson on Tuesday morning Morley sat near the back of the room, well out of range of chalk-throwing, and again his heart beat wildly, this time in pleasant anticipation of compliments from the teacher. His history exercise book lay modestly closed on his desk.

'So what were we doing last lesson?' Mr Griffiths asked, legs apart, rotating his shoulders forwards and then back-wards.

'Family trees, sir,' chorused some of the girls.

'Correct. So let's see what you've been up to.'

A boy and a girl were appointed to collect the books. The blackboard was full of notes under the heading 'Birming-ham Industries' for the class to copy into their rough books.

At his old-fashioned high desk in the corner Mr Griffiths went through the history exercise books, giving each only a brief glance. He frequently put a book to one side. Good or bad? Morley wondered. He waited excit-edly for the loud exclamation of pleased surprise when Mr Griffiths reached his book. Another one in the eye for Micky Plant. Rockfist Rogan, RAF! Ha!

Mr Griffiths was suddenly standing, going up and down on his toes. He slowly picked up a book and looked at it, eyebrows high. Morley half closed his eyes and held his breath. Mr Griffiths held the book up for all to see. The burnt-edged document! He'd done it! His eyes were wide open now. Yippee! His dad at the back of the room smiled proudly. Morley's delight was intense.

But only for a couple of seconds. *It wasn't his book*. It was similar but this one had a seal of real sealing wax on a real ribbon at the bottom. Had somebody copied?

Mr Griffiths put the book down, looked solemnly at the class and vigorously thumped his chest. '*Mea culpa, mea culpa, mea maxima culpa*. Ask the papists about that one,' he said in a stage whisper to a small boy in the front row, '*they'll* tell you what it means. I should have told you,' he resumed to the class, '*warned* you, *threatened* you. But I didn't. I'm obviously out of touch. Then of course I didn't take into account the damage possibly done you under the wartime privations of your previous education. Or the fact that you must obviously patronize olde worlde tea shoppes in your spare time.'

Morley didn't know what on earth he was talking about. Mr Griffiths picked up a number of books from the pile set aside on his desk and began holding them up one by one. Each bore a burnt-round-the-edge document, many lettered in old English script. All were more or less close relations of Morley's.

'How many pupils in this group?'

'Thirty-seven, sir,' said the fair-haired Catholic girl.

'And about ten, ten, *ten*, can you believe? Ten out of thirty-seven make me burnt offerings! You're not the first ones by any means: there've always been one or two. But *ten*.' He shook his head. 'Unbelievable. Did you all get together and conspire to torment me?' he asked in mock anguish. He addressed the tall boy who seemed to have no ears, whom Morley now knew as Hodge. 'I suppose you think burning round the edges makes 'em look more . . . historical, eh?'

Hodge grinned. 'Yes, sir,' he said.

It wasn't until the end of dinner time that Morley was able to start coming to terms with his disappointment and think afresh about his shining future.

*

He knew by his mother's laughter that Big Gwen was with her. She was always bright, generously disposed towards him and, it seemed, more interested in his activities in her company. He'd often wondered if it was an act put on for Big Gwen's benefit. Though frequently the effect lasted a short while after Big Gwen had gone home.

It was after school on Wednesday evening. He wiped his feet on the kitchen mat and went in. Still, he had to admit that Big Gwen made him feel better as well. She was handsome, always smiling, very shapely in a heavy-handed way and a highly suitable subject to have in mind for those who got up to nocturnal tricks.

'Hi, junior,' she said in the American she sometimes affected, caught from Russ, her daughter's boyfriend. Then, eyeing his school uniform as he took off his mac: 'My, don't *you* look swell?'

'Hello, duck,' said his mother almost as cheerfully. 'Yes, we just haven't got his blazer badge yet, have we? You're getting one soon, aren't you, duck?'

Morley nodded, hoping that she wouldn't ask him to put his cap on; thinking about its still badgeless state at the bottom of his satchel; ready to explain Babbage's continued absence.

'Gwen's got a present for you.'

'Wow!' exclaimed Morley.

'But you've got to guess before you can have it,' said Big Gwen playfully, hands behind her back.

Morley had no idea what it might be but wasn't at all averse to playing infantile games with Big Gwen. 'Scones,' he said, pretending eagerness as he remembered their slight disinfectant, turps or creosote flavour.

'Much, *much* better than that,' she said, fluttering her eyelids, thrusting out her generous bosom and swinging her body round from side to side like a huge little girl.

The chaotic erotic delights that danced in Morley's head made it necessary for him to edge round to the side of the table to conceal a sudden physical change. 'Some more Yankee wh-whiskey from Russ?'

'Warm,' she said. 'Give in?'

He nodded.

'Well, it *is* from Russ, all right.' She handed him a small brown paper bag spotted with paint.

Inside were two slim cartons printed in yellow and red. Films! 'Kodak, Verichrome Pan Film, 120, Made in USA,' he read, turning one of the boxes.

His joy was immense. The right size as well. But Russ would have remembered, he was like that. Morley had had the camera since the beginning of the war, a gift from his father for being brave and wearing his gas mask. Perhaps it was his in name only but he had the unquestioned use of it, although this didn't mean much as he'd never had a film. Films were practically unobtainable. He thought of the long queues he'd waited in without success; the rumours of films in distant suburbs he'd fruitlessly dashed off to; the promises made by Ron, his black-marketeer uncle, that had come to nothing.

Here was an opportunity to give Big Gwen an impulsive hug, but he didn't dare while his mother was there and anyway his condition intensified at the thought.

'Wow, cor, crumbs, th-thanks,' he said, and considered adding, Thanks awfully, as Nigel and Dick would undoubtedly have done.

'Well, it's Russ you've really got to thank,' said Big Gwen. 'He got them, but you've just missed him. He had to rush off about half an hour ago but he'll be back here on Friday night. D'you know, junior, he's been taking snaps of us for *hours*.' Big Gwen was looking particularly smart in a navy blue costume, only slightly marred by tiny, variously coloured specks of paint.

'Tell him what Russ wants to do on Friday,' said Morley's mother.

'Oh, yes,' said Big Gwen. 'He specially wants a picture of you. "My friend the famous English artist", he calls you. Isn't that cute, kid?' she said to Morley's mother.

Morley had done three paintings for Russ. His best, the last, was a landscape with Belbroughton village in the middle ground and an ivy-covered tree in the foreground. Russ had driven him and a slightly reluctant Beryl in the Chrysler to the viewpoint overlooking the village. 'I wanna tell the folks I was here on this very spot when the famous artist started this picture,' he'd explained to Morley. All the paintings had been carefully packed and posted off to his family in Milwaukee, where, said Russ later, they were now in specially made frames and greatly admired.

'And seeing you in that uniform,' said Big Gwen, 'well, you've got to wear it on Friday. Russ'll be thrilled to bits. He thinks it's so *English* that kids here wear uniforms for grammar school. And yours is a real art school uniform, isn't it?'

Morley nodded, thinking that now he definitely had to get his badges sorted out before Friday.

His mother said, 'That'll be nice, won't it, duck?'

# 14

It was Thursday evening. Thomas Donne's, the school outfitters in Corporation Street, popularly known as the Don, had got both badges for Balsley School of Art. There they were in the window fanned out below a youthful dummy (smiling despite lacking both legs) decked out in the complete Balsley School of Art uniform (except trousers). A rush of pride filled Morley as he surveyed the display. He wanted to turn round to people in the street and say, That's the school where I go. Only one person in forty or even fifty has the ability to go there.

He went into the shop, checked that nobody who looked as if they might be from the art school was there, became Dutch and effortlessly bought a cap badge. Then continuing in his Dutch role, he strolled along to Lyons in New Street for a cake and cup of tea.

As he drank his tea he read from *The Mystery of Swallings End*, his favourite Nigel and Dick book – his own copy. He had read it at least three times before but, having nothing else to read at the moment, it was still a great deal better than nothing. He continued reading it on the tram, trying not to worry about how he was going to explain to his mother which school badge went where without admitting he'd made a mistake. He forgot all about the bedridden man opposite Viceroy Close until he was well past.

At home he rushed up to his bedroom. It took about a quarter of an hour to sew on his new badge. He'd still not thought of an explanation; he trusted that something would occur to him when the time came. He put on his cap at a jaunty angle, then, keeping an ear open for her return, went into his mother's room to admire himself in the dressing-table mirror.

He stood where he could see himself almost full length. He stood very straight, slipped his hands into his blazer pockets and said in a BBC accent, 'And now at the foot of Cardiff Hill in Hannibal, Missouri, where Mark Twain spent most of his youth, stands a fine bronze statue of Tom Sawyer and Huck Finn. A fitting tribute to these famous heroes of fiction.' There was wild cheering. He pictured Miss Swealter with her fair skin, her teeth just visible as she smiled. 'Very well composed and expressively read,' she said in her lovely voice. 'I like the way you rounded things off. Charles, isn't it?' She knew his name! She knew his name! She hadn't mentioned Micky's!

Cheered by his performance and its reception, he felt ready to deal with anything. A couple of minutes later he heard the back door open. He left his cap on.

'Ah, *that's* better, duck,' his mother said as he came down the stairs. 'I always thought the other badge was *far* too big.'

He was only momentarily taken aback. 'Yeh, it was, you were dead right, Mom. Chap in the Don said other mothers had complained about how big the badges were as well,' he lied glibly, 'and how difficult it was to sew them onto the caps. He said *your* sewing was a lot better than most, your tucks were alm-most invisible – a shame to have to undo it.' He took his cap off. 'Yeh, this is the new badge. At least, they had them before the war, but they stopped making them. Just made do with the one badge, the big one. Some sort of econ-nomy drive. Some kids had it on their caps, some on their blazers.'

His mother seemed pleased at his flattery. 'Who sewed it on for you?'

'They did, in the Don,' said Morley, 'while I went for a cup of tea. At Lyons.' He didn't quite know why he'd told this particular lie: except that in some vague way, it would seem to lessen his involvement in the whole business of badges.

'Where's your other badge? The one you used to have on your cap?'

'Oh, it's in my satchel. I'll sew it on my blazer later.'

'Well, if you can manage it yourself, all right, duck.'

'Oh, yeh, won't be up to your s-standard, but I'd like to have a go.'

Morley sewed sitting on the bed in his room listening to *Send for Paul Temple Again*. The plot no longer made much sense but the programme was soothing company. And in a few moments his mother would switch over to *ITMA*. Life wasn't bad. School was turning out okay. There was the Wrighton Landscape Competition to look forward to. He thought about his two films from Russ; the photos Russ was going to take tomorrow night and send to America; art all day tomorrow; then Saturday when he had decided to visit his dad's old home – where he could now take photos. And soon he would have his school uniform complete. He sewed away happily.

There was a knock on the front door – or more correctly the side door. Not Big Gwen, mused Morley, she always came straight in through the back door. Not Frank, who was down the pub and wouldn't be in till much later; anyway, he had a key. Not Micky Plant, who almost never came round at night. He had exhausted all likely possibilities.

Wait, Nigel the boy 'tec urged Morley, didn't your mater go out a few minutes ago to fetch some coal?

Yes, said Morley.

Well, while she was out there she locked the back gate.

Of course, he'd heard the bolt being shot. She would lock it anyway before half nine – or send him out to do it – but as she was already out there getting coal . . . She'd lit a big fire earlier; he and she were to have baths later. Friday was their usual bath night, but in preparation for the photos Russ was going to take tomorrow afternoon, his mother had decided on baths tonight.

So it was probably Big Gwen, after all, knocking the door. One pleasant thought led to another.

He imagined being in the Pinders' loft watching Big Gwen in her bath through a tiny hole in the ceiling. He began to create the innocent circumstances that might lead to such an exciting situation.

He goes down to Big Gwen's to borrow . . . a suitcase. Big Gwen is about to have a bath as she's going out soon. You'll have to look for it yourself, junior; it's in the loft. The stepladder's out the back.

Morley is in the unlit loft cautiously moving along loose boards Percy has laid over the joists. There among a pile of junk is the suitcase. Nearby there's a pinprick of light coming through a small hole in the lath and plaster. He looks through and there's Big Gwen lying back in the bath soaping herself. Whoa-er!

Morley could just make out the buzz of muted conversation from downstairs. Pity the hole in his bedroom floor didn't give a view of the room underneath like the imagined one in Big Gwen's loft. Even though Big Gwen wouldn't be naked at the moment, she was still worth looking at. And he liked the idea of *secretly* looking at her. But sadly here the two holes, one in the downstairs ceiling, the other in his floor, weren't aligned. He oversewed the last stitch on his blazer badge two or three times, bit off the cotton, held the blazer up to admire, laid it on his bed, bolted his door and went over to the corner. As he pulled up the lino, the radio was turned off. Damn, he'd miss Tommy Handley. What on earth had happened? Everybody listened to *ITMA*. It even made his mother laugh and Big Gwen would never miss it. He put his ear to the hole. He could hear but it was an effort.

'. . . another thing, Mrs Charles. Do you know that although the war has been over only a little while, Canon Reilly says already attendance at all the Masses falls off a little bit every week? Would you not have thought the opposite? That people would now be showing a little gratitude?'

Sister Twomey! Didn't she know better than to call on people just when *ITMA* was starting? Sister called on the Charleses every three months or so. A vague tinge of guilt stirred as always in Sister's presence. Without really wanting to, he thought of her bald head beneath her coif. Nuns shaved their heads every morning, he'd heard, to show that they weren't vain.

'The canon says the youngsters are amongst the worst,' Sister was saying. 'Mind, that has always been the tendency, Mrs Charles. As soon as they go to non-Catholic grammar schools, or start work, it seems that their faith is put under a little bit of a strain and they have a little battle on their hands. Your little boy is now at an art school, I believe?'

'Er, yes, Sister,' said his mother.

'Well, wasn't he always the little artistic one with his little pictures? And did he have to pass the scholarship for his new school?'

'Oh, yes,' said his mother, 'art and, er . . .'

'You didn't want the little fellow to go to the Catholic grammar school, then?'

'Oh, yes, Sister, he took the exam for St Philip's but he didn't pass.'

'Ah, yes, I think I remember. But this is not a Catholic art school, Mrs Charles?'

'No, Sister. If there had been a Catholic art school, that's where I'd have definitely sent him. *Definitely*.' Morley could sense her awkwardness. 'But there aren't any, as far as I know, at least near here. Oh, did you notice the picture, Sister, in the hall?'

'Ah, no, I did not. Now, am I right in thinking that soon Mr Charles will be back from the war, Mrs Charles?'

Both voices now fell to undecipherable murmurs as Sister and his mother presumably went in to the hall to see the picture.

It was a watercolour Morley had copied from a small devotional picture of St Theresa the Little Flower his mother kept in her missal.

The murmurs in the hall continued. It wouldn't be a bad idea to make the hole in his floor bigger, thought Morley. His penknife was in his blazer. He worked as quickly and silently as possible, carefully avoiding the electric cable, putting the parings into his trouser pocket. He put his ear to the enlarged hole. Sister and his mother had obviously returned to the living room; he could hear Sister perfectly.

'. . . wondered whether to catch him after Mass and have a little word with him myself but he is always gone so quickly. And he is *never* at communion nowadays, Mrs Charles – not once in months have I seen him. Mind, there was just one occasion when I was not there in June, when I was away to Cork for a little while but . . .'

Morley pulled his head away; he felt faint, then realized he wasn't breathing. He bit his lip hard as if the pain would distract him from Sister's terrible revelation. God, now he was *really* for it. This wasn't anxiety about something that *might* happen: it *had* happened. Any minute now and his mother would call up, or come up to drag him downstairs to confront Sister. Even if she didn't, he'd have to face the music sooner or later. But first he had to think – fast. Trying to control his violent shaking and erratic breathing, he put on his blazer, crept downstairs and quietly let himself out of the side door.

# 15

The darkness outside was pierced with light from the street lamp next to the pig bin. Although it had been functioning for the last fortnight it still looked strange after nearly six years of blackout. But the novelty was lost on Morley. He strode up Woods Park Road to the corner, his mind completely seized up, biting great strips off the ends of his fingernails. Then he changed his mind, turned round and hurried down the road. A hundred yards down, he turned into the right of way that led to Marshfield Drive, the road where Micky Plant lived – not that he intended to visit him. He was just walking blindly, driven by the need to be well away from his mother until he could conjure up some sort of . . . what?

There was a couple cuddling against the high board fence that lined most of the right of way. The man was a soldier, his forage cap pulled out in feeble imitation of a Yank's. He had his greatcoat wrapped round his girl. The girl was giving little giggles and squeals but Morley was too distracted to be curious. He slowed down. This was the biggest challenge of his life, the stuff of his worst nightmares. And he knew why it had happened. Last Sunday, in spite of all the lessons that were constantly being flung at him, he'd as good as decided not to go to confession this coming Saturday but to leave it till the next, and again God had struck.

If you get me out of this one, God, he promised, I'll be in confession first thing *this* Saturday, *definitely*. And I'll go to Upfield to Canon Reilly, he bravely added. Then he remembered Father Smythe's frequent reminder from long-ago first communion classes: 'You cannot bargain or trifle with God.' No, sorry, sorry, sorry, Morley amended, I'll go whatever happens. *Definitely*. *This* Saturday. *And* to Upfield.

He was in Marshfield Drive, a road of privately owned houses; a superior world to his own municipal one in Woods Park Road. He saw Perky Beswick coming towards him, only yards away. Too late to avoid him in the now well-lit road.

'W-Warrow, Ec.'

'Warrow, Morle. Still doing the drawing then?'

'Well, yeh, you know, s-sort of, Ec,' was all Morley could come up with.

'Just been out with this tart. Lives down Marsh Avenue. Whoa-er! Works up the Kalamazoo. In the offices. We was in her air raid shelter. Let us have a good feel. Tits and twat and that. Whoa-er! Seeing her again. Tomorrow. Going up the flicks. Cowbag on at Upfield. Heard this one, Morle?'

Morley was desperate to get away, but forced himself to appear to be listening.

'There was this real neat tart. Russian. Called Tara Knickersoff,' said Perky, voice and face expressionless. 'She was in Lewis's. With her friend. They was looking at this underwear. This friend says, "Come on, Tara Knickers-off!" And this bloke . . .'

Morley's tense mind couldn't follow the story properly, though it seemed to closely resemble most of Perky's other recent jokes about tarts with names that were open to misinterpretation by passing blokes.

The joke seemed to be finished. Morley laughed politely. 'I'll r-remember that. For school,' he managed.

'Thought they was posh. At your school,' Perky observed.

'*Naw*,' said Morley, trying to convey in one word the wild, coarse nature of Balsley School of Art. 'Gosh, g-gorra rush, gorra meet our m-mom off the tram. She's gorrall these parcels.'

'This in't her tram stop. This is Marshfield.'

'Er, no, our mom's got this friend. W-What lives here. In Marshfield. She's bad in b-bed. This friend.' He was speaking in short flat bursts just like Perky.

'Here's another one, Morle,' Perky said, unmoved by Morley's urgency.

Morley gritted his teeth. 'I gorra –'

But Perky recited in his flat voice,

> '*Ever had your 'ole felt?*
> *Ever had your 'ole felt?*
> *Ever had your 'ole felt hat on?*'

Morley stretched his lips in a parody of a smile.

> '*To fight for the cunt.*
> *To fight for the cunt.*
> *To fight for the cunt-er-ry.*
> *To piss.*
> *To p–*'

Now there really was a tram. Morley could hear it clearly though he couldn't see whether it was to or from town. 'Really g-gorra go, Ec. That might be her tram. Er, neat p-poem, Ec.' Morley sped down the road and turned right, onto the main road and out of sight of Perky.

He was breathless, alone again with his enormous problem. Neglect of his religious duties was unforgivable. For his mother the Catholic Church was central to everything.

It was probably the life-or-death-seeming enormity of the situation that eventually got his brain working. He was walking along the greenish-lit Bristol Road South towards the Motor Works, the rhythm of his breathing gradually returning to something like normal. This needed a really courageous move, he decided, full of barefaced lies. He'd have to confess them all, of course.

He reached a café much patronized by motor workers, its windows uncurtained and steamy. It briefly flashed through his mind how pleasant it would be to be here free of problems, having a cup of tea and a Cornish pasty, late at night, with no one knowing where he was. He peered through the window. Twenty-five past nine, he could just make out from the clock on the wall. He'd better not be away too long; it might make things look even worse. He'd explain his absence by saying he'd been at Micky Plant's borrowing Indian ink for his homework.

He shuddered as he visualized his homecoming. His mother white with fury, full of shame that she'd failed as a Catholic mother. Her fingers itching to clout his head or hit him with anything to hand, the broom, the poker, the toasting fork. Then she'd spit out Sister's accusations.

His defence began to take shape. To begin with he'd have to look shocked. Then smile – understanding dawning. Shake his head, gently.

Mom, Mom, can't you see what's happened? She's got me mixed up with . . . Freddie.

Freddie, who?

Freddie O'Brian at church. You know that kid who was sick when we made our first communion. Freddie O'Brian didn't exist but Morley's first communion was a long time ago, long enough, he hoped, for his mother to have only a hazy memory of it.

Why should she get you mixed up with him?

Cause he *looks* a bit like me. He's older than me but he's small for his age. She was always getting us mixed up in confirmation class.

And then a subtle touch. Course, Freddie started work

last Easter; and, well, you know what happens sometimes when kids start work . . .

His mother, after hearing similar remarks from Sister less than an hour earlier, might give him credit for thinking along the same lines. But how do you *know*? she would say, not yet convinced.

He would be a model of frankness. Well, to be honest, I *don't* know, Mom, but its the only explanation I can think of. *I* go to communion every fortnight all right. But there's this kid, never a very strong Catholic, starts work, mixes with much older lads, lets things slide, stops going to confession and communion. Sister notices, but gets us mixed up.

His mother would persist. But Sister knows very well who you are; she comes here three or four times a year. She knows you do art, knows you go to the art school. We were talking about you only tonight.

Yeh, course she does. And she knows what Freddie does and about his family. It's just she gets us mixed up. You see, I didn't know Sister had come here tonight, otherwise I'd have come downstairs and then she'd have realized straight away who I really was. I wish you'd called me, then none of this would have happened.

It was thin but the best he could do.

He was entering his own road. He became aware that it was cold and windy. He was passing the Pinders' house. But thoughts of seeing Russ tomorrow and having his photo taken – even the gift of the films – failed to raise his spirits. The water he was in was far too deep and murky to contemplate life beyond the next half hour.

# 16

Morley called out twice but it was clear that his mother wasn't in. Nevertheless, he checked every room, half afraid that the news of his missed communions had caused her to faint with shock. Although the alternative that she was out looking for him to dole out punishment in the street gave him no more comfort. He went fretfully round the house again looking in the closet, wardrobe and under the beds, biting his lip when he wasn't biting what was left of his nails. He went into the bathroom and, without thinking, turned on the taps. He locked the door. A bath. Might help settle him down, then a splashing with very cold water to brace him – and as a sort of punishment.

As he lay in the bath his panic grew. Would his mother believe his explanation? He'd never, of course, mentioned Freddie O'Brian before. It was a very weak story. Much depended on the conviction with which he told it.

He decided to skip the cold splashing: he was miserable enough. A very bleak thought struck him. If his mother *did* believe his story, then he might be even worse off. She might rush off to the convent in Upfield and explain to Sister that she had mistaken her son for Freddie O'Brian. And Sister would tell her that there wasn't a Freddie O'Brian and she knew perfectly well who her son was.

He ground his teeth, closed his eyes tight, held his

breath, pressed his hands against his ears in a fruitless attempt to wipe out the whole of existence. But after no more than a few seconds everything rushed back with greater intensity, bringing a further depressing thought: he could have avoided all this if he'd kept his wits about him. It just hadn't occurred to him that Sister had been spying on him. The church was big and always full. He hadn't even been aware that Sister was always there at eight o'clock Mass. On the few occasions he had noticed her she was in the back pew, head bent in prayer. So on the other Sundays she must have been hidden behind one of the grilled arches at the back, keeping him under observation. If only he'd allowed for every possibility, he could have *pretended* to go to communion on some occasions. Gone up to the altar rails then mingled with the returning communicants; Sister couldn't have been watching him every second. Or he could have worked out something else –

'Are *you* in there?' came his mother's acid voice as she rattled the bathroom door. He leapt up in fright; he hadn't heard her come into the house.

'Out in a minute, Mom,' he called back with an effort at breeziness, but his voice sounded hoarse.

As he towelled himself he decided he'd stick to his story but make it vaguer and leave the name Freddie O'Brian well out of it, and just, well . . . hope for the best.

He was still wet under his arms and between his toes as he hurriedly pulled his clothes on. He continued drying his hair with the towel as he went in to the living room. 'Hello, Mom.'

'I'll give you "Hello, Mom", my lad,' his mother hissed. 'I wish to goodness I'd never let you go to that, that school. What you get up to, it's, it's . . .' She turned down her lips and shuddered.

It wasn't going as he'd rehearsed. 'W-Why?' he asked lamely. He'd started missing confession and communion months ago; it had nothing to do with going to the art school.

'You know all right, my lad, don't try and pretend with me.'

'But there's lots of Catholics at this school – lots more than Redhill Council,' he tried wildly.

'That's got nothing at all to do with it – that only makes matters *worse*.'

'What d'you mean, Mom?' he asked cautiously.

'Don't act daft with me, my lad. You could have passed for St Philip's if you'd put your mind to it.'

'I did,' Morley protested, even more confused by his mother's strange departure from the script. 'I d-did my best.'

'You? *You*? Do your best? Your mind's too full of rubbish for you to do your best – just like that pig bin. If you'd gone to St Philip's you wouldn't be doing this, for a start off.'

'It wasn't me,' he mumbled, 'it was a lad who –'

She wasn't listening. 'Evil-minded swine! But God isn't mocked; the wicked are always punished, you'll see. I've a good mind to go and see Canon Reilly on Saturday, and I know what *he'll* say all right.'

Morley felt sick and bewildered. She hadn't found out what he got up to at night as well, had she? It would be a relief to just give in, admit everything and accept the consequences. 'I really d-don't know what you're going on about,' he said, making a final feeble attempt.

'You! You lot, at school, drawing . . . girls.'

Her answer was so surprising that he was slow to catch on. 'We d-don't draw girls, the girls are separate for art lessons.'

'I'm not talking about *those* girls. The girls, the women, the women without no clothes on that you draw.' Her grammar was slipping as it often did when she got agitated.

He understood. The scruffs. He would have laughed with relief except that the charge of missed communions was still to come. 'Mom, Mom,' he said placatingly, 'course we don't; we don't draw girls or w-women at all, let alone girls without, er, wh-whatsits. Wh-Who was it told you that, anyway?'

'I've just come up the road with Mrs Nolan and she said you told her Reggie that's what you did.'

'Honestly. You tell me not to mix with him and that lot cause they've got no morals, then you straight away believe what he says. Without even asking *me*.' For a moment he felt virtuous and misunderstood but didn't push it too hard, he wasn't yet sure of his ground. 'Do you *honestly* think th-that's what we do at school, Mom?'

'Why did his mother tell me, then?'

'Well, I s'pose cause her Reg told her.'

'And you didn't tell her Reg that you did?'

Strictly speaking he hadn't. He'd told them they'd be drawing bare tarts *next* year. 'Look, Mom, Reg is a dirty-minded whatsit – *you* know that. Anyway, he goes and sees this picture about this French artist, er, painting this girl and that, knows I'm an artist – well sort of – thinks that's what artists do. He was going on about it last Saturday.'

'Which picture? Did you see it?'

'No, course not, it was an A film. Reg and that lot get in through the lav window round the back. Anyway, he was talking about it, this picture. He says, "I bet it's like that at Morley's new school." Just joking really.' He was amazed at the fluency of his lying once he'd got going; the film was as much an invention as Freddie O'Brian. Still, wasn't it lying to spare his mother's feelings?

'And it really isn't like that at your school?'

'*Course* not. Mind, I think they *m-might* do . . . those sort of drawings at the art college up town. I mentioned *this* to Reg. He might have got mixed up.'

'Well, I'll see to it that you won't be going *there*, then, for a start off.'

'No, Mom, it's for when you're sixteen or eighteen.'

'I don't care when it's for, *you're* not going, and that's flat. It's disgusting.'

He was tempted to point out that there were naked or, at least, near-naked figures in church – the stations of the cross, the cherubs and Adam and Eve in the mural at the top of the church; that these had been done by artists who must have drawn naked models at art college – but thought better of it. 'But I don't *want* to g-go to the art college, Mom.'

'Well that's all right then, because you wouldn't be going there even if you did.'

Morley could have allowed his indignation to soar but caution prevailed. For some peculiar reason she was keeping the charge of missed communions up her sleeve for the time being. It scared him.

'When did you see Mrs Nolan, then, Mom?'

She took off her coat, draped it across the back of the settee, took a packet of Minors from the mantelpiece, lit up, threw the packet onto the fire and sat down. 'Just came up the road with her.' She fixed Morley with an accusing stare. 'You went out. I called up the stairs to you.'

'Only popped out to b-borrow some ink, Indian ink from Micky. For my homework. Wondered wh-where you were when I got back.'

'Sister came, I went down to the tram stop with her, I tried to get some cigarettes from the pub on the way back, but they hadn't got any. This is my last one; I was going to save it till tomorrow –'

'Oh, it was *Sister* that came, then. I thought I heard somebody, thought it was Big Gwen. And was, er, she okay, Sister?'

'Yes, why shouldn't she be?' she asked sharply. 'She said she wanted a word with you.'

His fear grew. He swallowed hard and remembered to breathe. So Sister was going to have a go at him as well. 'What about?'

'I don't know. She said see her straight after eight o'clock Mass on Sunday.'

'And *you* don't know?'

'No idea.'

'M-Mom, shall I go and borrow some cigarettes for you? From Big Gwen?'

'No! You know I *never* borrow cigarettes; when they've gone, they've gone. I've learned to put up with things I can't have.' She gave him a withering look. 'I'm going to have a bath,' she said, as if she felt unclean in his presence.

He heard the water running and tried to not think of her undressing. Why wasn't she accusing him of missing communion? She hadn't hesitated to accuse him about drawing bare tarts. Was it so dreadful that she couldn't bring herself to even mention it? That Sister was being asked to do it for her, after Mass? Or was she tormenting him by deliberately not saying anything but making it clear that she Knew. So that not being able to stand it any longer he'd crack and confess. It was worse than the fiercest telling off. Worse even than being hit over the back with the washing stick, the broom or whatever else she could reach. He paced up and down the room in terrible agitation, wondering whether it was best to confess as soon as she came out of the bath to get it over with. Perhaps even cry. He hadn't cried in front of her for years. But, God, the shame of it. He went hot at the thought. The memory of it would be with him for days. Perhaps he could be less dramatic, mumble something like: Mom, I meant to say before, but I sort of missed confession and communion a few times. Looking suitably sorrowful. But what reason could he possibly give? That his stammer had got the better of him? Pretend he'd gone a bit funny in the head lately? No, that would worry her.

He could hear the water gurgling down the plughole. She'd go upstairs and then come down in her dressing gown and slippers. Light a cigarette. But she hadn't got any. That didn't help. He sat at the table, head in hands.

'Vile swine,' she spat, coming into the room a few minutes later, her head wrapped in a towel.

This was it! She couldn't hold back any longer. And she *had* found out about you-know-what. Morley meekly bowed his head, lowered eyes that were already smarting with tears and waited for the onslaught.

'Why the devil he can't hang his towel up like anybody normal, I'll never know. Slings it under the bath, wringing wet. Black as the grate as well. Looks as if he couldn't be bothered with a wash, just rubbed himself down with the towel. I only put it out clean for him on Tuesday. Ugh! Anyway, he'll be gone soon and the sooner the better, gormless sod! I definitely don't want him here when your dad gets back.' She was speaking as if Morley wasn't there.

Morley breathed a little more easily at the respite but still flinched at her words – as if *he* were Frank – then waited fearfully for her to turn her fury onto him.

She got up, looked in the mirror and brushed her damp hair with quick, vicious strokes. 'Dirty, insincere swine. Everything he does, everything he touches. Ugh. Tells lies, breaks promises.'

Morley inclined his head. 'Oh?'

'When his mother was seriously ill, May, was it? Anyway, before he went over to Ireland, he went to see Canon Reilly and Sister to ask them to pray for his mother. Promised the earth if she got better, Sister said. Oh yes, he'd go to Mass every day, High Mass on Sundays, communion every week, he'd go on a retreat in his holiday, he'd do work in the presbytery garden. Pfff! Well, you know, his mother *did* get better. And what's he done? Nothing! Well, practically nothing. Sister goes to all the Masses and she said it's all he can do to manage Sunday Mass. And then it's only the twelve o'clock one. Always comes in late and slinks out before the end. And she's never seen him at Mass in the week, not once. And he *never* goes to communion. Still, I could have guessed all that. Anyway, I don't know why she was telling *me*; *I'm* not responsible for him; what he does is up to him. *I'm* not going to interfere . . .'

Morley closed his eyes and felt a gentle roaring in his ears: the sound of all his terrors leaving him. His lungs expanded widely of their own accord and deflated slowly and smoothly. For several minutes while his mother continued listing Frank the lodger's misdeeds, he experienced pure bliss; the future became radiant with exciting possibilities.

'. . . that one of his sisters is a *nun*?' asked his mother, breaking into his thoughts.

'Whose is?' asked Morley.

'*His*. Who else d'you think I'm talking about?' But her manner had softened.

'Sorry, oh yeh, yeh, I know that, another one's training to be a teacher; at least that's what he *said*. Mind, he said he'd lived in America once *and* been to university for a bit before the money ran out.' Suddenly his head was bursting with a million things he wanted to say.

'Go and put the kettle on for us, duck. And there's still plenty of that whiskey from Russ left – it's under the wash boiler.' His mother was thawing rapidly now.

'Yeh, okay, Mom,' said Morley, startled. 'Why d'you keep it there?'

'So that *that* dirty swine can't get hold of it.'

# 17

Confession was over: Morley had kept his promise. For the first time in five months he was in a State of Grace. Outside, he breathed deeply of the clean and fragrant early autumn air. He walked down the drive of the Catholic Church of SS Peter and Paul in Upfield with a spring in his step, excitedly going over what had just happened.

'And on each of these occasions,' asked the canon, 'there were no others present? No old family friend you call Uncle Danny? Or a female cousin two or three years older than yourself you might have been showing off to?'

'Oh no, Father, *never*,' said Morley, eager to show his careful avoidance of these much more serious-sounding versions of the sin.

The canon cleared his throat. 'As a useful guide, my son, you must remember in future to do nothing whatsoever that you wouldn't allow Our Blessed Lady or your dear mammy to see you doing.'

The canon had said as much at his last confession but Morley wasn't sure whether the reference to his mother meant he had been identified, or whether this was something the canon said to everybody with the same sin.

'Now is there anything else, my son?'

Relieved that all had gone well – the canon had not even commented on the long interval since Morley's last confession – Morley felt generous and searched for some triviality to throw in. He remembered the yard or so of cotton he'd taken. It was hardly a sin in itself but he'd taken it with the intention of using it to deceive his mother.

'I stole some cotton, Father. From my mother's s-sewing basket. Bottle green,' he added scrupulously. 'Once.'

'Little enough, my son, but even so you had to be *re-minded* that you stole something. I sometimes think that stealing no longer seems a sin to some people. Even if you steal just one bit of paper from your place of work to write a letter to your ailing old daddy in Rathkeale, tis still depriving your employer of something. Ah, when I think of all those fellers making cigarette lighters at the Aero Works, there. Ah, but no, they will tell you, no, tis just a little perk that goes along with the job.'

His Act of Contrition over, absolution granted and penance prescribed (five Hail Marys, five Our Fathers and a Glory Be), Canon Reilly said, 'I hear you are a bit of an artist.'

Morley's heart lifted. Then sank; it was clear that the canon knew who he was, after all.

'Yes, F-Father,' he said meekly, 'well, sort of, Father. Well, I go to an art school, Father.'

'Ah, yes, so I am informed. And this is a non-Catholic art school that you are at?'

'I don't think that there are any *Catholic* art schools, Father,' he said, repeating his mother's lines, 'but I w-would have gone to one if there had been. *Definitely*, Father.'

'Ah, well, there it is. But tell me, child, do you know the crib we put up every Christmas?'

The crib had been a magic affair, arranged in the Lady Chapel with almost life-size figures; real straw strewn on the floor; ivy, fir branches and holly in profusion. Through an arched opening at the back of the stable was the starry night sky illuminating the roofs and domes of Bethlehem.

A big electric star shone on the Christ-child. But over the last couple of years its charm had diminished. Morley's developing artist's eye had noticed flaking paint and stains on the backcloth, areas of raw plywood visible on the stable and figures looking a bit knocked about.

'Now tis a fine crib we have there, Italian, a real work of art, as I'm sure you will agree. We got it in 1929,' the canon went on, 'but it has become a bit shabby over the years. It needs some freshening up. Now, as something of an artist, do you think that you're the feller to put things right?'

Morley blushed in the darkness. The canon was asking *him* to do a grown-up, professional job. A confessed wanker entrusted to repaint the holy crib! Wow! But that was the nature of forgiveness. 'Y-Yes, Father, I'm sure, thank you very much, Father.'

'Now, the stable building itself and the scene that's painted behind it need some considerable restoration, as well as one of the kings. His crown was broken by some clumsy eejit some while ago and glued up, but the cracks still show on him. Now will you tell me, what kind of paint you will be needing to put these matters right?'

The canon was expecting an art expert's answer. Morley did his best. 'I'm not absolutely sure, Father,' he said carefully. 'Different c-crib, er, companies who make these figures probably use different paints. I could find out. But I think poster paint would be okay, at any rate f-for the background and stable.'

'And do *you* have some of this paint?'

'Oh, no, Father, I've only got watercolour.'

'But do they have it at your school?'

'Well, when we do posters and showcards and that sort of thing, they give out sets of poster paints, one set between four of us, just to use in the lesson.'

'And these sets, child, how big would you say they are?'

'Well, Father, there are six jars about the size of, er, Nestle's milk tins in each set. They're in cardboard boxes, Father.'

'Six jars, you say, just six colours, that doesn't sound sufficient to meet every, er, requirement.'

'Ah, but Father, you don't even need six: you could make do with five, even four at a pinch, and m-mix every colour under the sun.' Morley was really feeling the expert now; astonished at the canon's ignorance.

'Well now, and what sort of subjects would you be doing with them, these . . . poster paints?'

'We've done a child's alphabet, and er, a design based on flowers and seashells, oh, and next week we'll be starting a travel p-poster, Father.'

'All very worthy – in their place,' observed the canon, 'but worldly, would you not say? Now if these poster paints could be employed – unofficially, admittedly – but justifiably . . . by yourself, to continue to advance your creative talents . . . You understand, child? Tis, after all, for a particularly worthy cause, the crib, would you not agree? Just a few wee jars of paint.'

# 18

Morley walked towards the tram stop in Upfield's High Street, imagining the murmurs of amazement when people saw the newly restored crib at Christmas time, looking even better than it had done originally. Perhaps there could be a small card saying 'Restored by Morley Charles'. He almost laughed aloud as he thought of the canon as good as asking him to pinch the paints from school. He would invent a reason why he couldn't and the canon would have to give him the money to buy some. He'd get them from the Midland Educational. He'd enjoy that.

He compared his present state with that of the terror-stricken lad of the other night. He relaxed. He thought of Sister. Of course. Painting the crib: *that* was what she wanted to see him about.

The tram he caught to town was an old-fashioned type; unglazed at front and back on its upper deck. He sat upstairs at the front, exposed to a refreshing stream of air. His adventure had begun. He looked at his father's boyhood address copied into his notebook from the birthday card: Clarence Street, Ashted. He'd have to enquire about which tram or bus to catch when he got to town.

He had his camera with him loaded with one of his precious new films. Eight exposures. He hadn't yet taken a picture. The first would be of his dad's old home. The sky was covered by thin cloud but it was very bright. One hundredth of a second at $f8$, he decided, after consulting the instruction sheet that came with the film. He wondered what sort of house his dad's would be. Superior to the one he lived in now? Detached? Old? Big? If it was big then it meant that he had come down in the world. He thought about his father's accent but couldn't clearly recall it. Certainly not so . . . carefully spoken as his mother. Though just as his mother had improved the way she spoke from when she was in service after she left school, his father might have roughened his accent up a bit.

The villa opposite Viceroy Close was on him before he had a chance to wave. He caught just a fleeting glimpse of the bedridden man reading a newspaper.

There was sootiness about Ashted; like Nechells, where his mother had been brought up. And Nechells, he was surprised to discover, was not very far away: he could see Saltley gasworks through a gap made by a bomb in the buildings down the road. They were quite near and could be seen just as clearly from Nechells Green, close to his gran's house.

The tram conductor had told him how to get to Clarence Street. It was a mere fifty yards from the tram stop, a very short street, one side entirely taken up with a high blue-brick factory wall. The other side started with a pub on the corner, a Co-op and a curious shop with 'Open' on the door but no name on the fascia and nothing in the window. Then a row of large villas with fair-sized front gardens. Built around 1870, Morley thought. Each had a name cut in stone beneath the upstairs windows. They were the names of girls in alphabetical order starting with R. Rachel, Rebecca, Sarah, Sylvia, Titania . . . A Rose Brae, the name of his dad's old house, obviously had no place there. After Ursula the houses were much smaller with tiny squares of front garden. None of these had names chiselled into their masonry but three or four had names on boards hanging from doorways or affixed to gates. Belle Vue, Fairfield, Seville, Morley read, but no Rose Brae here either. The street ended with a foliage-covered, fenced-off bomb site representing perhaps five or six houses. He sauntered back, trying to give every impression that he wasn't remotely interested in the houses he passed, while trying to take everything in. He saw a brick gatepost with a slim rectangular area cleaner than the adjacent masonry with two holes where there must once have been a name-plate. Possible, Nigel the boy 'tec would say. Further along was a house with a garden full of what looked like ancient rose bushes. Could be, allowed Nigel, but don't jump to conclusions, the other nameless houses may also have had names once. And don't forget the bombed houses.

Morley was back at the Co-op. What should he do next? What would he say if anybody asked him what he was doing? Perhaps an art student studying architecture. Yes, a Dutch art student studying Victorian architecture. He opened up the camera and adjusted its settings.

He looked back the way he'd just come. Just beyond Clarence Street, on the next corner, was a building with a domed clock tower. That, as far as onlookers were concerned, would be his subject. He walked on the factory side of the street pausing opposite the house with the old rose bushes. He looked down into the viewfinder and framed the building with the clock tower then, without turning himself, turned the camera to face his target. It was an awkward manoeuvre. He centred the house as best he could, held his breath, pressed the camera against his stomach and *squeezed* the shutter as he had learned from his reading. His first photograph! He repeated the process with the other house that might have once been Rose Brae. Trembling slightly with excitement, he folded the camera and put it back into its leather case.

He continued down to the end of the street and crossed over. The feeling grew that the house with the missing name-plate was his dad's. One last look. He glanced up and down the road: it was empty. He affected a limp and paused occasionally as if to recover. He intensified his limp as he drew closer to his goal, where he stopped to rub his hip, grimacing a little. Ready to explain, should it be necessary, that he'd got a shell splinter in his leg in the war, in Holland.

The house with the missing sign was number 14. It had a square of overgrown lawn with a dusty laurel bush in the middle. Then just as in St James Church in Balsley the other week, he had an overwhelming feeling of nostalgia; a yearning to have been here long ago, in his father's time. Just before the last war – or the First World War as it was now called. A newer, brighter, slower and yet more exciting world than now. He imagined his father as a child coming through the brown front door and down the uneven, blue-brick path, holding his mother's hand, off to school. Was his father's mother, his grandmother, even now sitting down with a cup of tea beyond that brown door with his grandfather? Dare he knock? No, he wouldn't have the nerve if he weren't Dutch. And if he did pretend to be Dutch, it might become complicated. Another time, when he'd worked out clearly what he should do.

About to limp his way up the road, he discovered he was being watched. A boy had come to the front gate of the house next door. He was eating a sandwich. 'Oi, son,' he said, his mouth full, 'what you doing, then?'

Why not tell the truth? He might learn something. He decided to speak with only a trace of a Dutch accent. Just enough to ensure confidence. Living next door, the lad would know his dad's family, he might even be his cousin – either way there might come a time when he would have to explain why he'd talked so strangely. 'I am looking for a family called Charles. Ve lost contact with dem years ago.'

'Ay?' asked the boy, the half-chewed bread and jam disgustingly visible in his mouth as he spoke.

Morley repeated the question.

'What?' asked the boy, frowning. He wore an old cap, well pulled down on his head. He hadn't much in the way of eyebrows and there was no hair evident below the cap either.

'De Charles family,' said Morley. 'I sink dey liff near here.' His Dutch accent came out much stronger than he'd intended as if to further protect himself.

'You talk funny, son,' said the boy thickly. 'I don't know what you're on about.'

*You* can talk, thought Morley, you sound even funnier. He tried once more. 'I look for de Charles family.'

The boy looked hostile. 'You trying to take it out of me, son?' Now almost unimpeded by chewing, his voice was a bit clearer and it sounded foreign. God, pray he wasn't Dutch. Memories of the park keeper assailed him.

'No, n-no, oh no, d-dentist,' said Morley, desperately. 'I been to the dentist. Hard to talk proper.' His accent and mode of speech were now closer to those he used with the scruffs. He puffed out his cheek, like a character in a comic with toothache, and rubbed it tenderly. 'Had the n-needle, cocaine, can't feel my mouth. Numb.'

The boy leaned threateningly closer. 'What you got there?' he said, looking at Morley's camera in its leather case slung over his shoulder. Morley suddenly realized that the lad hadn't got a foreign accent at all but something wrong with his mouth – like Raymond Kerr who served at Mass – a cleft palate.

He tried to think of something flattering to say to ease the situation. What a nice house you got! What a nice cap! Nice garden! But there was nothing nice. The lad had grubby clothes and probably no hair; the woodwork of his house needed paint; the garden was full of weeds and rubbish. William Brown or Tom Sawyer would have enjoyed such an encounter, welcomed the opportunity for a scrap. How he envied them. But he was neither. His nervousness increased, his stammer threatened but he wasn't sure whether he should armour himself further with being Dutch in case he annoyed the lad further. 'I g-gorra g-go now,' he said gently, edging away and trying to smile.

A woman came out of the front door. She was pale and thin. She had her arms tightly folded and shoulders hunched as if against icy cold. She looked fierce. She came down the path. 'I've had me eye on you, I have. What you up to? What you hanging around here for, anyroad?'

Morley had no choice other than to be Dutch. Without it he would be mute. 'I look for de Charles family: dey used to liff round here before de war.'

The woman gave him a hard look. Was she his dad's sister? Was there a family likeness? She stood alongside the boy on the other side of the gate, then put an arm around his shoulder. 'All I can say is you got a blasted cheek, you have, hanging around here after what your bleeding lot done. Look at them houses!' Pointing to the bomb site down the road. 'And our winders. All blowed out. And the roof round the back. In't even properly mended yet. Go on, get off with you afore I get the old man onto you!'

Morley retained enough presence of mind to remember to limp his way to safety.

# 19

Morley stood nervously at the stop waiting for the tram back to town, bruised and baffled by the woman's onslaught. Then it slowly dawned on him: could she have thought he was German? She seemed the sort of woman who would think that anybody who sounded foreign was a Jerry. He was half scared, half amused. On future occasions he would somehow have to make it clear from the outset that he was Dutch. And if he came back here again, he'd have to make sure he was disguised; wear his red lumber jacket, leave his cap off, wear an eye patch. He'd think of something.

He wasn't too keen on going straight home. He wanted to hang around the neighbourhood and wander in the footsteps of his father; perhaps find the park and the school his dad might have gone to. But the possibility of bumping into the hairless boy deterred him. And town had less attraction than usual as all he had was one and two-pence. After a cup of tea and a cake or two, and allowing for his fare home, there would be little left. He could, of course, go to his gran's in Nechells and hope she would have an errand for him, for which she usually gave him sixpence. And Walter, his uncle, who still lived with her, might be good for two or three bob when he was back from the pub.

A bright new thought struck him. Why shouldn't he ask Walter about his dad's family? His dad and Walter had worked together before the war. It was Walter who had brought his father and mother together – May had told him as much. Could he be persuaded to talk, though? Would there be an opportunity to see him on his own? Morley decided to count to a hundred and twenty slowly and if the tram hadn't arrived by then he would go to Grandma's. The tram came into sight at ninety-one but Morley on impulse broke with his decision and set off briskly towards Nechells.

He liked Nechells; it was almost like a second home. If not exactly picturesque it had more . . . atmosphere than the area where he lived. Nechells was grimy, thronged with people and smelt faintly of gas. It seemed to have everything you wanted crowded cosily together: library, baths, lots of shops and pubs.

At the entry to Grandma's yard Morley paused. Bullivant's clock said ten to two; Walter would probably still be in the pub. If he knew which pub, he could wait outside and waylay Walter as he came out. He'd heard the Villa Tavern mentioned. And another pub that used to make him smile . . . Grandma saying, Walter's still in . . . the Cowshed . . . the Pigsty . . . the *Beehive*. He decided to walk rapidly between the two; the Beehive first as it was nearer.

And there was Walter propped up outside the corner door talking to a soldier. 'Ay up, who's this, then?' he said, winking at the soldier. 'Don't see much of your sort round here,' he added, eyeing Morley's uniform complete now with badges in the right places. 'Come round for a quick half with us, have you? You'll have your mom after me, you will. It's the sister's lad,' he explained to the soldier.

The soldier grinned. He had a black eye and a bruised and cut cheek.

'He went and got hisself barred from here, silly bugger,' said Walter. 'For scrapping. You'd never catch me standing *outside* a pub, otherwise. Got barred from nearly everywhere else and all. You're a bloody loony, you are, Les.'

'Yeh, all right, then, but we'm wasting valuable drinking time, gassing. The lad can come and all if he wants.'

They turned the corner towards Saltley, Walter leaning heavily on his stick. An indirect casualty of the war: a motorbike accident in the blackout a week before he got his call-up papers.

The soldier's house was close by, at the end of a run-down terrace without front gardens. The door opened directly into the front room. They pushed through a heavy, dusty curtain into the living room. Walter flopped down on the settee, while the soldier went into the kitchen.

'He's all right, Les,' Walter assured him, as if Morley had found him wanting. 'Just fancies the wallop a bit too much.'

Morley was aware that he had been given an almost perfect chance to question his uncle about his dad well away from Grandma. Perhaps the soldier knew something as well. It might have been Meant, as his mother was fond of saying.

'What'll *he* have?' asked Les, nodding at Morley when he had returned with an orange-coloured crate of Davenport's.

'Same as us,' said Walter. 'I bet *you* was knocking it back all right when you was his age. So long as he don't tell his mom as I'd got anything to do with it.'

Morley nodded brightly. 'Thanks v-very much,' he managed.

Les proffered a packet of Gold Flake to Morley as if it was perfectly normal.

With the ale in one hand and fag in the other, Morley felt a real man of the world. There's more to Morle than meets the eye; he's a dark horse, that one, he heard imaginary admiring voices saying.

Walter and Les started talking about somebody Morley had never heard of. Morley cast around for a subject that might interest them. Could he make his new school sound really exciting? Then he became troubled about what sort of accent to use. He was gradually refining it by such tiny degrees that he hoped people would hardly notice. But it was a couple of months since he'd last seen Walter. He'd made progress since then and the changes might be obvious. Walter might make fun of him.

'Ar, I didn't catch on for a minute, it's old Albert's son, innit?' Les was looking at Morley with a twisted grin. 'He's coming out soon, in't he?'

Morley nodded.

Walter said, 'Les used to work with your dad and me.'

'God, wasn't he a lad?' mused Les. 'The things what he got up to. Remember when he dressed up like a wench at the Onion Fair down Aston?'

'You couldn't hardly forget,' said Walter. 'Drawers, whatsits, stockings –'

'Ar, and lipstick and that. And he got the voice right. God, he didn't do things by half, old Al.' Les laughed heartily though almost silently. 'Warrabout them two sailors chasing after him! God, I could a died. Mind you, I could a nearly fancied him meself.'

Morley squirmed in embarrassment. Other images of his father's exploits assailed him. A seaside pub in Weston: his dad eating the heads of flowers decorating the lounge; crying like a newborn baby with all the customers desperately searching for it; filtering his beer through his sock, pouring it into May's shoe and drinking it while standing on a table. May had told him all this with great relish. He pushed the disturbing thoughts from his head. Perhaps later he'd learn some heroic things about his father.

He became aware of Les examining him. 'He don't look much like him, as far as I can see,' he said.

'No, he don't look like anybody much,' observed Walter.

Morley had another gulp of his beer, took a deep breath and tried to think of something funny preparatory to saying something without stammering and came up with Canon Reilly asking him to pinch poster paints from school. He chose an accent he thought he might have used the last time he'd seen Walter. 'Did our dad *really* nearly play for Villa, then?'

It was Les who answered. 'Oh ar, definitely. Course he did. Well, course he *nearly* did. He had trials and that. Didn't he never tell you, then?'

'He might have, b-but it was a long time ago,' said Morley. 'I was, weren't never really sure. It never cropped up. I in't m-much good at football.'

'No, you don't much look like the sort,' said Les.

Walter said, 'Mind you, Les, he's a very bright lad and very gifted with his drawing and that.'

'Ar, I dare say. Well, so long as it gets him a job.' Les went into the kitchen and Morley could hear clattering and cupboard doors banging.

'He in't half a case,' said Walter, shaking his head. 'Mind, he played a good game of footer: left half. Your dad: centre forward. Me,' he looked ruefully at his battered leg, 'left back. I weren't a bad goalie neither, come to that. That was for the works team, Locke's, down Cuckoo Wharf.'

'Did you ever go to our dad's house?' asked Morley innocently.

'Ar, well, yes and no, really. They had this workshop place at the bottom of the garden, an old stable. All the houses had them. They got everything there, vice, bench, every tool you could think of. We used to meet in there, brew tea and have a smoke. There was a stove. It was like a meeting place, a den. One of his brothers used to come to start off with, and a lad from work, an Irish lad. We used to go in the back way, had to give a special, secret knock on the door, in fun, like. But that was all a long time ago.'

Morley kept quiet about having just possibly seen his dad's house. He tried not to appear over eager. It was likely that Walter had been told not to divulge things. Walter's brief description of the workshop, though, was enough for Morley to see the inside clearly. He could have drawn it. A hurricane lamp, the atmosphere fuggy from cigarette smoke, a big littered workbench, tools hanging on the whitewashed walls, steamed-up windows. He saw it snowing outside, the three or four young men not all that much older than himself huddled round a black, cast-iron stove, hands outstretched, hatching exciting plans. For a moment he was there. A curious nostalgia for a time and place he'd never known overwhelmed him again.

# 20

Les came back into the living room with some roughly cut bread. He put it on the table and poured more drinks. Walter blinked a few times, lay back on the sofa and fell asleep.

'Never catch him doing that in the pub after just a couple,' remarked Les. Without Walter, Morley felt very ill at ease. He wasn't at his best with strangers. Les was slight but tough, confident, and there was something a bit menacing about him. Morley was tempted to think of an excuse and leave. But then it would be back to Grandma's, a sixpenny tip if he was lucky and the main part of his mission left unaccomplished – and losing the chance of a few bob from Walter. He tried desperately to think of something to say, then discovered that there was little need: Les didn't seem to require any contribution from him. He talked away to himself and frequently laughed his shaking, silent laugh.

Les poked at the fire to expose an area of glowing coal. He put a slice of bread on a toasting fork and held it to the grate. 'You'd a thought she'd a left a bit of something nice, a chop or bit of salmon.' He lifted half his backside from the stool he was sitting on and let out a long, loud fart. He laughed to himself. 'I reckon that's better out than in.'

He had dark hair, brushed back flat, shiny with oil, and blue eyes. His smile, Morley noticed, was partly the result of a scar that kept one side of his mouth permanently lifted.

'Huh, only a weekend leave. And she in't left nothing . . .'

The room smelt of damp, soot and Les's fart. Morley, with several gulps of his second drink inside him, began to relax a little. Les didn't seem all *that* unfriendly, just the sort of man you had to keep the right side of. Perhaps Les knew all about his dad's family and hadn't been sworn to secrecy. After rehearsing silently two or three times, he cleared his throat and asked in an accent he might have used with the Reggies, 'When did you l-last see our dad, then?'

Les gave him a slow twisted smile. 'Ooh, let's think. Must have been a good two or three year ago. We was both on leave same time; went for a drink at the, strewth, can't remember.' He turned his toast over. 'Anyroadup, we was in this pub and there was these two blokes, civilians, going on about whether you could be in the army if you'd lost your eye or your arm or your leg or something. This bloke was going, "What about old whatsisname in the RAF, then, he got both his legs off."'

'Douglas B-Bader,' supplied Morley.

'And this other bloke, a real bigmouth, was going, "Yeh, in your *RAF*, I grant you, but never in your army, you tek it from me, I'm atelling you, never in a million years in your *army*. You find me a *serving* soldier with only one arm or similar and I'll give you ten bob – a quid." Anyroadup, your dad was tekking it all in. He goes up the bar with this limp, like, and comes back and says he lost a leg right at the beginning of the war, in France or somewhere, and they had him back in three month when he got fitted up with a false one. And he sits down and bangs his glass down on his leg. And it sounds just like metal. Bang, bang, he goes. "Aluminium," he says. Anyroad, this bigmouth buys us all a drink, well, two or three, more like; says he must have got it wrong, been . . . misinformed.' Les shook with laughter. '"Tons of blokes just the same," your dad goes. Says, "Course, it's only if you get your wound while you was *in* the army. Not if you got it in civvie street."' He glanced at the still-sleeping Walter. '"See," says your dad, "if you was in the army already, like, you'd've had the training, see. It'd be a waste to just get rid of you." And he bangs his leg again and keeps it sticking out stiff, like.'

In spite of mixed feelings about this particular stunt, Morley was intrigued. 'How did he make, m-mek it sound like m-metal, then?'

'When he was up the bar, he got this ashtray, shoved it in his pocket; this one,' pointing to a buttoned pocket halfway down his battledress trousers.

'And did, did our dad go and see his m-mom and dad? When he was on leave, like?' His accent was creeping rapidly closer to Les's.

'Well, he might have done, but it in't likely, is it?' He laughed his noiseless laugh. 'I mean, they din't exactly see eye to eye, if you know what I'm getting at . . . They was – how shall I put it? – Sod it, it's burning,' he said, pulling the toast back. He scowled at it and threw it on the fire and replaced it with another piece. 'So, I don't know, son.' For the first time he looked Morley directly in the eye. 'I only had a week's leave and I couldn't have seen your dad, ooh, more than a couple of times. Best you ask him when he gets back, ay?'

Walter stirred, rubbed his bad leg, grimaced and tapped his pockets for a fag.

'Ay up, back to the land of the living,' Les said. 'Here you are.' He held out his Gold Flake. 'Ay, remember, Wal, when we was down the Town Hall, when what-d'you-call-him, old Mosley come down and old Albert done his Hitler act? Let's see, must a been about 1935.' He scraped some margarine onto his toast. 'Want some?'

Walter shook his head.

'Remember how we all had them soot moustaches, like Hitler, out the chimney in that pub, the Woodman? Then old Al started doing Heil, Hitler and the goose step up and down outside the Town Hall, talking German, well, what sounded like German. And these Blackshirts come after us and chased us all down New Street.'

His dad's impersonation wasn't difficult to imagine; Morley had seen him doing it at the Pinders one Christmas at the beginning of the war. Nearly everybody else did it as well, even he, Morley, but his father did it best of all. But he didn't rejoice; he was back to a father who seemed to do nothing except make a fool of himself.

'M-Mosley?' asked Morley. He'd heard about Mosley but wanted to be included in the conversation.

'You know, that Nazi bloke.'

'England's Hitler,' said Walter.

'Oh ar, I was, w-weren't thinking, but I din't know he'd come to Birmingham, like, that's all.'

'Ooph, he had a big following here,' said Walter. 'The Town Hall was packed out. All sorts of folk you wouldn't a dreamt of.'

'And her from the wool shop,' added Les, 'and whatsis-name, that teacher from St Joseph's. Mind you, that was *before* the war, most of them changed their minds pretty quick soon as the war started.' He chuckled. 'And then, Fred, the keenest of the lot. Saved up and went to the Olympics, in Berlin. Wore a black shirt and black tie all the time when he got back. Everybody kept asking him whose funeral it was.' He turned to Morley. 'Did y'know you could buy black shirts off the barrows in the Bull Ring once upon a time?'

'W-Wow! Who was he, then, th-this Fred?' asked Morley, eager to show his interest.

'Oh, nobody you'd know,' said Walter. 'But you might know old Newton, at the ironmonger's in Nechells Park Road. He was another keen one, all right.'

'Remember after, when them Reds, real toughs they was, thought we was Mosleyites cause we was wearing them badges we pinched and come after us?'

Walter slapped his thigh in delight. 'God, them was the days.'

'Did they cat – cop you?' asked Morley, pleased that his dad's role had its heroic side after all.

'Naw, not us,' said Walter. 'We was like the wind, wasn't we, Les? Specially your dad; now he could a been in the Olympics, all right.'

Morley calculated: it was when he was three; his dad must have been twenty-eight! Naturally, his mother wouldn't have known.

Later, when Morley and Walter were approaching the entry to Grandma's, Walter stopped and said, 'I reckon that new school of yourn's a bit rough, then, son?'

'N-No,' said Morley puzzled. 'Why?'

'Naw, it's only just the way you was talking, a bit rough, like – like me. And there's me telling old Les when we seen you coming down the street in your smart new blazer as you went to this posh school and how educated you was and that. You let us down a bit.' He winked and grinned a bit drunkenly and punched Morley affectionately in the chest.

It had been a full and profitable day, thought Morley on his town-bound bus. Confession was out of the way. He'd been asked to paint the crib. He'd made a start in learning about his dad's family in spite of Walter and Les's reluctance to say much – which only deepened the mystery. He had a photo – *almost* certainly – of his dad's old house. Walter had given him a magnificent five bob and Les a tourist booklet of pre-war Warwick which had a nice watercolour reproduction of the Lord Leycester Hospital on the front. Grandma had given him sixpence for fetching some bread from the shop and a further threepence when he told her he'd been chosen to paint the crib.

He looked forward to communion tomorrow. And he'd make jolly sure Sister noticed him going.

# 21

Mr Griffiths dribbled a ball of screwed-up paper up an aisle on the boys' side of the room, paused, kicked it neatly into the waste-paper basket, shouted, 'Goal!' looked at his watch, frowned and yawned. He looked bored. Miss Swealter next door had taken her class to the Central Library. It was a quarter to twelve.

Morley was feeling a bit jittery because earlier in the lesson Mr Griffiths had thrown the chalk to a boy sitting right at the back in the next row to him, which Morley had thought safely out of range. He was reminded of being in the air raid shelter a few years back, hearing German bombers overhead bound for the nearby Motor and Aero Works and wondering if a poorly aimed bomb would fall on him. He was doodling ideas into his rough book for a border he intended putting round the notes of Birmingham Industries he had just finished copying from the board. Most of the others had also finished and the class was growing restless.

Mr Griffiths sat down, looked at his newspaper for a few minutes, yawned again, stood up, thrust his hands deeply in his pockets, bunching his gown behind him, opened the classroom door, looked out both ways in the corridor, came back and half sat on his chair. 'Who can write both quickly and neatly?' he asked.

A few hands went up, some hovered and went down

again. One pumped the air vigorously. It belonged to the apparently earless-from-the-front Hodge.

'Good. And does your skill extend to board writing?' asked Mr Griffiths.

Hodge nodded eagerly.

'Right, I want you to copy page 32 onto the board – you'll just about make it.' He turned the board over, erased the writing on it, gave Hodge a book called *Industrial Birmingham*, looked at the class and said, 'Copy what's on the board when he's finished,' and resumed his surveillance of the corridor.

There were some repressed groans. More copying: that's practically all they'd done this morning.

The fair Catholic girl who'd said 'parst' called out, 'Sir, talking of local history, you seem to know more about Birmingham than we do, yet you don't sound as if you come from here.'

Mr Griffiths turned back into the room. 'My adopted home. A, er, Brummie by adoption.' His superior smile broadened. 'We emigrated in the twenties. My father to a post at the university. But then there's always my professional curiosity in, well, wherever I happen to be, see.'

He seemed pleased at the interest. Mind, Morley thought, the fair girl was probably the most attractive girl in the group.

'And I'm still learning. It's Monica, isn't it? Now a question of you: you don't sound as if you come from Birmingham, either.'

'My father is always saying I *do*,' said Monica. 'Well, we almost do, but we actually live in Solihull.'

'Ai say,' said Mr Griffiths in a comedian's posh voice, 'Solihull, eh? So you're less of a Brummie than I am!'

Monica smiled and said, 'Sir, you worked here before the war, didn't you?'

'For my sins, yes, and a few months into the war.'

'And were the children then better behaved than us?'

'Never noticed any bad behaviour to speak of, then or now – at least, not in my classes.' He squinted at his watch.

Hodge's board writing had slowed down. About another ten minutes to go, Morley calculated. Another diversion was called for. Almost without thinking he blurted, 'Sir, you knowing all about B-Birmingham – the history – was there any fascist activity here? Before the war. My uncle was saying –' He broke off, almost afraid at his temerity.

He was uncertain whether the question interested Mr Griffiths: his grin seemed dismissive.

Then Monica said, 'Oh, yes, sir, *I've* often wondered about that. You know, if we'd had a Hitler here would people have followed him as they did in Germany? My father said they wouldn't have.'

Mr Griffiths' grin softened. 'In my view, he's essentially right, but that doesn't mean that there wasn't a vigorous fascist movement in Britain. People in high places too. Aristocrats, politicians, businessmen, as well as working-class people. And Birmingham was certainly no exception.'

He rotated his shoulders forwards and backwards, spotted a vacant pupil's desk at the front and settled on it, throwing his gown clear, crossing his feet over the back of the chair. 'There was a fascist HQ and bookshop in Handsworth as late as 1940. Lasted about a week. Closed down because of threats – from women, would you believe? They said that they'd smash the place up, along with the organizer, if they dared stay open. Grove Lane, if anybody knows the area.'

'Honestly, sir?' This was a dark slim girl called Peggy who, in Morley's view, was nearly as attractive as Monica.

At the blackboard, Hodge was flexing his fingers as if to relieve them of cramp.

'Oh, yes. There were even attempts to secure premises

just up the road from here, in Moseley – highly appropriate, Oswald Mosley, the name of their leader, of course.'

Morley wrote Mosley down and was conscious of its similarity to his own name.

Hodge said, 'Yeh, I've heard of him, sir. Wasn't he hung, sir?'

'*Hanged*,' said Mr Griffiths sharply. 'Your pictures are hung, men are hanged. No, he's still alive and kicking. He was interned, though, for a few years during the war.'

'I thought that meant buried, sir,' said Peggy.

'That's *interred*,' said Mr Griffiths. 'Good heavens, I'll have to have words with Miss Swealter to give you all extra English.'

There were playful groans. Then Mr Griffiths resumed talking enthusiastically about the fascists until the bell went, extra copying from the board forgotten. Which was just as well, as Hodge had only managed two and a half almost illegible sloping lines.

On his way out of the classroom, something that seemed greatly significant flickered briefly at the back of Morley's mind. But all his attempts to grasp it failed.

# 22

The following evening, with his homework done and nothing new to read, Morley lay curled up on his bed close to the warmth of the airing cupboard half-heartedly extending his vocabulary from the dictionary section of *Monroe's Universal Reference Book*. He had just learned the meaning of 'resonate' when his eye was drawn to 'respect'. He knew what it meant well enough but felt oddly compelled to read it. 'An attitude of deference, admiration, esteem,' it said.

The word depressed him, reminding him that respect was something he got very little of. That if he had more respect, he'd feel more confident and that would reduce his stammering. And if he were respected, his shortcomings would hardly matter. They were all pretty trivial anyway and could be easily remedied. Look at Monty with his funny nose and speech impediment: he was respected all right.

He thought of Hoskins, a senior boy, regarded as the most skilled artist in the school, painting a backdrop at the back of the boys' drawing room. He was a lanky youth with a prominent Adam's apple and somewhat receding chin. He spoke quietly and rarely. But he was respected. Respected by the lads who assisted him and by Mr Sitwell, who asked him questions about the work as if Hoskins were the teacher. Even Mr Plume treated him almost as an equal. Morley had watched the scene developing with awe. It was the interior of Herod's palace, for the Christmas Nativity play. There were glazed tiles that really gleamed, columns and arches that looked three-dimensional. He, Morley, was also gifted in art, but then so was everybody else at his new school. So one way to get the sort of respect he wanted was to become a better artist than Hoskins; the best artist there had ever been at Balsley School of Art.

He saw quite vividly a scene in the staff room at some time in the future. The headmaster, Mr Boldmere, Mr Plume, Mr Sitwell, Miss Swealter and Mr Griffiths – his mocking smile missing for once – excitedly talking about the exceptionally high standard of his work. Mr Griffiths claiming that he'd recognized Morley Charles' special talent from his early homework.

Morley got up from the bed. He took out his history exercise book and looked at his ill-fated family tree despondently. He looked at the work that he'd just finished, notes on Birmingham Industries sandwiched between two friezes of factory chimneys, canals, cars, bikes and jewellery. Okay, but hardly the work of a future genius. His geography exercise book was no more inspiring. He'd have to make far, far more effort. Fame had to be earned. Then one day . . . His thoughts leapt to the future again. His paintings were in the Art Gallery – no, the Royal Academy. He was being interviewed on the wireless. His accent would match that of the interviewer. Next day the school would be buzzing with the news. All his relations – perhaps even his dad's family – would be listening. Even the scruffs. What would the scruffs think of his accent, though? But that was a detail.

And yes, he'd lay it on really thick about his humble origins to show he was no snob and how far he had come. He'd talk about the slum in Nechells where his mother was born and his gran still lived. The evil-smelling water which lay in a hollow in the brick-paved yard and always mysteriously reappeared even when you swept it two or three yards away to the drain.

Some of the things that were stumbling blocks at the moment would come in handy when he was famous. His name, Morley Charles, would sound really impressive. That he was a Catholic would be no bad thing. And it would be okay to have an eccentric father.

While he was perfecting his art, he would also perfect everything else. From now on, he'd use every opportunity that each minute offered to shape his famous future. Morley became euphoric.

But it was short-lived. Hadn't he had the same ambitions only last week? And had he made any progress since then? Was he even a *little* more respected? He sighed. Hardly. Yet he knew clearly what needed doing . . . He was struck by a piercing revelation: *you have to remember to do it.*

He cut a postcard into two. Then after ten minutes of practising in his rough book with a broad pen and Indian ink, he carefully lettered 'Remember' on each half. He propped one notice against his loudspeaker; the other he pinned to the airing cupboard underneath the Nazi flag. Then in 3B pencil he wrote the same word on the inside flap of his satchel and very lightly here and there throughout all his school textbooks.

Very pleased with himself, he went downstairs and rummaged through the left-hand drawer of the dresser where he kept some of his art things. He took out a packet of ten chalks in assorted colours that he had bought the previous week. Embarrassed immediately afterwards at the absurd use he planned for them, he had banished them to the back of the drawer. But now with the path to his brilliant future more clearly defined, embarrassment had to be brushed aside.

In his bedroom he took out a chalk, threw it in the air

and caught it effortlessly. He repeated the exercise half a dozen times with similar success. He began to almost look forward to when his turn came to be chalk monitor. He'd catch it with style, casually looking up and putting his hand out at the last fraction of a second. He might glimpse the fair girl, Monica – and some of the other girls – smiling at him with admiration. But he needed much more challenging practice to get to that standard.

'But what I still don't understand, nipper,' said Frank the lodger, throwing chalk from the table end of the living room to Morley sitting on a chair at the other, 'is why it's got to be chalk, why can't they use a wee ball like a ping-pong ball?'

'Well, it's just that it's the custom for one thing. And it needs a lot more skill for another, cause you've got to catch it without breaking it, see,' Morley explained. 'A lot of old English schools have these quaint old games. There's one at Eton and at Rugb-by. In our school it started forty years ago. Games were banned because somebody had stolen a cricket bat and everybody was kept in this hall on games afternoons until the thief owned up. It went on for weeks. And gradually this game with the chalk, er, d-developed to, er, overcome boredom and that and became a . . . tradition.'

'Ah well,' said Frank shaking his head, 'I'll never understand the English and that's for sure. Okay, nipper, just another five minutes then I'm finished and off to me devotions. I'm late as it is.'

# 23

Apart from Grandma and Walter, Morley had told nobody that he had been asked to renovate the crib. He hadn't mentioned it to Micky Plant because he was a Congregationalist and might sneer; even say cribs were graven images. With the scruffs he'd have to explain what a crib was and even then they would say, So what? He had been itching to tell his mother but he'd kept it to himself, in reserve for when it might come in useful. And now that time had come.

His mother, just back from Big Gwen's, was looking at the table top. 'What the devil's that?' she demanded.

Morley followed her gaze to the tasselled chenille cloth, the white tablecloth half covering it and the lone table mat from Frank's late tea. Here and there and showing up particularly vividly on the ginger-coloured chenille were yellow, pink and white chalkdust and tiny fragments of chalk. Frank's ability to catch had been worse than Morley's.

'It's all over the damned window ledge. And the floor. *And* by that chair as well,' his mother said. 'It's not some of your paint?'

'N-No, Mom, it's not paint,' said Morley truthfully.

'I bet it's *him*,' she said acidly, referring to Frank the lodger.

He was tempted to tell the truth, but typically it was something difficult to explain. Although allowing her to think it was Frank was likely to rouse her to fury. A freak explanation was called for. 'It's funny, that,' he said. 'There was some on the tram.'

'So it was *you* that brought it in, then.' Accusing.

'Oh no, it wasn't near me. But these chaps were going on about it. One had got it in his hair and that. Oh, and then there was some blowing about down by the Hen and Chickens, but it didn't touch me.'

'What on earth is it, then?' Her tone conveyed that he should be an expert on the subject.

'Isn't it that qu-queer wind that blows from Siberia sometimes . . . in September? Brings sort of peculiar dusts and that. I've read it somewhere. I know, Ripley. You know, in *Believe It or Not*. It blew in dead goldfish once; they were all over the place. Another time it was frog-spawn, then sand, then' – losing his thread – 'there was, were these giant f-footsteps going over all these roofs in the snow and –'

'Never mind about all that, how the devil did it get inside, in here?'

'Well, I opened the window.'

'What on earth for? It's got bitterly cold outside.'

'B-Because you keep on saying I'm pale. I mean, you tell me to sleep with the window open,' he said wildly. 'I thought I'd open this one as well for a bit – you know it was a bit stuffy – and it must have blown in. And then, well, his socks.' She'd understand that, all right. He bit his lip: he'd been doing his best to steer her away from thoughts of Frank's misdeeds.

She seemed about to say something, shook her head and went to work with the crumb tray and brush.

It was his cue. 'I was having a chat with Canon Reilly the other day, Mom, I meant to tell you.'

She was all attention though her expression indicated she feared the worst. 'You haven't been –'

'He wants me to paint the c-crib,' Morley rushed in.

'A picture?'

'No, the real thing, repainting all the statues, the stable, the scene behind – everything.'

'Why should he want you to do that?'

'Well, he said it's got sh-shabby over the years and he needed an artist to put things right.'

She stopped, put down the brush and tray. 'That's really lovely, duck. I am pleased. Why didn't you tell me before?' She took off her coat.

'You seemed, er, a bit preoccup-pied. I didn't like to –'

'Well, I hope I'd always have time for what's important.' She sounded apologetic. 'That's what Sister must have meant last week when she said she wanted to see you. I'd forgotten all about it.'

'Yeh, she told me after Mass but Canon Reilly had asked me already.'

She went into the kitchen to swill her hands. 'May and Grandma will be pleased.'

Morley didn't admit that he'd told Grandma already and been rewarded for it.

'There's a bit of cheese and some chutney behind the gas meter, duck,' said his mother, 'hidden away from *him*. Get them for me, will you, and I'll cut us some bread. And there's still plenty of whiskey left; you know where it is.'

Morley brightened. Another little celebration when his mother's almost permanently bleak mood briefly lifted.

As they ate the bread and cheese and drank whiskey mixed with lemonade, his mother's face relaxed. 'What did Canon Reilly actually say to you, duck? And when was it? And were you the only one he asked? I thought that that nun from the convent was very artistic, the one that writes out the prayers so nicely.' Her interest was tumbling out.

'It was after confession last Saturday,' said Morley. 'He

asked me about the art school and that.' He felt curiously virtuous since it was actually true. Too late he remembered that last Saturday was not his proper week for confession; any departure from routine was asking for trouble. He was about to amend his story – but perhaps his mother hadn't noticed. He let it go. 'He asked what sort of paint I'd need. Said that some of the figures need repainting and one of the kings' crowns had got broken and needed restoring. And that the stable and Bethlehem scene behind need redoing. Must have been Sister Twomey told him that I was at the art school.'

'What did he think about you going to the art school?' She sounded slightly anxious.

'Oh, fine, I mean he would know that there's an . . . enorm-mous connection between art and the Church. Haven't you noticed the mural at the end of the church and the s-stations of the cross, and that church by May's with all the Italian mosaics? They were all done by artists.'

He thought of her disgust the other day about drawing nudes at the art college and added mischievously, 'The canon asked was I going to make a career out of art and would I be going on to the art college after I left the art school. I said I probably w-wouldn't,' he added in a martyred tone. 'Canon Reilly said it was a pity.'

Her mouth dropped slightly. He'd got her cornered. 'Well, we'll just have to wait and see. But school's still going all right, duck, isn't it?'

'Not too bad. My art's all right. The English teacher complimented me on my work and said I'd read really expressively.' He wondered whether he could nudge his mother into divulging more information about his dad's family but that might put an end to her good mood. He savoured the secret knowledge of standing outside what may have been his father's house and taking a photograph. Then he had the unpleasant feeling that his mother could read his thoughts. He changed them very quickly. 'Has Sister found somewhere for, er, Frank yet?' he asked.

'She thinks there might be a place in Upfield, at Mrs Delaney's. I know her a bit. Big woman with a funny chin, always looks as if she's sticking it out.' She gave a short laugh. 'Can't help it of course, poor devil. They're a big family but I think only one or two of them are at work. I think they've already got one lodger. There isn't a husband there so they could probably do with the money.'

'What happened to him, then, the husband?' asked Morley.

'I've never asked,' said his mother, as if she weren't one to gossip, 'but there was talk that he was locked up at the beginning of the war. Then they moved up here from London probably because of the scandal.'

'What had he done, the husband?'

'I've no idea.'

'*Interned*, I'll bet. Our history teacher was on about it yesterday. I bet he was a Nazi collaborator. There were loads of Irish interned, as well as English people like M-Mosley and his lot.'

'There are some *wicked* devils about,' his mother said, her face suddenly darkening. 'As if we didn't have enough to put up with fighting the Germans without our own lot shoving in their two pennyworth. But they'll be punished, you'll see!'

'Yeh, yes,' said Morley hastily, 'they will all right, Mom. Ha, Lord Haw-H-Haw's already been sentenced to death. He won't get out of that; he'll be hanged all right.' He tried to think of something to restore her good mood. 'Did Russ send the photos he took of us off to America?'

'I dare say that's what he's done if that's what he said.'

'Just think, Mom, there'll soon be a photo of *you* and *me* in America. "The English artist and his mother," Russ said. I'll do another picture for him soon for those films he gave me.' He visualized a spot at the foot of Walton Hill in autumn splendour, leaves carpeting the ground.

His mother drained her glass and briefly smiled a wide relaxed smile, which made her more closely resemble her glamorous sister May. 'I could do with another one of those. Pour us out another drop, duck, and have a drop more yourself.'

His mother's good mood had lasted till bedtime. Perhaps she would be like this all the time when his father got back, he thought, as he lay in bed deliberately deferring sleep.

He thought about the photographs he had taken on his first film – only one exposure left now. Russ had offered to get his film developed and printed at his base when he heard that the chemist's would take a fortnight. Morley's last photo was of the scruffs round the bin with Kelp acting stupidly with his tongue hanging out. Still, they'd seemed impressed at his having a camera. And watched with interest as he dealt with apertures and speeds and afterwards wound on the film, carefully checking its passage through the little red window.

'See,' Perky had said, joining the group and seeing the camera. 'Told you. Save you time. No need to do the drawing. No more.'

He looked forward to taking more pictures on Saturday, when he and Micky were going to walk to Clent. He began to drop off, then stirred, alerted by a fleeting thought, which seemed important. But try as he might he couldn't pin it down – just like the other day.

# 24

Perhaps the real reason that Morley had taken the Ensign to school on Friday was just to show that he was the owner of a folding camera. He was, however, anxious to finish off the film, and took a picture of the front of the school at dinner time. During afternoon art, searching for a brush that had got itself lost in the depths of his satchel, he deliberately parked his camera on the desk for everyone to see. Then he took the camera out of its case, peered into the case and shook it, as if hoping some lost item would drop out. Without actually looking round, he got the impression that nobody was taking any notice. But at break, when he was watching a group from his own year playing polly-on-the-mopstick and debating whether he ought to start playing himself, Dawkins approached him.

'It's an Ensign, isn't it, your camera?'

'Yes,' said Morley, pleased his bit of showing off had paid off. 'Only just started using it. This Yank friend m-managed to get me some films.'

'Nice jobs, Ensigns,' said Dawkins. 'We've got one, an old model. But Dad lets me use his Baldamatic now.'

Morley nodded knowledgeably, hoping a trio of their classmates also watching polly-on-the-mopstick nearby were listening.

'It's got an Xener $f2.8$, 45 millimetre, four-element lens.'

'Neat,' said Morley.

'Ten-speed Synchro Compur shutter, up to one five hundredth of a sec,' Dawkins went on.

'What about films?' Morley asked, seeking a safe haven.

'Thirty-five mill.'

'Yeh, I guessed that, but wh-where do you get them from?'

'Ex-RAF stock. Dad gets it.' He seemed impatient with trivialities. 'Coupled rangefinder and built-in exposure meter – coupled with the shutter, of course.'

Morley nodded tightly. 'Course.'

'Automatic parallax correction –'

'Super. Has it got a case?'

'Yeh, the usual ever-ready. Oh, this'll interest you: luminous moving range and viewfinder. The frame moves as you focus, keeps your subject exactly centred.'

'W-Wow!' He felt defeated. The trio of lads from their class were having an animated conversation that suddenly sounded far more important than photography.

Dawkins said, 'D'you use it much? I mean why did you bring it to school?'

Morley struggled to find a superior reason to compensate for his less than superior responses so far. 'Oh, on the way home, got to take a picture of the Old Crown Inn, you know, in Deritend, for this Yank, master sergeant, this friend who got me the films. He's nuts about old English inns.'

'Mm,' said Dawkins, 'I'd go to Stratford and the villages around. Tons more to choose from.'

'He's got plenty of country inns already,' Morley lied. 'It's just that he partic-cularly wants one from Brum cause that's where his girlfriend lives.'

'What sort of film have you got?'

'Kodak Verichrome Pan, 120, American,' said Morley airily. One of the three nearby boys sniggered.

'Yeh, should be fine. Dad and me sometimes go into the countryside at weekends to take photographs, sometimes take a tripod for more serious stuff.'

Morley already had Dawkins earmarked as a possible friend; here was an opportunity to put things on a firmer footing. 'I'm going to Clent tomorrow with Plant, Micky Plant. His dad's going to get him a film if he can. Come with us if you like.'

Arrangements were made. They would meet at the tram terminus – safely away from Morley's municipal house – at ten o'clock, bringing sandwiches.

'What filter are you using – for the Old Crown?' asked Dawkins. But at that moment the polly-on-the-mopstick line collapsed, throwing two bodies between Morley and Dawkins, and Mr Griffiths came out and blew the whistle for the end of break.

Morley sat at the living-room table idly drawing cartoons. He had done them all many times before: Hitler, Mussolini, Donald Duck and other Disney characters, Churchill, Desperate Dan, and Our Ernie from the *Knockout*. These drawings were much admired by the uninitiated. But he knew that they were just mechanical copies of other artists' work. He pulled himself together. *Remember!* If he was going to be good at everything and become famous and get respect, he'd better get down to it and devise his own cartoons. He took some coins from his pocket and started a caricature of the king. But after five attempts all he had were two pictures that looked like the king but not like cartoons, two that were certainly cartoon-like but didn't resemble the king and one that looked like neither.

He found a penny bearing a portrait of the old king. He was easier because of the beard, but again the technique eluded him.

He wasn't getting far as a cartoonist, he reflected glumly.

This on top of learning that he wasn't so much of an expert on photography either. Photography was one of the things that earlier, he had decided, had singled him out as interestingly different. Someone with a folding camera and films, who had actually printed his own photos.

Morley had learned how to print photos in Science Club at his previous school. From the closet in his mother's bedroom he had got out the wooden box containing his dad's chemicals, gaslight paper and negatives; stuff that until then had meant very little to him. In his bedroom – already conveniently provided with wartime blackout curtains – using his mother's meat dish and tin tray, he had happily printed some of his dad's negatives of countryside scenes until all the gaslight paper had been used up.

Morosely, Morley shoved a new threepenny bit under the paper and, holding coin and paper firm, gently rubbed over it with the side of the pencil lead. A faithful likeness of George VI appeared. His father had shown him the trick when he was five; he had been amazed. But anybody could do it. He looked at both sides of the cartoon-covered paper in disgust, crushed it into a tiny ball and threw it onto the roaring bath-night fire.

Morley was bored. Self-improvement had lost its urgency. The notices he'd made to remind him to *Remember* irritated him. With photography still on his mind, however, he wandered into the front room and took down the coronation biscuit tin that contained the family's photographs from the top of the china cabinet, and carried it to the warmth of the living room. Going through the photographs was a mildly pleasant diversion he indulged in occasionally. They were all familiar. Himself as a baby, toddler and infant schoolboy; his family and relations; the beach at Weston – his only seaside holiday; some views of the Lickey Hills and unknown countryside. Many taken before he was born. All taken before the war – apart from the photograph with foreign-looking fancy edges of his fooling-around dad and a mate posing in front of a tank. No pictures of unknown people who might be his father's family, of course. They would have been destroyed long ago.

An exciting thought struck him. Could there be an overlooked *negative* of his father's family? He rushed upstairs to the closet in his mother's room, found the several wallets of negatives in the box and took them downstairs. He felt secure: his mother had gone with Big Gwen to see a neighbour in the Cripples Hospital in Upfield and wouldn't be back for some time; Frank was at his devotions. One by one, he carefully held the negatives to the light. They corresponded to the photos he'd just been looking at – except for three. One showed a man on a motorbike – almost certainly Walter; the second, a group of seated figures; the last, a slightly blurred image of two laughing girls sitting on a farm gate – his mother and May, he was sure. He turned back to the seated group and held it up in front of the white ceiling lampshade. He examined it in detail, as Nigel the boy sleuth would have done. Five black-faced men dressed in white were sitting very uprightly on chairs. No, four: one was a woman. The man in the centre wore a white uniform cap. There were grey-curtained windows to the right and left of the background and between these a small framed picture. Of course, the faces weren't really black but white, and the clothes weren't white but black.

And now those elusive thoughts of the last few days came into focus. Blackshirts! Mosleyites! These black-clad figures were his dad's family . . . with a mate. The woman was Joyce, his aunt! *That* was what had caused the rift! What had his mother said? Different ideas, enough to fall out over. And yes, Les, Walter's mate, had talked of a Fred, the worst of the lot, who had saved up to go to the Berlin

Olympics. Fred, short for Wilfred, the name of his father's brother. What else? His mother's anger when he'd mentioned collaborators. Gosh, his dad's family had probably been interned. No wonder she had kept things secret. The shame of it. The danger if people found out: bricks through the window – or worse! God, it all fitted. And Mr Griffiths talking about how widespread fascism was in Birmingham. He looked at the photograph again. The man on the left, who was bald with a moustache, looked older than the others: was he his grandfather? He screwed up his eyes. On the cap of the man in the middle were two badges. The upper one was – yes, the lightning flash! The British equivalent of the swastika.

He had Nazi relations! He was thrilled. Now that certainly distinguished him from the crowd. Not something you could go around bragging about, though. At least, not yet. But with the war over, wouldn't it come in jolly handy when he was famous? How impressive it would sound on the wireless and in the papers after his latest painting success: Charles' war-hero father loyal to his country's cause, to the extent of cutting himself off from his despised fascist family. He looked at the negative again. If only he could get hold of some gaslight paper and print the negative, he would get his first proper look at his unknown relations.

Slow down, said Nigel the boy sleuth. If your father was supposed to have despised his fascist family so much, what on earth was he doing taking a photo of them in all their fascist paraphernalia?

Maybe his dad hadn't taken the photograph. Or, if he had, could it be that he had once been a fascist himself? No, no, he couldn't have been . . . surely.

What else had Griffiths said? That at the beginning, Mosley's British Union of Fascists had attracted a number of . . . eminent intellectuals and people with strong social consciences. Yes, his dad might well have had some sympathy to begin with. And been willing to take the photo. But had quickly changed his mind like the others who, Griffiths said, condemned the violence connected with the party, as well as what was happening in Nazi Germany. It was *then* that the break with his family must have happened. Things fitted even better than before.

Morley had stumbled on a dangerous family secret. He felt very important.

# 25

Morley waited for his new friend Dawkins at the side of the green, cast-iron urinal opposite the asylum, well hidden from passers-by in Eachley Lane. It was highly unlikely that his mother would come this way if she went to the shops: there was a much shorter route that missed out this part of the lane. He was simply playing safe. It was his proper week for confession and he'd just given his mother every indication that that was where he was off to before going walking with his friends.

Apart from this slight anxiety, he quivered with delicious excitement whenever he thought of his momentous discovery of last night. He felt he had grown in stature. He wasn't as other people. He smiled a secret superior smile as he listened to Harry Braithewaite, a patient from the asylum, addressing a small group of people nearby who, hoping to go to the Lickey Hills, had caught the wrong tram.

'See, Redhill and Redwell sound nearly the same, see. And I reckon what you went and done up town was, you seen a Redhill tram and said, "We'm agoing up the hills so that's got to be the tram for us all right." But it in't. You should have gone and got the Redwell tram.'

'Ar, we've grasped that all right, *now*,' said a man with a walking stick and thinning hair, with two small boys, 'but how do we get there now, like?'

'It's a good job you come across me, cause I can tell you

a short cut,' said Harry. 'Now then, you goo up there' – pointing up Eachley Lane – 'past Woods Park Road, past Marshfield Drive till you come to the library –'

'Whoa, whoa, just a minute,' said a fat woman with a faint moustache and a man's voice who was properly dressed for hiking, getting out a notebook and taking a little pencil from its spine.

Harry repeated everything slowly while the woman wrote it down, then added, 'After the library, there's a dairy, a sandpit and a shop, but don't tek no notice of them, just carry on till you come to a place called Elmwood where they lock up naughty lads.' He looked down at the two little boys. 'So you better behave yourselves by there else they'll shut you up and all. Mind out for the bricks they chuck at you over the wall. After that, you have to goo over this canal. It's very deep and mucky. There used to be a bridge . . .'

Morley had heard other versions. Sometimes the route was through a quarry, a swamp or a wood with an unexploded bomb, or whatever took Harry's fancy.

A tram drew up at the terminus. Dawkins descended, followed by a couple who gazed around uncertainly as if they also had caught the wrong tram.

Glancing back for any sign of his mother, Morley hurried over to greet his new friend.

Dawkins, like Morley, was in his school uniform with an open mac. He had an RAF respirator bag over his shoulder. 'I didn't bring the Baldamatic,' he said.

'Ah, you brought the Ensign, then?'

'No,' said Dawkins, 'Dad's gone away for the weekend. It seems he took both with him, so I brought Mother's Brownie.'

By the urinals, Harry Braithewaite had lost his original group and was going through his performance with the young couple who had got off the tram with Dawkins.

Morley ushered Dawkins round the concealing side of the tram shelter, explaining his caution with the fiction that there was a kid who was following him around. 'He's all right, b-but he's only eight and he always pesters you to come with you. I've just seen him hanging about over there.'

Dawkins nodded. 'How far away do you live?'

'Not far, up that lane.' He pointed through the tram shelter.

Dawkins peered round the edge of the shelter. There were half a dozen large, turn-of-the-century houses along one side of Eachley Lane. Without actually claiming as much, it would do no harm if Dawkins got the idea that he lived in a similar one.

There were also telegraph poles along the lane, the lines to some of the houses clearly visible. 'Ah, so you're on the phone,' said Dawkins.

'No,' said Morley truthfully, but couldn't resist adding, 'What with the war, you know. We're still w-waiting to have one put in.'

'I could have met you at your house,' said Dawkins, 'see where you live. And you wouldn't have had to wait for me at the tram stop.'

'Oh, well, the walk we're going on is in the other direction,' said Morley quickly. 'And my mother's got one of her bad headaches, nothing serious, so you know, w-well . . .' A thought struck him. If Micky came he might somehow let out that Morley lived in a municipal house and had a lodger – spoil things. Perhaps it would be better if Micky didn't come. 'Where do you live, then?' he asked. He suddenly remembered that Dawkins had already told him the day before. 'I mean exactly.'

'Harcourt Road off Hagley Road – Norwich House,' said Dawkins.

Morley visualized Dawkins' drawing of his house from

the other week in art. Very wide, with three storeys, an elaborate front door, two sets of tall gateposts, a coach-house at the side.

At nearly half past ten, it seemed certain that Micky wasn't coming. It was probably because his father couldn't get him a film and he'd feel left out. They walked up Cock Lane. Round the first bend, Morley breathed more easily. He felt comfortably removed from the world of his mother, confession, municipal houses, lodgers and scruffs. It was an opportunity to try out a new self.

'You said your father had gone away this weekend,' he said.

'Yes, he's often off to some conference or other. But this weekend it's a medical school reunion. He's a quack.'

Morley gulped, impressed yet slightly dismayed. 'A doctor?'

'Surgeon at the Eye Hospital.'

'W-Wow,' was all Morley could manage. 'What school did you go to before Balsley?' He was half hoping it wasn't too grand.

'Oh, just the local council school.'

Relieved, Morley remarked, 'I should have thought you would have gone somewhere a bit smarter, like Hamilton House. Even Rugby or Eton,' he added flippantly.

'Well, if you count a prep school at Malvern, I suppose, I did, once,' Dawkins said almost apologetically.

Malvern: a posh, certainly boarding school. 'When was that, then?'

'Until just over a year ago. I got glandular fever, was in hospital for ages. When I got out, Mother suggested that I went to the local school for a bit to be near home and while my future was decided. You see, when I was in hospital I read some books on art and did lots of drawing and painting and got really enthusiastic. All I wanted was to go to the art school. So after some humming and hahing,

Mother and Dad finally agreed. Until then it had been taken for granted that I would be going to Malvern College.'

They had left the straggle of houses that marked the edge of Birmingham and were now in a narrow, twisting lane approaching Gannow Green. The Waseley Hills were spread in front of them and there was a farm on their right. The wind was in their favour as the air was fresh and redolent of the countryside. There was no indication that the sprawl of the Black Country was within walking distance and the Motor and Aero Works less than a couple of miles behind them. Morley glanced back and saw the green dome of the asylum rearing above the trees, but after two more twists of the road it too had disappeared. Autumn was well under way; its colours invited a painting. A girl on a horse smiled at them.

Morley's spirits rose further. In their school uniforms, equipped with cameras and walking through this pleasant, unspoilt stretch of countryside, he felt he had joined the idyllic world of Nigel and Dick the boy 'tecs. A crisp sunny Saturday morning like this in the boy sleuths' world always meant something thrilling was about to happen. Perhaps it would for them.

But by the time they had reached the Manchester Inn, less than a mile further on, Morley's buoyant mood was beginning to sink. He was brooding about Dawkins' background, which seemed to grow grander every time he opened his mouth. Too grand. And, as he had feared, Dawkins was proving to be a know-all.

If only you knew, Dawkins, if only you knew that you're talking to someone with a dangerous secret, said Morley to himself. He pictured his Blackshirt relations: enemy collaborators, a threat to national security. Beat that, Dawkins! He reminded himself of his plans for self-improvement. It wouldn't be too long before it would be Dawkins being impressed and doing most of the listening.

They reached Romsley and walked down what was little more than a track with caravans on one side and Calcot Hill rising up in front. Then, after a sharp bend in the track, from behind a high hedge, a soft, high-pitched, bird-like voice called out, 'Morle, Morle.' Or, as Morley fancied, Maul, Maul. It followed them for some yards and Morley knew it boded something unpleasant.

Dawkins' bland face looked questioningly at him.

There was some laughter that sounded oddly familiar. Then, at the next opening in the hedge, two convulsed Reggies tumbled out into the track. Of all the people Morley would least want to come across . . .

'Had you there, Morle,' said Reggie Kelp.

'We followed you all the way from them caravans,' said Reggie Nolan. 'We come with Alf in his van.' Alf worked at the ironmonger's in Redhill and delivered paraffin and other goods to the scattered inhabitants of the outlying countryside. 'We followed you all that way down this lane and you never seen us once.'

Morley's spirits dropped lower. He had always assumed that he was good at tracking, certainly as good as Nigel and Dick, who were forever following suspects or avoiding being followed.

But now he had more serious things to worry about. Had the Reggies overheard him talking to Dawkins, in an accent considerably different from the one he used with them? He thought back. Perhaps not: Dawkins had been doing all the talking.

Worse, though: how was he going to talk now? Forcing himself to grin at the Reggies to show what a neat joke he thought it was, he coughed and held his throat and said thickly and only just audibly with lots of throat-clearing, 'Seem to have lost my voice.'

Kelp looked from Morley to Dawkins and back. He said, 'He's got the same clothes on as old Morle.'

'Course he has, you twat,' said Reggie Nolan. 'They go to the same school: it's their uniform.'

'Oh, yeh, that daft drawing place.'

Morley felt helpless. Dawkins seemed unmoved.

'Where you going, then?' asked Nolan.

Morley coughed and muttered, 'C-Clent.' He prayed ferociously that the Reggies wouldn't tag along.

'Wouldn't mind going there myself,' said Reggie Nolan. 'They got amusements and a caff and hills and that. How far is it?'

Morley's heart sank. 'C-Closed down . . . other week,' he whispered, 'amusements.'

'How do you know?' demanded Kelp.

'*Bromsgrove Messenger*,' Morley lied. 'Burnt down.'

'Get out of it,' jeered Kelp.

'Did,' insisted Morley in his curious whisper.

'Why *you* going there for if they got burnt down?' asked Nolan, eyes like slits.

Morley glanced uneasily towards Dawkins. But he was merely standing to the side, politely smiling. He was afraid Dawkins would answer for him, displaying his near-posh accent, explaining that they were going to photograph the church. God, he might even mention it had some exciting Norman features or something! Dawkins might impress some but not the Reggies. Barely taller than Morley, he was a little round-shouldered, inclined to plumpness, with a pink, somewhat baby face. He *had* to keep his mouth shut.

'Got to see this chap,' Morley blurted.

The Reggies turned at the toot of a vehicle's horn. Round the corner of the track came a van. 'J. HENTY & SON, REDHILL, Ironmongery, Paints, Wallpaper & Household Goods' was painted on the side.

'I'm gonna go with Alf,' said Nolan. 'I in't struck on walking all that way and back if they in't got no amusements.'

'Ar,' said Kelp, 'anyroad, ole Morle's voice'd get on me nerves.'

The van pulled up alongside. Alf leaned out of the window. 'You two coming or not? We in't finished yet. Got to goo down the Bell.'

The Reggies piled into the back of the van and closed the doors. They pulled derisive faces at Morley and his new friend through the windows until the van disappeared round the next bend.

# 26

Morley sighed with enormous relief at the departure of the Reggies. But explanations were called for. 'It's happened before,' he whispered, stroking his throat tenderly. He thought rapidly. An ordinary throat infection seemed a bit soft. 'We were fruit picking . . . last year . . . and the lorry taking us crashed. I was thrown out . . . Not too . . . badly hurt. But there was a big piece of rock . . . it caught me in the throat.'

'You ought to carry water with you and some Fisherman's Friends,' advised Dawkins.

'Yeh, should have done. Usually do . . . have cough sweets. But lately it's been much better.'

'Well, at least there's plenty of water around.'

There was, you could hear it gurgling from every direction. There was a ditch at the side of the lane they had just entered.

'Don't touch that,' Dawkins commanded. 'You'll have petrol, horse muck and Lord knows what in there. Try down there,' he said, pointing through the barbed-wire fence on the other side of the road where there was a fast-flowing stream at the bottom of a muddy slope. 'Straight from the hills, pure, untainted.'

Morley had no choice but to do as Dawkins suggested. With Dawkins' help he crawled under the wire, squelched through very soft ground and gingerly stooped and scooped ice-cold water to his mouth and pretended to drink.

They continued walking, Morley making a variety of exploratory noises in his throat before deciding a few minutes later that his voice was more or less restored. 'Those weird kids . . .' he began tentatively.

'Oh, yes, who were they? They seemed to know you,' said Dawkins.

Morley had it all worked out. 'Loonies, from the asylum. Not d-dangerous. They let them out to help the delivery chap on Saturday mornings. Air raid victims, parents killed. Sent them a bit funny.' His slight hoarseness was genuine from the recent strain he had imposed on his voice.

'And what were you saying about going to Clent to see someone?'

'Well, you just have to humour them, simp-plify things, and there actually is a chap who came to live in Clent. He was our art teacher. Ross-Armitage, the well-known artist. Might see him, you know, painting – if it's not too cold for him.'

They had reached the top of the hill. The wide sprawl of the Black Country lay beneath them; the smoke from its many factory chimneys spiralling into a long, smudgy cloud.

'Yes, I've heard of him,' said Dawkins. 'Impressionist sort of style, plays around with complementary colours. There's something about him in a book we've got. Ah yes, I know, Frederick, isn't it?'

Morley gritted his teeth; Ross-Armitage was *his* property. He had taught him art for a couple of years. 'That's right, F-Frederick. He helped me a lot, gave me a c-couple of brushes. And some oil paints and coloured ink – pre-war.' The gift of the inks and paints wasn't true. 'Oh yes, very well known. He was commissioned to do some land-scapes for Shell – the petrol company. And he taught at the art college in Margaret Street. Very famous.'

'He was associated with the Newlyn School if I remem-ber right.' Dawkins turned his smooth, immature face towards Morley. 'And you say he taught you in *your* school? What school was that?'

'Redhill,' said Morley, truth being the only option.

'And he was your teacher? You had a special art teacher?'

'Y-Yes,' said Morley, a bit stung. 'I mean he was retired. Came back to teaching to help out, you know, the war effort what with all the m-men teachers being called up. Then, because he was an expert, he gradually took over all the art in the seniors. He used to live quite near the school but now he's moved to Clent.'

He hoped that they wouldn't meet him now. Mainly because he was afraid Ross-Armitage wouldn't remember him, and secondly because Dawkins might go on about the Newlyn School with him – whatever that was – and complementary colours – whatever they were. 'F-Fancy you knowing all about him.'

'Well, you said yourself he was famous, and he was born in Edgbaston, not far from us, in fact. He was a war artist in the 1914–18 War. *Gas Victims*. That's it. Wasn't that his most famous picture?'

Okay, okay, shrieked a voice in Morley's head, swallowed a bloody encyclopaedia or something? But he nodded grimly, annoyed at his ignorance. Dawkins hadn't even met the bloke! He was tempted to even things up by claiming that he'd often painted in Ross-Armitage's studio at Redwell and been on painting expeditions with him. But decided against it.

They were descending a slope at the bottom of which Clent Church nestled among trees. They stopped to take a photograph. It turned out Dawkins didn't have a film.

'There was *definitely* one in,' he said. 'Mother said.'

Wasn't it all a bit queer? thought Morley. Not just one camera Dawkins couldn't get hold of but two! And now no film. What would Nigel have made of it? 'Why did your dad need *two* cameras?' he asked, sounding innocent but feeling a little triumphant.

'I asked Mother about that. She thinks he took the two of them just to be on the safe side. Perhaps the film in the Baldamatic was near the end so he took the Ensign as well. After all, he wouldn't have known when he went off yesterday that I might want to use it today.'

'Yes, course. But it's a shame, isn't it, about there not being a film in the B-Brownie as well?' Morley allowed just a touch of sarcasm to enter his voice.

Dawkins shrugged, not in the least put out. 'I reckon Dad must have taken it out to put in the Ensign.'

'But would a film for a Brownie fit an Ensign as well?'

'Oh, yes, this Brownie model takes a 120, same as the Ensign.'

It was all so reasonable that Morley felt ashamed of his suspicions. But there was something else. 'How do you get films out of cameras b-before they're finished – I mean, the light getting in and that?'

'Easy – in the darkroom. Or a changing bag if you're careful.'

Morley was satisfied. He took a picture of the church, then a second one from a different viewpoint, making a point of seeking Dawkins' advice on settings to compensate for having doubted him. In his humility he even asked what a changing bag was.

Morley took two more photographs in Clent and learned more about Dawkins: that he had a sister at Cambridge; that they had a car – an Alvis; that his father was too old to have served in the war. It struck Morley from time to time that Dawkins was working on coarsening his accent slightly to fit his social descent into Balsley School of Art.

They were struggling up the last hill on the way home. It had become much colder; both lads had their macs buttoned up to the chin, collars turned up. Dawkins was breathing heavily, Morley was delighted to note, and was saying little.

Morley said, 'My father's getting demobbed in two or three weeks. A few months ago, we thought he'd been killed. Got the telegram and everything.'

Dawkins looked interested. Morley was encouraged. 'It was in Holland. Then about five days later we heard that it had all been a mistake, that he was just wounded.'

'What – happened – exactly?' Dawkins panted.

'Dad put this Jerry machine-gun post out of action. They were by this canal and all their tanks were burnt out. C-Centurions. There were German Tiger tanks over the other side of the canal out of action as well. Dad swam across the canal with a couple of grenades in a place where he couldn't be seen from the other side. He chucked them into the machine-gun p-post. There was this terrific explosion and all these dead Jerries flew out. All killed. At least he thought they were. But when he was swimming back, this Jerry who was dying managed to get a shot in. Dad's mates pulled him out of the water.'

All this had come into his head almost of its own accord soon after hearing of his father's supposed death. Later he had done a watercolour of the imagined scene at the canal. He had run the event through his mind innumerable times. Then, as he had heard nothing to the contrary, it became, for him, the truth. He was fully expecting to see the furrow made by the bullet across his dad's shoulder when he came back. He hadn't told Micky Plant or the scruffs this story, just in case: they lived a bit too close to home.

They had reached the top of the hill. 'Oh, just thought, don't say anything to Micky Plant, yet. He feels a bit sort of inferior that his dad wasn't in the war – no need to be, his dad was in a reserved occupation, but you know . . .'

'Course,' Dawkins said understandingly.

'Anyway, later on, an officer came to see our, m-my

mother, to explain that there'd been this mistake and what had actually happened.'

'A – war hero. I know the son – of a war hero,' puffed Dawkins. He was clearly delighted.

Morley wondered whether to follow with the story of his dad's stand against his fascist family. He was even more sure of his ground here, but it might get around. And how would Dawkins – and other people – take it? Another time.

Dawkins was getting his breath back. 'Which medal did he get? An MC or was it a DSO?'

'DSO, I think,' said Morley rashly. Then more cautiously, 'Although I'm not quite sure, I don't know whether it's been sett-ttled yet. This officer said something but . . .' He was floundering.

'I should think the DSO too, but I don't really know,' Dawkins said, then added modestly, 'Not too good on medals.'

Morley was also hazy about medals. He'd never given the subject of his father's getting a medal any thought at all. He was out of his depth – did soldiers get medals in the field or later from Buckingham Palace? Afraid of further awkward probing about his dad, Morley changed the subject. 'Oh, just thought, what picture did you s-submit for the Wrighton Competition, er, Dawkins?'

'Something I did when we were in Dorset in July. This little town we were motoring through – Shaftesbury, I think it's called.'

Motoring! Oh, yeh, naturally. And has to be bloody Dorset, said Morley to himself, forgetting that this was the world of Dick and Nigel and the Famous Five – a world he'd always wanted to be part of.

'Really quaint, very steep street. Did a couple of pencil drawings on the spot and made watercolours later. I was reasonably pleased with one – the one I handed in. I'd put some figures into it. You know the sort of thing: old shepherd coming up the hill with his dog, old woman looking out from the doorway. Dad said it was a bit sentimental but there really *was* this old chap coming up the road with his dog.'

'Ah, figures. Good idea, figures,' said Morley, thinking of the figureless Redhill Farm entry he had handed in last week, and deciding he'd do another entry as soon as possible, complete with figures.

# 27

Searching for a subject for his next Wrighton Competition entry, Morley made a detour through the Spunk-bag Woods on his way home from eight o'clock Mass. It was an area much favoured by the Yanks to take their girls to; and picturesque if you were blind to the dumped rubbish and the Durexes underfoot. The woods themselves had less to offer than Morley had hoped, but coming out on the other side, framed between the thinning trees was a view of a sprawling farm with Frankley Beeches as a backdrop. This was more like it. The sky was overcast, making tones a bit flat like his last picture, but the composition was far more interesting, the colours richer and more varied. In the final version he would add a figure – maybe two.

He worked in pencil in his pocket sketchbook, adding notes on colour and tone values. Then, about to leave, he remembered that fame was not won lightly. He found a better viewpoint and made a larger drawing of the farm, this time flanked with a couple of close-up trees. He assigned each of the main tones in the drawing a number: nought for the lightest, ten for the darkest.

It was only when the lowering temperature made his fingers numb that the desire for the warmth of home became stronger than the desire for fame.

His mother was in her coat, arranging her hair in front of the mirror, about to leave for High Mass when he got back. 'Big Gwen just brought your snaps up,' she said through teeth clenching hairgrips. 'I'll see them later. I'll have to dash.'

Morley gazed at the yellow photograph wallet lying on the table, hardly daring to breathe. Done already! His first film. He'd only given it to Russ on Friday afternoon.

He deliberately put off the thrilling moment of seeing the first of his first photographs by slowly hanging up his mac by the loop, making sure the sleeves were pulled out and hanging his cap absolutely centrally above it. He went into the bathroom and washed his hands, combed his hair and examined himself in the mirror in the hope that the face that would one day look out from newspapers, magazines and newsreels across the land looked better than the last time he'd looked. He had a reasonable colour from his walk.

Then, hoping for the best but fearing the worst, he rushed into the living room. He made himself sit down. He noticed that the wallet had tiny green, still-sticky spots of Pinder paint on it. He half closed his eyes and laid the prints face downwards on the table. He picked up one at random. It was a disappointment: a very blurred picture of Chadwich Manor. He selected another: the scruffs grinned up at him, Kelp with his tongue sticking out and eyes crossed. Then the house in Clarence Street with the laurel bush. His heart beat in alarm: would his mother recognize it? Best hide it – and the other one. A second view of the manor, this one much sharper. The other Clarence Street picture, also very sharp. Next, his mother in the garden smiling a bit tightly, wearing a hat that May had given her. Balsley School of Art with a blurred cyclist going past. And finally Beacon Hill looking much smaller and more distant than he'd have expected.

The thrill was over. He went through them again. Would the thrill of first seeing his dad also wear off quickly? He spread out all eight photos. Nothing that would win a photography prize. The best was the second attempt at Chadwich Manor, although the house was small with far too much sky and foreground. He masked these off with the backs of other photos, then used two more to mask the sides. Although only about a quarter the size of the original, it made a very successful picture – much better in every way than the sketch of the farm he'd just made from the Spunkbag Woods. The sun gave it dramatic light and shade and a slightly tumbledown brick bridge spanning a narrow stream added interest in the new foreground. Say that he enlarged that and made a watercolour of it instead of his farm sketch to enter for the Wrighton Competition. Would it be cheating? After all, it wouldn't – dreadful sin – be copying from someone else's painting or photograph. The photograph was *his*. And he'd have to supply the colours himself.

But squaring up the part of the photograph that he needed would be fiddly: the area was so tiny. And he was loath to spoil the photo with pencil lines. Simply copying the photo freehand would take ages. He thought of the pantograph that Ron, his uncle, had given him when he'd passed for the art school. Using that wouldn't be cheating either, would it? Just a tool for enlarging things. No less honest than squaring up, just much quicker. Tomorrow was the final day for entries. He'd secretly scorned the pantograph and only used it once before – then only to play around with.

The pantograph produced rather crooked lines but they were in the right places and easy enough to correct. By nine o'clock that night he had a finished watercolour of Chadwich Manor complete with farmer looking over the parapet of the bridge. The model was Frank the lodger leaning over the back of the settee. He, at least, had been produced without the aid of pantograph or photograph. Morley gazed at his picture admiringly. It was loads better than his two previous entries. And it had the advantage of the figure. The prizes would be awarded on the Friday after next. A few days before his dad came home. If only he could win first prize.

That night, to increase his chances of doing well in the Wrighton Competition, instead of praying in bed as usual, Morley knelt down to pray. He told God he was sorry that he'd done you-know-what about seven times since his last confession. He hoped it wouldn't spoil his chances of getting the first prize too much, but that if it was God's will then he would gladly settle for the second or even third prize. He asked God to protect his father and mother and to make him a better person. He hoped that Micky Plant wouldn't get a prize at all. And that if Dawkins won a prize it would be a lower prize than his . . .

He realized his praying had degenerated into wishful thinking. He cancelled the last bit and said he was sorry again.

# 28

It was geography. The class was copying notes from the board. Morley looked up from his rough book, caught Mr Griffiths' eye, heard him call, 'Coming over,' saw the chalk sailing towards him. He found his hand plucking it from the air, fingers snugly closing round it in the most natural way in the world. There it lay safely in his hand, unbroken. It was only immediately afterwards that his heart beat fiercely with delayed shock. But he'd done it! He carefully avoided showing the elation he felt and tried, without moving his head too much, to gauge the class's reaction to his achievement. There was none. Still, nobody had sniggered, which made him feel pleasantly normal. The thing was, he thought excitedly, he'd done it without thinking. He hadn't had time to think: his hand had just caught it of its own accord. That was the secret: Don't Think. Perhaps not thinking would work with other things as well. Mind, his mother and others were forever telling him to do the opposite. He went over what had happened. No, he hadn't been clumsy, had caught it quite casually. Definitely hadn't made a fool of himself. Pity Dawkins was absent and had missed the performance.

Heart still racing, he continued copying Mr Griffiths' board notes, which included the city's proposal to widen parts of the Bristol Road. Would that mean that 144, the house of the bedridden man, would be demolished if they went ahead? His house was right in the middle of one of the bottlenecks. On the other hand they might widen it by pinching a strip from the grounds of Viceroy Close, the luxury flats opposite. Although the flats . . .

'Chalk! Chalk! Wake up, chalk monitor.'

Morley threw the chalk back, not as skilfully as he'd have liked, but near enough for Mr Griffiths to have to do no more than stretch out a languid hand to catch it.

Morley sent up a desperate prayer that he would catch the chalk just as easily the next time and the times after. It was so important that nothing ridiculous should happen to him just before his dad got back. He imagined his dad asking how he was getting on at school and having to answer, Okay, fine. And his dad looking pleased, not knowing that his son was a laughing stock.

Perhaps he could apply his discovery of Not Thinking to playing well at football this afternoon. Even get chosen for a team, if he yelled, Me, me, me! insistently enough, instead of allowing himself to be overlooked and left to kick a ball around with the Untouchables, as Mr Griffiths called the leftovers. Perhaps he could score a couple of goals. If he could catch the chalk, why not? His dad would be pleased at that all right – on top of winning a prize in the Wrighton Competition. All-rounder Morley Charles, he was already reading in a future newspaper.

He recalled prize day at St Cuthbert's in *Nigel Accused*. Nigel the boy 'tec walking off with tons of awards and trophies for games and athletics and a special prize for bravery for rescuing his chum Dick from the icy, fast-flowing River Reade. The cheers of Nigel's schoolmates threatening to break the ancient glass of St Cuthbert's windows. The proud, restrained smiles of Nigel's pater and mater; Dick's grateful aged guardian . . .

He saw a prize-giving at Balsley School of Art. The boys' drawing room, the largest space in the school, crammed with parents and distinguished visitors: the Lord Mayor; teachers in gowns; his mother and father very impressed with this strange, superior world this son of theirs had somehow entered and was at home and successful in. He thought of all the awards he was likely to get. He might get May and Ron to come. Ron who looked like Ray Milland, with a smart accent to match – although 'Put On' was his mother's description. Started being posh when he worked on men's hats at Lewis's when he was seventeen, she'd said scornfully. And glamorous, glamorous May who also looked like a film star. Gosh, his classmates would be goggle-eyed. *And* the teachers, particularly Griffiths. So this is your aunt, Charles? Well . . . So long as she didn't open her mouth. Morley winced. He loved May's warm laughing voice, but everything you weren't supposed to do in speech May did, and in the broadest of Brummagem accents. She clung fiercely to the way she talked, had told Ron that's the way she was and that was that. Now if only May could speak like his mother, nicely though without a trace of poshness. Or his mother look a bit more like May with the same expressions and friendliness. And if his dad could look a bit more like Ron . . .

His dad. What would Dawkins make of his dad? Wouldn't he be expecting somebody very different? Much more . . . impressive. Perhaps his dad wouldn't be able to come . . . because of shift work, he thought hopefully and guiltily. And perhaps he wouldn't ask May to come after all. Pity . . . He suddenly visualized the whizzing return of the chalk.

He tried to concentrate on copying the plan of the Bristol Road from the board. That's how he had been when he caught the chalk: Not Thinking about catching. But not thinking of something wasn't easy. Every so often he couldn't resist looking up. He swallowed hard; Mr Griffiths had finished writing; was contemplating what he had just written; hand at his side fiddling with the chalk. Any second now.

Mr Griffiths turned and called, 'Chalk monitor!'

Morley dithered. Should he put his hand out now or casually at the last moment?

The chalk whistled though the air and hit Hodge, who at that precise moment was in the process of standing up. Hodge clapped a hand to his eye and yelled, 'Ahhhh.' The class laughed.

Mr Griffiths had to stand on tiptoe to examine Hodge's eye. He said, 'You'll live,' and sent him to the secretary who looked after the first-aid cupboard. The chalk lay in two pieces. Morley picked them up and laid them on his own desk. But chalking on the board was over for the lesson. Mr Griffiths went bowling his way to the communicating door at the back of the room to talk to Miss Swealter.

Frank's bedroom windows at the back of the house were wide open in spite of the cold evening; his mattress hung out of one of them. Frank had finally gone. The kitchen was filled with steam and the wringer swung upright ready for action. Morley's mother was viciously prodding the contents of the wash boiler with the washing stick.

She said, 'Hello, duck,' without losing her disdainful expression and added that he'd have to wait for his tea. First she'd got to get *his* bedclothes wrung out and onto the line quickly otherwise she would heave as she was always on the verge of doing when she was doing *his* washing. 'We've got sausages!' she called out, as he made his way upstairs.

In his bedroom he examined his muddy football boots and regretted that he hadn't made much of an effort to get picked for a team and had as usual kicked a ball around for an hour and a half with the Untouchables. Still, he believed he'd played better than most of the others. And he was definitely miles better than Dawkins – when he was there.

He wondered why Dawkins was away. Perhaps it was a return of his illness, the one that had kept him away from his prep school. A long illness. What was it? Glandular fever. He looked up glandular fever in *Monroe's Universal Reference Book*. Yes, it could last for months. But could you get it twice? Trust him to make a friend only to lose him almost immediately afterwards. And Douglas Dawkins had been a friend of just about the right . . . calibre, even if he was a walking encyclopaedia. He'd taken it for granted that certain other lads were out of his reach: the mostly tall, strong and athletic types who had already formed cliques, closed to such as Morley. Later, though, when he was famous . . .

There were others. Short-trousered Babbage, who was even thinner and shorter than Morley and went around with Lode, who was covered in spots – new ones erupting all the time. Glasses-wearing Hunnington, who looked okay but had such a quiet voice that Mr Griffiths had once said he needed to get a new battery; and another time had rolled his newspaper into a funnel and put it to his ear like an ear trumpet and said, 'Will you please repeat that, caller.' Then lanky, likeable Hodge, who had become a bit of a butt. None of these could Morley consider as friends. Associating with someone with a defect would make him even more conspicuous.

He glanced at the geography notes made this morning in his rough book and wondered how best to present them in his exercise book. Something brilliant and original. Perhaps a sort of triptych. The title and some suitable drawings or maps on the closed front. Text inside, in columns like a newspaper. In a very modern style. Not bad. He would think it over carefully later. On the window ledge was Frank's lighter. He put it in his pocket.

His mother called, 'Tea's ready.' He went downstairs.

'I saw Frank's lighter in my bedroom,' said Morley.

'Oh, yes,' said his mother, 'I put it there. He said you could have it. Said you'd find it useful for something or other that you do at school. I didn't really know what he was going on about. Said he could easily make another one at work.'

Morley felt moved. Frank had always been generous, was often good for a shilling or two when he was drunk and somebody else was around to witness his generosity. He was always very friendly.

'He was always very friendly, I suppose,' said Morley's mother as if reading his thoughts, 'even if he did get on your nerves. And he always paid up on time and never complained about anything. Still . . .'

# 29

So anxious was Morley to avoid anything unpleasant happening before his father got back that he went unhesitatingly to Canon Reilly for his next confession. No more messing about, no distant parishes, no putting it off. Anyway, he wanted to see the canon about the crib painting. His mother knew this much so wouldn't be suspicious – as it wasn't his week for confession – if she saw him in or around the church.

He confessed to self-abuse nine times. It passed without comment. He finished his list of sins. He thought of the Wrighton Competition and the means he had used for producing his entry. He'd already decided that his methods were legitimate but . . .

The canon was asking, 'And is there anything else, my son?'

Better be on the safe side. 'Father, I ch-cheated a bit at school, Father. I, er, sort of copied something.'

'Either you did or you didn't, child.'

'I copied, Father,' said Morley manfully.

'Well, now that we have that clear, did the fellow you copied it from willingly supply you with the answer or did you have to use some sort of pressure?'

'Oh, no, Father, nothing like that. It was, well –'

'There would be less need for copying if those with the gift for it would willingly help others; not everybody has the knack. Algebra is a tricky kind of subject. Though I question its importance. Even Flynn, who was top in it, surely has no use for it now.'

Morley was about to protest but it was just too difficult to explain. Anyway copying algebra seemed far more sinful than using a photograph in art. So he wasn't getting off lightly.

Absolution and penance over, the canon said, 'Let me see, now, you are the young artist who is going to repaint the crib, are you not?'

'Yes, Father,' said Morley, glad that the priest hadn't forgotten.

'And you have managed to obtain suitable materials?'

Morley's half-truthful answer was well prepared. 'Well, you see, Father, I think I said that the work needs p-poster paint and we only have poster paints *occasionally* at school just for certain lessons. And they *always* count the boxes at the end of the lesson. I mean, they wouldn't let us leave the classroom if there was anything m-missing. And with materials and equipment being so scarce and everything and –'

'Yes, yes, yes, I think you've made the situation abundantly clear,' said Canon Reilly. He sniffed. 'Well, if you can't, you can't, but would they not have *given* you some if you had asked for it and explained its purpose?'

'I-I tried that, Father,' Morley lied. He had anticipated this question and thought the lie not very serious now that confession proper was over. Anyway, it was a lie that the canon had forced on him. 'I asked the teacher taking us for heraldry and he said he would if he could, but that the headmaster was extremely strict about materials and that sort of thing. The other day somebody dipped a blue brush into the white and there was the absolute d-dickens of a row –'

'Well, if you've done all you can, then I suggest you see Mr Fisher in the church hall and ask him to let you see the crib. Then you can assess what's needed. Buy what paints are required, make sure you get a bill and it's presented to me for reimbursement. Start the work as soon as you like.'

'Yes, thank you, Father,' said Morley, about to take his leave.

'Oh, by the way, child,' said the canon. 'You know, you're getting to sound a bit fancy in the way you talk these days. Do they teach you that way of speaking at your school?'

'S-Sort of, Father,' said Morley uncertainly, blushing in the darkness, aware that he had been chancing a more refined accent than usual with the canon.

'Now please do not misunderstand me, I'm all in favour of those striving to speak grammatically and extend their vocabulary. That's fine. But don't be ashamed of what you are, child. Almighty God is no more impressed with those of his children who choose to speak in a lah-di-dah fashion than those who do not – even though others might be.'

Having found Mr Fisher and been shown the crib, Morley felt confident that he could do the job. Even restore the crown of the king with plaster of Paris, or even Plasticine; once it was painted no one would be able to tell. The only other flaws in the figures were a few areas at the bottom of the drapery where the white plaster showed through a little. The stable and backcloth would need a lot of work, though, a lot of paint. The money would have to come from his mother. He would be Dutch when he bought the paint.

In spite of the chastening about his accent, he felt freshly exultant about the responsibility of being entrusted to paint the crib. He hadn't told Douglas Dawkins about the honour. The very lad – the *only* lad – who would understand and be interested. Dawkins could even come over and watch him working. So long as the canon didn't see him: a non-Catholic with a somewhat fancy accent.

He wondered again if Dawkins was really seriously ill. Although it was more likely something quite ordinary: a cold or flu. Two or three others in his group had been away already with colds. Perhaps he should write to him, or call round. Or even telephone – if he dared. He'd only used a telephone once before – to ring May. Leave it for a few days: he'd only been away since Wednesday, after all.

He whistled his way down the remainder of the drive and walked to Upfield Library faintly hopeful that there might be an unread Nigel and Dick book.

Girls as well as boys filled the huge boys' drawing room on the following Friday morning. It was the occasion of the Wrighton Competition awards. There were nine prizes, three for each year, and Mr Wrighton himself would soon be presenting them.

Richard Wrighton's glasses were very thick, making his eyes look tiny. His lips were red and slightly shiny and made you think of lipstick. He had been a pupil at BSA before the 1914–18 War. He had gone on to Birmingham College of Art in Margaret Street and then to the Royal College of Art. He had designed posters or illustrations for the BBC, the GWR and the LMS and several government departments. Smiling a lot, he continued talking enthusiastically about his achievements.

Get on with it! thought Morley, frantic hope and hopelessness mixed. An enormous yearning for recognition swept over him. He imagined his walk to the front of the room, hundreds of eyes following him. Climbing onto the platform; shaking hands with Richard Wrighton. He saw himself framing the certificate himself in passepartout, and hanging it in his room alongside his first communion picture and his swimming certificate (This is to Certify that Morley Charles plunged in and swam one width of Upfield Baths). Ah, but soon he would have a father back who could frame it for him properly!

Mr Wrighton hadn't finished. Wasn't it difficult to believe

that he'd once been just an ordinary pupil at BSA? 'Just like you,' he said and paused. 'Although not so much like *you*,' he said to the girls and laughed loudly. He said that this was his first appearance at BSA since 1941. That Mr Hitler had had other plans for him in the intervening years. Plans, though, that had to remain hush, hush – tapping the side of his nose. But now here he was, large as life and twice as ugly. He laughed loudly again. But he wasn't going to spend all morning jawing, as everybody was anxious to know who the prizewinners were. He'd spent all yesterday afternoon with their worthy staff making terribly difficult decisions from the very high standard of entries submitted.

The third-year prizes were announced to thunderous cheers from the back of the room where the seniors were sitting. Hoskins, who was painting the backdrop of Herod's palace, came first. The second prize went to one of the boys who'd accosted Morley in the yard on his first day. There was a huge grin on his tanned face as he swaggered back to his place. A remarkably calm-looking, fair-haired girl, who Morley immediately took to, strode confidently to the front for the third prize. Mr Wrighton held her hand for longer, it seemed, than necessary.

In the second year, a boy in a grey chalk-striped suit came first. A nervous lad who kept his eyes downcast throughout was second. The third prize went to a small boy who tripped climbing onto the dais. There was a good deal of laughter. He laughed back and held his prize and certificate above his head in triumph.

Morley's pulse raced. He undid his doubly crossed legs and planted his feet firmly on the ground. He did his best to make his expression neutral, in preparation for the dramatic switch to utter amazement if he was announced as the winner of the first prize. But it wasn't to be.

'First prize, Raymond Egliss,' announced the headmaster.

A tall, athletic lad strolled to the front, one hand negligently in his blazer pocket. There were loud but respectful first-year cheers. Mr Wrighton seemed equally respectful and whispered something at length to him. Egliss smiled easily.

Two more to go. Morley held his breath.

'Peen-lope Freeman,' said the headmaster. There were titters. He looked fiercely in the direction of the titterers. The deputy head was instantly at his side, mouth close to his ear.

'Ah, yes, this typewriting.' He shook his head. 'Penelope Freeman,' he said, pronouncing it nearly correctly.

A girl, plump and cheerful with glasses much like Mr Wrighton's, smiled her way up to the platform.

Morley's legs were tied in a knot again and his mouth was open. He straightened himself out and feigned the suppression of a yawn.

'And last and finally, third prize . . . Edwin Hodge,' read the headmaster. There were ragged cheers as Hodge loped towards the dais.

And that was it. Morley let out his breath. Bitterly disappointed, resentful at daft Hodge's success – though relieved that it wasn't Micky Plant.

# 30

'Well, I didn't get a prize, so what difference does it m-make?' asked Morley.

'You *might* have done,' said Micky Plant. 'Giving in *three* pictures.'

'So what? You know as well as I do, we were *told* that we could. Sitwell said so and it said in the r-rules on that paper we got. Anyway, *you* gave in two.'

'You knew that, though, but *you* gave the last one in without *telling* me, without *showing* me: giving yourself more of a chance. I mean, I might have done another one as well, seeing that *you* had. What sort of mate does that? Behind my back.'

'It was just that I gave the last one in the other Monday – it was the last day. It was a last-minute decision. I just happened to do another painting over that weekend – of Chadwich Manor – and it seemed b-better than the other two I'd given in. I didn't have *time* to show you: we didn't come in on the same tram that day. It wasn't a secret.'

'You didn't ask *me* to go with you to Chadwich Manor. I bet you went with that new mate of yours: Dawkins.'

'No, I didn't, I didn't go anywhere: it was from a sketch I did, oh, ages ago, and f-forgot about,' lied Morley, thinking guiltily of the photograph and the pantograph. 'I almost didn't finish it, actually.'

'Ai almost didn't finish it, ectually,' mocked Micky. 'Getting a bit posh in your old age, in't you, Morle? Caught it off old Dawkins?'

Morley shrugged, aware he'd overdone it a bit. But Micky's taunts didn't bother him too much. Micky had made it clear that he was jealous of his friendship with Dawkins. He felt quite pleased.

They were sitting on a low garden wall near the tram stop waiting for the tram home. Morley wondered why on earth he'd told him about his third entry. Micky would happily squabble for the whole journey home. But Morley wasn't in the mood. The weekend was here; he had, to some extent, overcome his disappointment at not getting a prize; he had things to think about.

People were moving towards the middle of the road. A tram was coming. But the wrong one: a number 70 to Redwell and the Lickey Hills. Morley decided to board it. It would mean a quarter of an hour's walk at the other end but he might be rid of Micky. 'Coming?' he asked brightly.

'Naw, too much of a slog,' said Micky, as expected, taking a *Champion* from his mac pocket and settling himself back onto the wall.

Morley looked through the window of 144 as the tram went past. For the first time, the bed of the bedridden man was empty. Morley thought of Dawkins. He had now been away for eight school days. Might he, after all, be seriously ill? Yet he still hadn't got in touch. The nearest Morley had got to enquiring about his chum's health was to put aside two pennies in his top pocket and familiarize himself with how to use a telephone in the phone box opposite the school – with the intention of ringing the next day, which had been Tuesday. And now it was Friday. He couldn't imagine Nigel or Dick behaving as he had done. He had no excuse.

*

There were two telephone boxes between Redwell, where Morley got off the tram, and home. He couldn't put it off any longer; it must be tonight. The first box was about two hundred yards down Eachley Lane. He rehearsed again what he would say.

I'm Morley Charles, sir, – or should he say 'doctor'? – a chum of your son's, from school. I'm enquiring about his health. He took his notebook from his pocket and found his hand was shaking. 'Edgbaston 214,' he read. The telephone box was already in view; he was nearly there. He took a deep breath and looked at the distant Waseley Hills, trying not to think. He hoped Dawkins' mother would answer; he would feel easier talking to a woman. I'm Morley Charles, Mrs Dawkins, a chum of Douglas's, I'm enquiring . . . He tried it again. He was sure that he would stumble over 'Mrs Dawkins'. Perhaps he should miss it out.

The phone box was occupied by a plump, youngish woman wearing a feathered hat. She stood first on one foot then the other talking so loudly that Morley could hear occasional words. He slowed down, walked fifty paces past the box and retraced his steps. She was putting more coins in. There was a strong similarity with confession, he thought wryly. Special boxes that you had to go into and talk. And which made you anxious. The woman looked as if she was a fixture.

He walked towards the second telephone box outside Hiller's General Stores. In the future, he thought, when he was famous, he'd be phoning every day, talking to all sorts of people. Using a phone would be the most natural thing in the world. There'd be a telephone at home . . . or rather the big house they'd be living in. One in his room as well. He remembered the Dutch colonel in the film *Rendez-vous Rotterdam* dealing with *three* telephones. Yelling orders, demanding more supplies, arguing with government departments. Running the war. And here he was, nervous of asking about his chum's health. You milksop, accused Nigel the boy 'tec. Where's your spunk?

Taking a deep breath and squaring his shoulders, Morley opened the door of the box. He picked up the receiver and put in his twopence. One penny went straight through. He tried it again. He examined it. It had worn a bit thin: the machine wasn't having it. He tried it once more, joy mounting as he now had a genuine reason to put the phone call off. Hiller's isn't closed yet, said Nigel, go and swap your penny. Or, if you're in such a funk, buy something: you've got a shilling and sixpence. Buy a pencil or a rubber. Morley pressed button B and retrieved his good penny.

He bought a pencil. Armed with three additional pennies he went back to the box and inserted two. EDG 214, he dialled, reading from his notebook, his breath laboured. Brrriiinnng, brrriiinnng. He saw a burly, frowning man with a pince-nez walking through lots of rooms, up and down stairs. He considered thinking of something funny but somehow fear seemed a necessary accompaniment to the situation. Perhaps they were having tea and would be annoyed at the interruption. Should he say, Sorry to bother you? He would try his hardest with his accent. Would Dawkins speak in a more refined way at home? he wondered.

'Edgbaston 214,' said a woman's cultivated voice. He pressed button A. He saw a tall, thin, bony woman.

He took a deep breath. 'Can you tell m-me please . . . I hope it's not serious,' he said, completely forgetting what he'd planned. 'Is it gl-glandular . . . again. I mean w-will he b-be coming back soon? I, er, am his friend, er chum, Ch-Charles, I –' His voice failed him.

The resemblance to confession grew stronger as he waited for a reply.

'I haven't the remotest idea of what you are talking about, young man,' the woman, said sharply. 'And I trust you have made a genuine mistake and are not playing an ill-considered prank.'

Morley went cold. He hadn't dialled properly. Just like him to get the wrong number.

He was about to replace the receiver when the woman said more pleasantly, 'Oh, I think I understand. Please wait for a moment.'

He hadn't stammered so much for ages. He gritted his teeth. She must have thought he was a gibbering idiot. He imagined his father outside the box shaking his head sadly.

There was a man on the line. 'I understand you are a friend of my son. It was thoughtful of you to have rung up. He has had a very nasty bout of the flu but he is nearly recovered now. He is sleeping at this present moment but I will tell him as how you were asking after him. Very kind. And your name, young man?'

'Morley Charles, sir.' Damn, he should have said 'doctor'.

Douglas's father repeated, 'Morley Charles, Morley Charles. Very kind. Goodbye and thank you.'

Morley kicked at a tuft of grass outside the telephone box. 'Prat, cunt, idiot,' he said under his breath. 'What a shitty, pathetic performance. Nought out of ten.'

But you did your duty, said Nigel. And Dawkins' father was very grateful. And your chum will be pleased. Remember, you've only ever used the telephone once before.

True, thought Morley, somewhat consoled. He heard himself explaining laughingly to Dawkins, You'll never guess, when I rang you up, I could feel my old throat problem starting up. I must have sounded like a right old loony at first to – was it your dad's secretary? – but then it suddenly wore off. Will you explain to her and apologize?

# 31

Morley's father was coming home today, Monday: not at the end of the week as earlier expected. They had had a telegram on Saturday. Morley's mother was rubbing lavender-scented leather polish onto the back and arms of the chair where Frank used to sit, her face bearing a slight look of distaste. She was wearing a new-looking pinafore and a touch of rouge and lipstick. Her mood kept changing. Sometimes she looked sour and troubled as if even now her husband would be killed in an accident on his journey home. The next minute she would be humming as she busied herself in the kitchen. On a couple of occasions, when she passed Morley doing his homework at the living-room table, she tousled his hair affectionately, a gesture he remembered from long, long ago. Once she smiled so widely, he could have mistaken her for May in profile.

There was a lot of coming and going: his mother going down to Big Gwen's for something; Big Gwen bringing something up; Big Gwen's husband Percy coming up with a couple of slightly paint-smeared chairs and being told by Big Gwen to take them back as they'd already got plenty: this wasn't a party for the street; Little Gwen from over the road bringing a dented pre-war tin of pineapple chunks that she wasn't quite sure about but that Morley's mother could have with pleasure.

Morley was having the day off. His mother had written

a note: 'Morley was not able to attend school yesterday due to a heavy cold that he developed on Friday.'

'You can hardly have a heavy cold just for one day, duck, can you?' she said, smiling.

She would tell it in confession, he was sure. A very small sin. But it wasn't every day that your father came home from the war.

How moving it sounded: *your father coming home from the war*. His eyes smarted. He thought of the picture in Grandma's parlour. A sailor approaching an open cottage gate; tall, powerful, sunburned. His beautiful wife gently smiling, brown hair tied back, hands together under her chin. A child of about three clinging shyly on to her skirts. A boy with a hoop in a sailor suit, perhaps a bit younger than Morley, standing to attention a little to one side, giving his dad a salute. *The Return* it was called. A boy without a brace, a father who was tall and handsome and incapable of ever being ridiculous.

Morley was idly working on an essay in his rough book called 'An Embarrassing Experience'. As all his embarrassing experiences were too painful to even think about let alone write about, he was adapting a true story of an accident that befell May at Lyons. With lots of pauses and crossings out, he continued:

> The heavily laden tray shot out of my hands. Mashed potato shot into the air and descended like a bomb on to the shoulder of an unfortunate lady in a smart cream two-piece costume, the sausage skidded across the floor like a boy on a slide, peas like bullets shot from a gun found targets in every direction, gravy formed a huge puddle on the floor . . .

Every so often an enormous surge of nervous excitement coursed through him at the thought of seeing his dad again. He wandered down to the front gate and looked up and down the road. He looked up to admire his banner. It was made from two sheets of precious quarter-imperial cartridge paper divided in half down their lengths and joined together with gummed paper on the back to form a long strip. 'WELCOME HOME, ALBERT', it said in the sans serif lettering they were being taught at school. The banner was drawing-pinned to the windowsill of his mother's bedroom. He went inside to continue with his essay.

'Gravy formed a huge puddle on the floor,' he read. A *huge* puddle? What bloody crap, what was he thinking of? And he'd used the word shot three times! And the terrible similes. And what were the plate and tray doing while all this was going on? He'd really go down in Miss Swealter's estimation if she read this. He thought tenderly of her small teeth biting her lower lip.

He'd have another go at it later. He roughed out an illustration to accompany the account: a tilted tray with its contents flying all over the place. He thought of the dead Jerries flying out of the machine-gun post his dad had chucked the grenades into. He started drawing dead Jerries. His mother came in from the kitchen; he was aware of her looking in the mirror. He stole a sly glance to see her patting her hair. She seemed to be trying out expressions. Perhaps she too was thinking of *The Return*.

It was after half past twelve. His dad could be here any minute. His mother shooed him away: she needed the table for the food she had prepared. He went upstairs to work in his room. He preferred to be here, he decided: he would feel awkward when his father met his mother. Although the chances were that Big Gwen would be with her – and probably Percy if he took the afternoon off. He looked at the 'Remember' notice leaning against his loudspeaker but the message seemed meaningless at the moment.

There was the sound of a car stopping outside. His dad might have got a lift, of course. He dashed on tiptoes to his mother's bedroom and looked down, keeping well away from the window. But it was Maureen's dad's works' van next door.

He went back to drawing airborne dead Jerries. He drew some stiff as ramrods, some spreadeagled, others minus helmets and uniforms, some in several pieces, spurting blood. What, he wondered, would really happen to people in such an explosion? He'd covered nearly two pages of his rough book with dead Jerries when he heard a motorbike. Again, he stood several feet away from his mother's window, anxious not to be seen.

And there he was, his unfamiliar, familiar dad. The tears came back in a rush. He sniffed hard. Back from the war. *The Return*. The tears increased. The war hero. The anti-fascist. The almost-Villa player. He rubbed his eyes with his sleeve. His dad stood very upright as he'd always done. His greatcoat looked too long. 'It's the smallest they do,' he'd once joked, 'and they still had to shorten it.' Still only one stripe, Morley noticed with disappointment. Surely if he'd done something so courageous . . . Even the motorcyclist, also a soldier, had two. The motorcyclist said something and pointed up to the welcome sign. Morley moved back. His dad looked up grinning. He turned to his mate and shook hands; then swung his kitbag – to which were attached several bulging brown paper parcels and a standard lamp – over his shoulder and walked up the path, disappearing round the side of the house.

There were shrieks from the living room. Big Gwen's. Morley crept downstairs and hovered outside the door for a while, wondering how he should greet his dad. Perhaps he should give him a salute like the boy in *The Return*, he thought dryly. On his last leave his dad had given him a hug, but then he'd only been eleven. When Nigel's father had come back after a long absence he'd clapped his son on the back and shook his hand. Deciding not to think, he went in. His dad looked tired, his face lined. But there was his old wide grin, the white but slightly irregular teeth, the dark hair that looked as if it had been permed. Morley struggled hard to hold back the tears.

His dad punched him lightly in the chest, then frowned. 'Who's this, then? Don't think I recognize the regiment,' peering at Morley's blazer badge. 'Must be one of yours, Gwen. Ours is only a sprat.' He grinned again. 'You've grown, son. Blimey, if you're not careful you'll soon be as big as your dad.' They all laughed. Morley was almost tongue-tied and very aware of his brace, which his father had never seen. Would his dad notice the change in his accent?

Big Gwen mentioned his school, how good he'd become at art, that he had done the banner outside, done paintings for Russ, Beryl's GI boyfriend, that had been sent to America. His mother talked about him in startlingly glowing terms. How he was going to paint the crib. The nice friend he'd made at school. He hadn't even told her about Dawkins: Big Gwen must have told her. If his dad had already heard some of these things, he didn't let on but nodded his approval, or said, 'Well done, son.'

His dad sat in the newly polished armchair smoking, a glass of beer in his hand, sighing and nodding contentedly. He told of his ride from town on a motorbike that threatened to fall to bits any minute; how they'd had to keep stopping to fix something; how they'd been overtaken on the Bristol Road by three old men shuffling along to the Traveller's Rest.

'How did you know they was off to the pub, then, Albert?' Percy asked, frowning.

'Well, I didn't at the time, but when we eventually got to the pub ourselves, there they was, just staggering out, going back home again,' said Morley's dad with a straight face.

'You'd have been better off walking,' said Percy.

'Well, I had to after that cause the bike packed up for good and I had to push it the rest of the way here. And, blimey, he wasn't half a weight – the bloke who gave us the lift.'

'You didn't push him up here, all the way up the hill?'

'Well, it seemed only fair, he didn't *really* have to come all the way to the house: it was right out of his way.' Morley's dad's face remained deadly serious.

Big Gwen, Morley and his mother exploded with laughter. Percy belatedly joined in but still looked puzzled.

It all came back: this teasing of Percy. Everybody nodding seriously as his dad's story grew ever more improbable, watching Percy's face growing ever more confused before they could hold back no longer and fell about. Once or twice his dad grimaced and rubbed his right shoulder. The war wound! So he had been right. Morley was amazed that he'd so accurately pictured where the bullet had struck. Was he . . . psychic? But he didn't dare ask about it. You didn't. It was understood. All in good time, his dad might tell them.

The afternoon passed swiftly. There were egg and cress sandwiches, cheese, pickled onions, tongue and ham, a pork pie, tinned salmon; crusty, nearly white bread from heaven knows where; Family Ale and Nourishing Stout in abundance; a bottle of Jack Daniel's from Russ; cigarettes galore. Morley's dad had brought Player's, and Minors – his mother's favourite. Morley was allowed to drink and when he lit up a Minor nobody stopped him. 'So long as it's just the one, then, duck,' said his mother. Neighbours dropped in and admired the flower-painted clogs on the mantelpiece and the ornate gilded standard lamp his dad had lugged all the way from Holland. His dad was the life and soul of the party. Morley pictured him looking grim, chucking the hand grenades into the German machine-gun post; shaking his fist at his father and brothers and walking out of his house, never to return; face purposeful, playing foot-ball – on trial for Villa.

The drink made him feel mellow. He wore the oversized German steel helmet his dad had brought him, happily aware that he looked ridiculous, eager for people to laugh at him. Suddenly everything in the world was okay. His dad was another James Cagney: small, funny, not good-looking, but bright, popular, respected, tough when the need arose. A dad to be proud of. Who wouldn't be proud to have a dad like James Cagney?

It looked like rain. Steadying the helmet with one hand, Morley went upstairs to detach the banner from the window ledge. He would put it up again tomorrow, hoping that it would get about that *he* had done it. Even the scruffs might be impressed.

Morley stood at his bedroom window gazing at the backs of the houses in Marshfield Drive, one in particular. Two weeks ago, on the curtains of an upstairs window, he'd seen the shadow of a woman taking off her brassière. He had looked every night since but without any luck. Suddenly he wanted nothing to do with that sort of thing. It didn't seem . . . proper with his dad just back.

Had it been the happiest day in his life? he wondered. Perhaps it had. Although he no longer had anything half so exciting to look forward to. He thought rather half-heartedly about his future fame. He'd think about that tomorrow. God, school tomorrow. His spirits dropped. When you'd had a day off, going back to school was even worse than going back after the weekend. He spotted a *Dandy* on top of his magazines. He hadn't bought one for ages: he'd found this one on the tram and read it already. He'd read it again in bed. There was something com-forting about the *Dandy*.

## 32

Morley was back at school. So was Douglas Dawkins. A strangely elusive Dawkins who kept his distance throughout morning lessons and was nowhere to be seen at break. Morley felt uneasy wondering if, while he had been away yesterday, Micky Plant had said something about his dad, his ex-lodger, his house, his mother's job or anything else that conflicted with what he might have said to Dawkins on their walk to Clent. Perhaps Dawkins was embarrassed. Perhaps he wanted nothing more to do with . . . a fake. He'd only been friends with Dawkins for two or three weeks – less, if you excluded Dawkins' long absence – and now the friendship seemed to be over.

Then, as Morley was heading towards the canteen just after twelve o'clock, Dawkins buttonholed him. 'Er, come on, I bet you'd rather have chips. I know I would. Let's go to Fryer's: they're better than Morrell's – the treat's on me.' His manner was awkward.

Morley nodded gratefully, wondering how he could best undo the false impression he had created on their walk.

It was cold and overcast. They walked briskly to Ladysmith Road and Fryer Tuck's fish and chip shop, saying little.

It was comfortably warm and steamy inside. Waiting to be served, Dawkins said he had heard about Morley's dad's return from Micky. Had he changed much? he asked. How were his injuries? How about the medal? What had been his civvie job?

Morley was highly suspicious: Dawkins was trying to catch him out. He said evasively, 'Dad was t-terribly tired when he got home and, and his wound was playing up so we let him rest. We didn't ask too many questions ab-bout what he'd been through, or his plans.' He thought of his dad's single stripe, his pre-war job at the Motor Works as a fitter and the story he'd told of his dad's heroism. He regretted the airs he'd put on and the little thought that he'd given to the consequences. He could hardly invite Dawkins home for tea; and he still hadn't worked out what to do about school events – those that parents were invited to. There was a strong impulse to come clean. But that could make things worse. How much did Dawkins actually know?

They walked across Highgrove Park, kicking their way through the fallen autumn leaves, silently eating their chips, Morley wondering what on earth to say.

Dawkins finished his chips first and said, 'Dad told me you rang up asking how I was.'

Morley nodded, his mouth full.

'It was thoughtful of you. But you must have guessed . . . something.'

'Such as?'

Dawkins looked rueful. 'His manner, the way he talked . . .'

Morley thought back. He'd been so disgusted at his poor performance on the telephone perhaps he had missed something. 'Well, he was very polite. Erm, seemed p-pleased that I'd rung up.'

'Anything else?' Dawkins asked.

Morley closed his eyes and took himself back inside the phone box outside Hiller's shop. There was something.

'Not quite how I imagined he'd sound. Didn't really sound like a doctor.'

'In what way? Say what you like: I won't get upset.'

'Well . . . saying everything very carefully. *Too* carefully. A bit unnatural.'

Dawkins gave a tight smile. 'Yeh, near enough. What about the woman you spoke to?'

Morley winced at the memory. 'I, er, had a bit of my throat problem. I was stumbling over my words and coughing. I don't know what on earth she thought of me –'

'No need to worry about that. Who did you think she was?'

'Well, your mother, for a second, then I thought she must be your dad's secretary.'

'And pigs might fly. Look, I'd better put the record straight: it'd probably come out sooner or later, anyway. Practically everything I said when we went on that walk was . . . made up. Dad's just a handyman and chauffeur – and sounds it; Mum's a housekeeper. They work for a chap called Grice-Evans – he's an eye surgeon. The woman you spoke to was his wife. I just acted as if I was their son. They've got a real son, eighteen, in the RAF.'

Morley felt resentful, wondering if he had been taken advantage of, until he realized that Dawkins would have to keep up the same pretence with everybody else at school – and his own problem was solved.

'I shouldn't have given you that telephone number. It was stupid,' went on Dawkins. 'Mind you, I was planning to say later that the number had been changed – or disconnected or something – to be on the safe side. But then I got the flu and you rang before I got the chance. I just wanted to impress you a bit at first and then I got carried away. Still, as it's turned out, it was a blessing in disguise: stopped me before things got completely out of hand.' He looked at Morley with a twisted, questioning smile, seeking understanding.

'Did you go around t-telling other people at school?'

'I might have let the odd thing drop, but it was only on the walk with you that I got a real opportunity. Still, just telling one person is as good as telling everybody: things get around.' He looked anxious. 'I s'pose you mentioned a few things to Micky – it'd only be natural: he is your mate.'

Micky had taken little interest when Morley talked about Dawkins. 'I didn't say all that much,' Morley said. 'Have you always done it, Douglas, pret-tended things?'

They had wandered into a street of terraced houses with no front gardens. The coal-cellar grating of each house was protected with two dwarf brick walls topped with a slab of reinforced concrete. Cellars had become air raid shelters. They were like the ones in Les's street in Nechells. Morley chucked his screwed-up chip paper into one of the enclosures.

'I s'pose no more than anybody else,' said Dawkins. 'But it was really just before last Christmas when I first played being the doctor's son. I'd saved up a year or two for this stamp album – twenty-five bob it cost – and when I got it home I found two of the pages were all creased. I could have cried. I knew they'd say *I'd* done it if I took it back: you know what they're like with kids? And I hadn't got much faith in Dad – he's a bit, well, cap in hand. So I pinched one of Grice-Evans' cards and marched into Wainwright's in Broad Street. There was a different assistant – which helped. I showed him the card and said in a really posh voice how cross my father had been when he found out that a reputable dealer had palmed him off with a damaged album, on the first occasion he'd dealt with them. I didn't half lay it on. Philately, his only relaxation after being up night after night performing ops on air crews.' Dawkins smiled, obviously pleased with the memory. 'And it worked. They got the manager and he swapped it. He said, "Please convey my apologies to your father," and gave me a set of explorers' stamps free.'

'And after that you carried on with it all the time – being the doctor's son, with everybody?' asked Morley, the fellow masquerader.

'Oh no, just when it was useful. To get out of a scrape. Like when I got caught scrumping cherries: that sort of thing. Occasionally for a lark.'

'I can underst-stand all that all right,' said Morley wholeheartedly, dying to confess to his role as a Dutch boy, but feeling embarrassed about why he did it and afraid Micky would get to hear of it. 'But why pretend at school? It's so risky.'

'I didn't plan to,' said Dawkins. 'I didn't go round talking all *that* posh; I just spoke . . . carefully. What started it I s'pose was when we had to draw our houses that time. Actually, it crossed my mind to draw a smaller house, so mine wouldn't look out of place. I remember you – and one or two others – looking at my drawing for some time. It made me feel, well, superior. One kid said what a lucky old so-and-so I was to have a house like that. I didn't tell him that we've only got three rooms.'

He shrugged. 'I'd imagined that most people at the art school were a cut above me, like you. It was you, in a way, that got me *really* going –'

'Me?' Morley was startled.

'Yes, *your* house drawing. I only got a quick glimpse of it; it wasn't exactly massive but big enough, pretty grand. Then your name . . . and the Ensign camera. And waiting to have a phone put in. And your brace. The doctor's daughter had a brace. Had to keep going to this expensive special dentist. I mean, I didn't exactly think of you as top drawer, as my mum would say, but comfortably off, a much higher class than me. You didn't boast about anything. It was more your manner. And your accent. It changed around a bit. I got the idea that you deliberately made it rougher sometimes – you know, to be a bit more like the other kids – but when you were with me, you talked more naturally, kind of thinking I was the same sort.'

Surprised and pleased with Dawkins' impression of him, Morley said, 'Well, what about *your* accent, and your . . . choice of words and, and knowing so much about everything: you could pass as a real public-school kid, all right.'

'Well, you sort of catch things in a household like ours and the doctor's kids were always very friendly and spent time with me when I was younger.'

'What about your competition entry? You said you'd done the sketch in . . . was it Shaftesbury?'

'True. Dad drives the doctor all over the place in his line of work and that time I went as well. Nice chap. Let me use his cameras and even drive his old car once.'

'The glandular fever?'

'True as well. I didn't make up more than I had to – well, apart from swapping my identity.' He shrugged. 'Ah, well, should have struck me at the start that most of the kids at school come from just ordinary backgrounds – with a few exceptions.' He looked directly at Morley. 'I wasn't surprised that your dad was an officer.'

'I didn't say that, did I?'

'You said he would be getting a DSO. At least, I think I said he would and you agreed.'

'Y-Yes,' said Morley uncertainly.

'Well, a DSO is only awarded to officers. Ranks would get a DCM or a Military Medal.'

'I know a bit about army badges and that but not medals. I wasn't –' He made up his mind. 'Dad's only got one stripe.' Then he added defensively, 'Very tough and brave, my dad, but a bit of a rebel, not one for discipline – or pr-promotion, come to that. But he really was wounded on active service.'

'A lance-corporal!' exclaimed Dawkins. 'Mind, a lance-corporal can be just as brave as anybody else. Braver.'

Dawkins' pleasure was so gratifying that Morley added, 'We live in a municip-pal house. I, er, my drawing that time was a bit, well, exagg-ggerated. Where I live's just *past* that road I pointed out to you.'

Dawkins beamed.

Morley went further. 'Mom's a kitchen assistant in a hospital.' He nearly said loony bin, but that was going too far.

Morley suddenly realized that he didn't know where they were. Neither did Dawkins. They had strayed well beyond familiar territory. They might be late for afternoon school. But Morley didn't care. He felt cleansed, a sensation not unlike coming out of confession. His friendship with Dawkins was intact. Without having to rehearse, he turned to him and said happily, 'You aren't half a bl-bloody lying hound, Dawkins.'

'You're not too bad yourself, Charles, but you could do with a lot more coaching – and I know just the chap to give you some lessons.'

# 33

Micky Plant was a rare visitor to the Charleses after dark. But here he was being elaborately polite to Morley's mother, saying how he'd heard that Mr Charles had been demobbed. That she must have been so pleased to see him safe and sound after all this time. How he himself was looking forward to meeting him. So many had been lost, he added, the son of their next door neighbour, a school friend of his father's . . .

Morley had half emerged from his bedroom onto the landing after hearing the knock on the door. Smarmy bugger, he thought amusedly, Micky couldn't half lay it on when it suited him.

And how were Micky's mother and father? asked Morley's mother. Morley knew that Micky's superintendent dad and matron mother didn't acknowledge his kitchen assistant mother when their paths crossed at Redhill Asylum. But one day when they were rich, after he'd become famous . . .

He wondered why Micky had called. Probably curiosity about his father. He was relieved that his father was out. Micky could meet him some other time when he was sure he would be out of his uniform with its single stripe. Still, he was pleased that Micky had come: he was a friend – of sorts.

'He's upstairs, Micky,' said his mother, her voice free of its usual tightness. It made Morley feel warm and secure.

'Warrow, Morle,' said Micky, sounding as coarse as a few seconds earlier he'd sounded well bred, 'what's all this then?' he said, looking at Morley's history homework. It was a double-page watercolour of an industrial landscape of canals and factories. It was painted in very pale tones so that the superimposed black text was easily readable. 'Making a big palaver about nothing, in't you? It's only history.' He sprawled out on the bed, unmindful of his boots.

Morley knew that Micky's affected coarseness was to make him feel feeble and effeminate. But at the moment he felt ready for anything. 'Oh, that, nothing special.' He plucked the first artist's name to come into his head. 'It's just that Graham Suth-therland said the way he got successful was by doing his very best every time he put pencil or brush to paper – whatever it was. He said it can put you back *weeks* if you do things thoughtlessly or rush things. I read it.' He knew that attributing his own ideas to others gave them more conviction.

Micky was silent as if what Morley had said wasn't worth commenting on. Morley saw him looking in the direction of the 'Remember' card lying against the loud-speaker for some moments, but he said nothing. Then he smiled. 'Ay, Morle, that's a pretty neat mansion you live in – when you're not living here. Wouldn't mind living there myself. Six bedrooms –'

'What are you going on ab-bout?' asked Morley. But light had already dawned.

'Oh, just been looking at some pictures. Saw your house painting, the ones we did a few weeks ago. Blimey, Morle, you've got a vivid imagination all right, I'll say that for you – or you're half blind. It's dishonest really when you don't live in a house like that at all,' he added unctuously.

'Whereabouts did you see these p-pictures, then, Micky?' asked Morley, playing for time.

'Ah, now, that would be telling,' said Micky irritatingly.

Morley knew exactly what to do. He affected a yawn, scratched the back of his head and looked with apparent interest at his homework.

Micky said, 'I left my *Champion Annual* behind in the boys' drawing room. I had to go back. Shitwell was there sorting out this work. They were all spread over the desks; he was putting them in order. And there was yours, with this great big arched front door and these stained-glass windows and everything.' He laughed derisively. 'Blimey, Morle, you haven't even *got* a front door!'

Morley took a deep breath. He was ready. 'That's exactly what I said to Sitwell. I said drawing the front of our house was just too easy because it hadn't got a front door. He said draw one from somewhere else, one you've actually seen because it's a memory test. So I drew the front door of the doctor's on the corner of Eachley.'

'You could have still drawn your side door; shifted it round the front.'

'Same reason; too plain. N-Not much of a . . . challenge.'

'But you drew the next door house as well.'

'Started too small and too far over on the right,' Morley said innocently. 'It was just to fill the space.'

'But that stonking big tree. You haven't even got a . . . sapling in your front garden, let alone a tree.'

'It's a close-up of a tree on the other side of the road. That's where any half-decent artist would have drawn it from.'

'I reckon you were just trying not to show that it's a municipal house.'

'Think what you like, Micky,' Morley said, 'but who was I supposed to be impressing? I *told* S-Sitwell it was a municipal house . . . And the tiles; you only find tiles like in my drawing on municipal houses. It's a dead giveaway, a well-known fact. Go outside and have a look.'

Micky didn't lose his triumphant smile. 'Ay, I saw that mate of yours' drawing of his house as well. Big as bloody Buckingham Palace. I know you said he lived in a big house in Edgbaston, but this was ridiculous. Three or four floors, great big entrance with pillars and that. There's something fishy about him, Morle. Trust you to get yourself a funny mate.'

'He's okay. Anyway, you talk to him as well. And he's been around with both of us at dinner times.'

'Have you ever been to this house?'

'Not yet.'

'No, I don't reckon he'll ask you either cause I bet it's really a slum house down a yard. Ever noticed his satchel? Well, it's not a satchel, it's an RAF respirator bag. And his blazer looks worn and as if it's been altered; and I don't think he's got any footer boots.'

The boy sleuth in Morley was annoyed because he'd made nothing earlier of what now seemed significant clues. 'But there's other kids with respirator bags and I didn't get *m-my* footer boots till the other week. And there's one or two kids who haven't even got blazers yet.'

'But he's supposed to come from a posh, well-off family.'

'Ah, but it's those sort of families who don't always bother t-to keep up appearances: it's sometimes the poorer families who scrimp and save to buy stuff for their kids to try and show that they aren't poor.' He was pleased with this observation that had just come out of the blue. 'And, *and* it was in the paper the other day that Princess M-Margaret Rose used to wear her sister's cast-offs.'

He realized he'd taken a wrong turn: Dawkins *didn't* come from a posh, well-off family; it was pointless to pretend that he did now that Dawkins had come clean. Nevertheless, he ought to be defending Dawkins' reputation and showing he was a friend worth having. 'Still, in Dawkins' case, I reckon that they did find things really difficult; it's not his fault that they can't always afford new things.'

'Oh, so he's poor now. A poor kid with a dad who drives an Alvis, who's a famous doctor, who lives in a mansion, who's on the phone. That's what *you* told me.'

'No,' said Morley with a great show of exasperation. 'Drives an Alvis *for* a famous doctor. He's a chauffeur.'

'But you never said that.' Looking suspicious.

'I did, all right,' said Morley without flinching.

'What about his great big house, then?'

'Well, course he lives in a big house: they live on the premises; his mom's a housekeeper. What's wrong with that?'

'But he still talks kind of posh, thinks he knows everything, gives you the idea he's lord muck sometimes.'

'Well, I suppose he is posh,' said Morley, anxious to wipe the sneer off Micky's face and reluctant to allow Dawkins to lose all his middle-class value. He remembered 'Derek's Defiance' in the *Hotspur*, the story of a wealthy family suddenly reduced to wretched poverty. 'Dawkins' dad was an army doctor but he got badly wounded, had to come out of the army. He couldn't carry on with his civvie job because of his wounds . . . and shell shock and that. This other doctor he'd known when they were students gave him a job as his chauffeur.' He'd overdone it. He'd have to coach Dawkins on his changed circumstances.

There was a faraway look in Micky's eyes. 'But I could have sworn you said . . . and there was something Dawkins said as well . . . about –'

'Trouble with you, Micky, is that you never b-bloody well listen,' said Morley boldly.

# 34

'For thine is the Kingdom the power and the glory for ever and ever,' chanted the assembled pupils of Balsley School of Art. Morley was silent. Had the other Catholics missed out this bit as well? he wondered.

'Amen,' said Morley, now rejoining the rest.

Canon Reilly was emphatic. 'Your Catholic duty is quite clear,' he said in confirmation class. 'You should not participate in *any* Protestant – or anybody else's – act of worship. And you must certainly not attend non-Catholic funerals, weddings and baptisms unless there is some powerful family reason; in which case you should ask your mammy to see me about it first.'

Joseph Kinsella asked, 'What about assemblies at school, Canon? We got to go. They won't let you off, Canon.'

Canon Reilly shook his head. 'Ah, this is a sad, irreligious country. So, if you have to go, you have to go. But,' he thundered, wagging his finger, 'be sure that you don't sing their hymns or say their prayers. Pretend if needs be but don't have your heart in what you are doing. Their liturgy is in error.'

Sister Twomey had a more relaxed attitude. 'When they say the Our Father it would do very little harm if you joined in but make sure you use the proper Catholic version. Theirs might sound very similar but there are little differences here and there; it's not the genuine thing at all.

So be quite sure you don't say "Our Father *which* art" with the little Protestant girls and boys. You must say "*who* art". And you must say "*on* earth", not "*in* earth". And you must *never ever* continue with "For thine is the Kingdom"' – Sister flushed as if she were in grave error herself for uttering it – 'and the rest of it. You must finish at "But deliver us from evil".'

'What do we do while the others are saying "For thine is the Kingdom" and that, Sister?' asked Joseph Kinsella.

'Ah, well, Joseph Kinsella, you could be saying a little prayer, in your own words, for the little Protestant children,' suggested Sister.

Morley laughed at the absurdity of it, but still obeyed Sister's injunction, though nowadays he drew the line at praying for the little Protestant children.

He became aware of the headmaster's voice: '. . . walking round the streets, eating greasy filth out of newspapers. In your school uniforms just like the riff-raff!' He paused uncertainly. 'I won't have it. I will not have riff-raff in my school. You either consume your dinners in our canteen or, if you must, you go to a respectable establishment where you sit, are seated properly to eat! We have our good reputation to keep and sustain.'

The headmaster stood in front of his table to deliver his homilies. The boys directly in front of him moved back a little or inclined their heads to one side as his excitement grew and a fine shower of spit began.

He swept his eyes round the assembled school. '*I* know why boys go to these greasy shops and purchase greasy filth,' he said in triumph, his Birmingham accent grown stronger. '*I* understand boys. *I* was a boy myself once!' The boys in the front row ducked further. 'Boys are really still little savages underneath with only a thin layer of civilization on top. Given half a chance they go back to their savage and primitive ways. They *enjoy* eating with their fingers like the primitive savages. But you don't really want to be like, resemble the savages, do you? It's common! We live in a civilized society. We're not pigs eating out the trough.'

If they wanted chips again they'd have to watch out for prefects, thought Morley. He liked chips, particularly May's; she only used dripping. Mind, cottage pie was nice. And bacon and eggs, and winkles, shrimps, whelks. He listed all the foods he liked, then those he disliked. He hated cooked swede. Would he eat a spoonful for sixpence? No, definitely not. A shilling? No. Half a crown? He found he was holding his breath steeling himself for the ordeal, almost heaving. Probably for three shillings.

The headmaster was talking about something else. 'All right, another example. Let us say you went to the Art Gallery up town and stole that painting called the *Last of England*. D'you know the one I'm on about? A picture of emigrants leaving England by Holman Hunt.'

The deputy headmaster rose and whispered something.

'See, boys and girls, you wasn't paying attention, were you? It took Mr Boldmere to spot my deliberate mistake. Ford Maddox Brown was the one who really painted it. Anyhow, you run off or abscond with this picture worth thousands of pounds. You'd be a criminal or a lawbreaker, all right, wouldn't you? No doubt, no question about it is there? Ay?'

There were murmurs of assent.

'All right then, what if you didn't steal the painting but done, did an exact copy or replica of it, put your own name on it and sold it to some rich or wealthy American for hundreds of pounds. And this American didn't know anything about . . . Ford Maddox Brown and as how it was him who did it first, did the original, like. How about that, then?' He paused.

The school was quiet for a few moments, then someone

at the back ventured, 'Sir, if this picture was an exact copy and just as good, then –'

'Never mind if it was just as good!' shouted the head-master sharply. 'For a start off, it *wouldn't* be, *couldn't* be. I'm telling you!' Several boys in front of the head put up protective arms or stepped back a foot or so. 'What I'm going on about is have you committed a crime, a criminal offence?'

There were mumbles of 'Yes, sir.'

'Yes, sir, indeed. You would have committed forgery. You'd be a forger, a counterfeiter.' He looked around the room. 'Now then, it pains and hurts me to say it but some-times we get forgers here. Even here at Balsley School of Art! Scholars passing off famous artists' work as their own in important competitions. Well, not all that famous or I would have known about it all right. I can't be ex-pected to know all the work of every artist or painter that ever lived, can I? Ay? I didn't know *all* the work of this man. Now compare these two pictures.' From the table behind him, he picked up a calendar opened at August 1938 and held it up to the assembled school. He tapped it. 'Here we are, Theodore Crane, 1851 to 1927.'

The calendar bore a reproduction of a cornfield seen through an open farm gate with a village in the distance. It was familiar; Morley had seen an almost identical version displayed in the entrance hall: Edwin Hodge's Wrighton Competition entry.

The headmaster picked up Hodge's version and held it up beside the calendar. 'I shall be dealing with the young forger, counterfeiter who done this after assembly.

'Now then, on a more cheerful or happier note, in the opinion of myself and the other art staff, the proper third prize in the –' he picked up a piece of paper from the table '– Junior Section of the Wrighton Landscape Competition goes to, is awarded to . . . Charles Morley.' He whipped off his glasses and looked over the heads of the first few rows of pupils as if they didn't exist, before the deputy head drew his attention to Morley's upstretched hand. The head beckoned urgently with two hands as if he were guiding a motorist parking in a tight spot.

And before he had time to get flustered, Morley was on the dais shaking hands with the headmaster and receiving a large white envelope from the deputy head, to quite respectable applause.

Happily, they had got his name the right way round on the certificate.

'Let's have a dekko, then,' said Micky in the yard at break.

It read:

> The Wrighton Landscape Prize Competition
> Third prize in the Junior Section awarded to
> Morley Charles
> For his entry: Chadwich Manor

'Well,' said Micky, 'fame at last, Morle. Yes, Chadwich Manor. Course, you've had a lot of practice drawing mansions, haven't you, Morle? No, joking' – as Morley's expression began to change – 'well done. Sure you didn't copy it from a calendar, like Hodge, though?'

'What did Hodge say?' asked Dawkins, shivering a bit in the chill, damp air.

'Said he didn't know he was doing anything wrong,' Micky said. 'Didn't trace it or anything. Just copied it. Said he thought it was just the same as sitting outside and copying the scene in front of you.'

Morley felt a flicker of guilt as he thought of his photo.

'Barmy twerp,' said Micky. 'Doesn't seem particularly bothered. Look at him now.'

Lanky Hodge was playing polly-on-the-mopstick with

some beefy second years. He was running with great lolloping strides, buttonless shirtsleeves fluttering loose. He took a flying leap over the bent-over backs of half a dozen lads, fetching up clumsily against the wall.

'Good job he didn't cash in his prize,' said Micky. 'Let's see, Morle.'

Morley had been presented with a second, smaller envelope not long after assembly. Inside were National Savings stamps to the value of ten shillings in a slightly creased savings booklet, stained slightly with what might have been brown sauce.

During the course of the day, Morley was congratulated by Mr Sitwell and three boys. Fair-haired Monica gave him a smile. And such was the confidence that his prize had generated, he smiled back without blushing. He had an overwhelming desire to talk, preferably about his entry and prize, but was also prepared to talk about anything else.

He had declined Micky's invitation to go into town after school, as he wanted to hurry straight home and tell his mother and father his good news. He was about a couple of hundred yards from the Outer Circle bus stop when he saw the bus sail across the crossroads. He wouldn't make it. He slowed down.

A breathless Dawkins caught up with him. 'Sorry I missed you – had to see the secretary. Kept me waiting. Couldn't find my fountain pen. Got it when I passed for the art school – from the doctor. Anyway, Plume found it – handed it in.'

'Ah, that's where you were,' said Morley. 'Meant to say before, Douglas, if you're not doing anything tomorrow afternoon, c-come over to ours. There should be plenty of stuff to eat and drink. One or two relations will probably pop in.'

Douglas pulled an apologetic face. 'Ah, really love to but Dad's driving the doc to some hospital in Leamington tomorrow and it's in the Alvis; first time it's been properly out since the war. The doctor's been promising for ages that I could go with them. Probably be out most of the day. It's a Vanden Plas, short-chassis tourer.'

'Wow!' said Morley dutifully, eyes wide, mentally switching off.

'Yeh, full synchromesh gearbox *and* independent front suspension.'

'Neat,' said Morley, rewrapping himself in thoughts of his prize.

'I mean,' said Dawkins, 'if it had been only the old Austin Berkeley –'

'Course.' But Morley was already miles away, answering questions from a group of newspaper reporters.

Yes, the first one was only a third prize a couple of years ago at school, then later there were some seconds and firsts and now this RA prize. His voice was confident and unstammering.

Yes, I'm a Catholic.

Oh no, not Irish, English: my maternal grandfather was a convert.

Mother? Yes, born in a slum, not ashamed to admit it. Father was from a more prosperous family. Oh yes, a war hero. Put this German machine-gun post out of action. No, not an officer. Never quite . . .

Perhaps the time would be ripe to throw in his Blackshirt connection. My father's family were fascists, would you believe! Quite high up. No, not Dad, of course, he was a staunch patriot. He walked out on them . . . Perhaps he could add a light touch. Most families have a black sheep but we seem to have got half a dozen!

He was struck with a dazzling new thought. The reason his dad had only one stripe and hadn't been decorated for bravery was that he had been penalized because he came from a fascist family.

# 35

It was unlikely that Morley would have gone to confession anyway. But when his mother made the startling announcement that she wasn't going, it clinched it.

'Just go up the village for us, duck, to get your dad a few things. I would have got them myself in Upfield but I'm not going to confession today what with people likely to drop in on us from all over.'

Although it wasn't his proper week as far as his mother was concerned, it was two weeks since he'd last confessed: he was due. Even now he should be making some excuse to leave the house. Still, what was good enough for his mother . . .

Returning home from Redhill Village about three quarters of an hour later, he saw May and Ron's green Hillman outside his house and Russ's olive-drab Chrysler outside the Pinders. Not a sign of the scruffs, he noted happily. The side door was open; he went into the hall. From the living room came shouts and laughter. He hesitated at the closed door. Just a quick look first. He dashed upstairs as silently as possible. The certificate was propped on his window ledge. He picked it up, read it and smiled.

The sounds of hilarity from downstairs grew in volume. He pulled up the lino in the corner and put his ear to the hole. This was the second such gathering since his dad had come home; there was no doubt of his dad's popularity. He could hear May and Big Gwen fairly clearly, a deeper rumble of male voices and his dad asking, 'Any more for any more?' in an Arthur Askey voice. There was the usual thrill of hearing all this in secret; it was like being invisible. Then, afraid of being caught lying spread out flat on his floor, he got up quickly, dusted his knees and took a last look. *'Awarded to Morley Charles.'*

Fortified by the study of his certificate, he went into the living room. The air was thick and blue with smoke. The room was packed. Even Reggie Kelp's mother was there, wearing a shabby fur coat, lots of powder and bright orange lipstick that went well beyond the edges of her lips and emphasized the gaps in her stained teeth.

He was greeted enthusiastically. 'Congratulations, old son,' said Ron; 'Well done, junior,' said Big Gwen and Russ together. Beryl Pinder almost smiled. An old man he'd never seen before sitting in Frank's armchair grinned, nodded and puffed ferociously on his pipe.

'I only came th-third, though,' he said modestly.

But they wouldn't hear of it, third or no, it was an important prize. 'And remember,' said May, 'it's a proper art school. *All* of them's gifted at his school. And he come third out the lot of them.'

'I won a prize once,' said Percy Pinder. '*First* prize mine was. In a raffle. At the seaside. Bournemouth, wasn't it, cock? Marvellous invention. One of them alarm clocks that makes your tea for you then wakes you up. Only our one never did – quite.'

'Only because you took it to bits,' said Big Gwen. 'Anyway, nobody wants to know about any of that. This young man *earned* his prize because he's got talent.'

His dad gave him a small glass of sherry. There were no chairs left but May grabbed a cushion from behind her back and told him to sit down beside her on the floor.

He enjoyed the proximity of her long nylon-clad legs. Sitting directly in front of him was Big Gwen with her equally shapely but much sturdier legs, hers coloured with gravy browning or some such stain. She crossed them just then and he glimpsed a slightly wobbly fake seam, done in – was it eyebrow pencil? He could have done a much straighter and neater line. Perhaps he would offer – one day. He felt aroused and crossed his own legs to disguise the fact. He laughed to himself and felt almost at peace with the world.

May tousled his head and said, 'Comfy, love?' Then to Morley's dad: 'Carry on about that chap in whatsit, then, Alb, what you was billeted with.'

'Yes, near Eindhoven. He had a long funny Dutch name but he made me call him Papa,' said Morley's dad, topping up the glass of the old man in Frank's chair. 'Anyway, as I was saying, I'd got these couple of eggs this first morning. I showed him one. He looked as if he hadn't seen an egg in years. I shouted, "*And* it's fresh, Papa! *Fresh*! Understand? I only *laid* it this morning."'

A titter rippled round the room.

'Course, he didn't know what I was on about. I shouted, "I'll just lay another, Papa, to show you."'

Most of the room was listening now.

'What did you do, Albert?' breathed Big Gwen.

'Went like this.' He strutted round the room like an exultant hen, clucking realistically, flapping crooked elbows up and down, thrusting his head forward and back.

Everybody laughed heartily; Morley resigned himself and joined in. Yes, James Cagney might well have done something similar.

His father's clucking became drawn out and contented-sounding; then he put his hand between his legs from behind and withdrew an egg. He held it out for everyone to see, like a conjuror.

There was uproar. Morley glanced at his mother; she was shaking her head but laughing quietly.

'You daft old piecan,' said May delightedly.

Big Gwen was shaking, tears rolling down her cheeks. Her slightly paint-spattered skirt rode up a little; Morley could see the smudged uneven edge where the gravy browning finished. Russ was banging the table. Even posh Ron was laughing, a quiet, dignified laugh.

The old man in Frank's chair coughed and chuckled in turn, his pipe still tightly clamped between his teeth as if he was afraid of losing it. His eyes were large and looked as if they were about to pop out of his head. Who was he? Morley wondered.

'I should have thought that the fowl would have laid the egg *first*,' said Percy Pinder, '*then* gone around doing the squawking.'

'Shurrup, Percy,' said Big Gwen.

Reggie Kelp's mother and Little Gwen left together, and a little while later Beryl Pinder and Russ. Morley went with them to the door. 'Swell dad you got there, Morley. One of the best,' said Russ.

Back in the living room, Morley tensed and relaxed his leg, stiff from sitting on the floor. He sat at the table and out of the corner of his eye studied the old man in Frank's chair. There were stains, burns and shreds of tobacco on his cardigan; his off-white moustache was stained yellow above his lip. There was something about him. Had he seen him before somewhere?

His dad was busy topping up drinks. For the first time there was a lull in the conversation. Morley tried to think of a suitably neutral subject. 'D-Did you learn much Dutch, Dad?' he asked.

'Ar, a bit. But not as much as the German I'd picked up. Mind you, they sounded pretty similar.'

May asked, 'How did you pass the time, then, when you was with this old man?'

'Drinking mainly. Well, I had to, he kept on forcing it on me.'

'I'll bet!' said May.

'Strue. I put up a shelf for him and mended the door on his greenhouse and did a few other odd things. And he kept giving me this sort of gin he'd made. I got the idea he was keeping it for something special and it turned out to be me. Strewth, it was strong: you could have stripped paint off with it! But it was all he'd got to give. Wouldn't have been polite to refuse, would it? And then I had to get hold of some beer to sort of pay him back.'

'Course you did!' said May. 'What else did you do?'

'Pointed at things and said their names. He kept showing me things round the house and out the window and saying, "In *Engeland*, Albert?" And I was always going, "Yes, yes, *ya*, *ya*, Papa." I mean, they were just ordinary things: a Monopoly game, a wireless, a camera. And the petrol station and the picture house across the road – oh, yes, funny that it was called the Rex like the one here in Redhill, and next door to it was a Bata shoe shop – just like home.'

His dad's Holland didn't sound at all like the Holland in May's *Pictorial Book of Knowledge*, thought Morley gloomily, or the Holland he imagined he came from when he was Dutch. Monopoly? The Rex? Bata shoe shops?

'W-What was the house like?' asked Morley, hoping, nevertheless, for quaint stepped gables, blue tiles on the walls, views of windmills and dykes. Everything very different: very foreign, very Dutch.

'A bit like this one,' said his dad.

'N-Not different at all?'

His dad closed an eye. 'Not a lot. Newish like this; brick, same tiles on the roof as ours. Oh, they didn't have a fire in a grate; they had a sort of stove instead. And the windows opened inwards – made it easy for cleaning.'

'Didn't he ever point to *anything* different, this old man – something you'd *n-never* seen in England?'

'No, nothing I can think of: everything he'd got, we'd got, or I'd seen somewhere or other over here. In fact, I had to pretend every so often just to liven things up a bit.'

Morley was bitterly disappointed. But the Real Holland must exist *somewhere* and his dad must have seen some of it. He'd ask him at length some time. He fell silent while the others plied his dad with further questions about his time with the old man. It was as if this was the most important period of his dad's five-year war. Probably because it was a safe subject.

His dad explained how he had pretended he'd never seen a lavatory before and got the poor old Dutchman to show him how to use one, that in *Engeland* they had to dig a hole in the garden. That they didn't have stairs in *Engeland* and had to go to bed up a ladder.

Morley studied the old man in Frank's chair. What would Micky Plant think if he came round – which was quite possible on a Saturday afternoon. He might think he was a relation. Scruffy devil, he spoilt the general effect. He looked round at the remaining company: May and Ron looking as much like film stars as ever; his now quite attractive mother; handsome Big Gwen; Percy looking all right in his sports jacket with only two or three tiny paint stains marring his yellow waistcoat; his dad thankfully out of his lance corporal's uniform in a striped sports shirt and cord trousers – his James Cagney-kind of dad.

May was saying, 'But I mean, he must of realized that you was only joking, Alb. I mean you might of tricked him the once but he weren't daft, was he?'

'Oh, no. It was just a bit of a laugh. But he did expect me to lay eggs every time somebody came round, to show me off a bit, like. I had to try and explain that I was only a two-egg-a-day chap and I only laid before nine.'

Morley's mother came in from the kitchen with a tray of tea. She gave the old man a searching look. Morley looked at him again: smallish, snub nose, the way he leaned back in his chair, hands behind his head, like his dad. He *was* a relation. A lot grubbier and older than the man in the negative but negatives were deceptive. And it had been taken years ago. And he'd probably been interned. Still, he should have guessed much earlier: it was his grandfather, his fascist grandfather.

# 36

Very sluggishly Morley became aware that it was dark and slightly chilly and that he was lying fully clothed on the top of his bed. When he tried to sit up, his surroundings refused to move about him in the accustomed way. There was a strange taste in his mouth. He stood up gingerly on the heaving floor and made his way to the window. He leaned on the sill, chin cupped in hands, and pressed his forehead against the cold glass. It gave some relief. Automatically, his eyes sought the window of the brassière-shedding woman but it was in darkness. Not that he was much in the mood for that sort of thing. He looked at his certificate, just discernible in the darkness, with little interest. He was suffering from a hangover, he gradually realized, but felt too rotten to rejoice in such a manly achievement. He had no idea of how much he had drunk: he'd just casually topped up his own glass whenever he'd been asked to fill somebody else's. He had had sherry, port and some gin that he didn't like but had finished rather than waste it.

He yawned, sat on the edge of his bed and wondered whether to go downstairs or carry on resting. His loudspeaker was silent and he could hear no voices from downstairs either. Perhaps his mother and father had gone to Big Gwen's.

The events of the late afternoon drifted into his mind. Micky coming and meeting his dad for the first time. Saying that he ought to be on the wireless after hearing one of his stories; refusing a drink – his parents were strict teetotallers – impressed, though, that Morley was allowed to.

He thought about the old man, who had left quite suddenly, happily before Micky's arrival, without saying anything, just smiling, nodding, protruding eyes swivelling around the room, spluttering and still fiercely hanging onto his pipe; bits of ash and tobacco dropping from his scorched and holed cardigan.

'Well, *he* din't have a lot to say for himself,' May had said.

'No, not much.' His mother smiled broadly. 'Somebody you used to work with, Alb?'

'Never seen him before in my life,' said his dad. 'I thought he was somebody to do with Gwen, or he was a new neighbour or something.'

'Oh, no,' said his mother. 'Gwen asked *me* who he was. Naturally, I thought he was somebody *you* knew. Who the devil was he then?' She looked puzzled, then laughed and laughed as if she would never stop. His dad and May joined in.

'Well, I must say he did all right for himself,' said his dad. 'Must have drunk three parts of a bottle of port, at least, not to mention the beer he drunk when he first come.'

'Perhaps he goes in *all* the houses what's got welcome home signs up outside. Lot cheaper than going down the boozer,' said May.

They all fell about laughing again.

So he wasn't his grandfather. Morley was relieved: he'd banked on a much smarter, cleaner grandad, one with a . . . military bearing, as befitted a fascist.

Several drinks later, just after Micky's departure, Morley had felt a bit queasy. His mother had given him an affectionate squeeze and suggested he have a rest.

Now there *were* voices from downstairs. Quiet voices. His dad's and his mother's. He felt slightly embarrassed. The voices grew slightly in volume and there was a peal of laughter. May! Or could it be his mother? She'd done a lot of laughing today. Moving very cautiously, he shot the bolt on his door and lifted the lino. He paused, remembering the overheard conversation between his mother and Sister Twomey; aware that eavesdropping could lead to no good. There was another peal of laughter. Much louder. If it was his mother, he wouldn't listen but if it was May, well, he'd see. He put his ear to the hole. It was May. She must have moved to the table: he could hear her with startling clarity. Perhaps just a moment or two.

'. . . hurt at all now then, Alb?' May asked.

'Naw, only a bit of a sore shoulder – but that's mainly cause of my ruddy kitbag. So apart from that, good as new, look!'

There were muted thumps and grunts.

'Okay, okay, I believe you,' said May, laughing at whatever his dad was doing. 'You'll be doing yourself another serious injury if you carry on like that. Anyroad, what was it, then, Alb, what put you in th'ospital? Oops, sorry, you needn't tell us if . . .'

God, his dad's wound. Trust May to ask straight out. He frowned, bit his lip and braced himself. He didn't want to know. He already *knew* and wanted it left that way. And he didn't want his dad to tell May. He had to stop him. Heart thumping loudly, he almost fell downstairs in his haste. He went into the living room rubbing his eyes, hoping he looked a sleepy picture of innocence.

'Hello, love,' said May. 'You've had one or two over the eight, you have, you naughty lad. Growing up too quick, you are. Shall I make you some cocoa? Or how about cordial?'

Morley said, 'Nothing yet, thanks.' He was conscious

of the warning glance May threw towards his dad. He changed his mind: he now wanted to know what had caused his dad's wound. Get it over and done with.

His dad was smiling slightly vacantly and scratching the top of his tousled head. Morley was irresistibly reminded of Stan Laurel. He was warming himself in front of the nearly dead fire. His trousers looked much too large and terribly baggy. He'd changed: hadn't he spilled some drink on his others earlier?

'Well, it wasn't a Jelly – lorry, Jerry – lolly,' he said. 'Ay, May, try saying that when you've had a few.' He looked as if he'd had a lot more than a few. 'No, Jerries had gone ages ago. It was most likely a Dutch lorry – or a Dutch van. That's good: Dutch van.'

'What are you going on about, Alb?' asked May.

'Well, *you* asked me what put me in hospital and I'm telling you. It was a lorry.' He swayed. 'Least, I think it was: I never seen it.'

'Alb,' said May seriously, 'perhaps leave it for now.' She glanced at Morley. 'Esther'll be back –'

'Sorright, I'll stop when she comes.'

May said with a sad smile, 'You won't say anything to your mom, will you, love?'

Morley had had years of not saying things to his mom. He shook his head.

'Never seen it, this lorry,' said Albert, a faraway look in his eyes, 'but knocked me out cold all right. The old man told them at the hospital.'

May had lost her caution; she was all attention. 'Don't sound much like you: getting yourself knocked down, Alb. Still, I bet you'd been on the pop, hadn't you?'

'Naw, not so you'd notice, it was the fresh air mainly that did it. As a matter of fact, I was having a bit of a dance at the time.'

May shot a brief glance at Morley sitting at the table,

his legs crossed twice, his face wearing a fixed grin. 'Ar, *now* we're getting somewhere. Being a bit naughty, was you? Who with, some little whatsit girl, Dutch girl? What was she like?'

'No, worse luck, had to make do with myself.'

'So where was you? And how does a lorry come into it? Was it a party in the street?'

'It was in the street all right. I was doing this tango on this kerb, pretending it was a tightrope, like. Like this.' He hummed a tune that Morley recognized. He did a highly exaggerated version of a tango up and down the length of the room without faltering, until he bumped into the table. 'Whoops,' he said and flopped onto the settee.

Morley would have found it terribly funny if it hadn't been his dad. May laughed loudly. Morley gritted his teeth, forcing himself to believe that this had nothing to do with his dad's war wound, hoping even at this late stage that somewhere there was a sniper around.

'Sounds pretty normal so far – for *you*. But what started you off?'

'Just acting daft, really. It was the last night when I was billeted with the old man. We'd sort of celebrated. It started to rain. I pointed out the window and I said, "Look, look! Water coming out the sky, Papa! Look! Never in England, *niet in Engeland*." I opened the front door and looked outside. I pretended to be scared at first. Then I looked up, you know, as if I was getting a bit braver, like; put my hands out to catch it, stuck my tongue out to have a taste. The old chap was in the doorway looking at me. I reckon he nearly believed me. I said, "Good, *goed*, Papa." And I could hear the wireless playing this tango; so naturally, well – you know me, Fred Astaire Junior – couldn't resist the music. You should have seen him laughing. Then this lorry must've hit me. Most likely, I fell in the road, or he come too close to the kerb . . . I dunno.'

'You went to a lot of trouble to mek him laugh, Alb. You only generally act the goat like that when there's lots of people watching.'

It was true, Morley reflected; his dad, he'd noticed, liked a big audience for his wilder antics. He sighed deeply. His hangover was retreating. He resumed his forced smile.

'Well, it got to be a sort of game really, a challenge to make him crack his face, cause when he wasn't laughing he'd got a face as long as Livery Street and that's putting it mildly.'

'Why?' asked May.

'I reckon it was just when he was looking at me.' He dropped his jaw, crossed his eyes, bent forward and dangled his arms.

May shrieked. Morley tried hard to chuckle.

'Naw . . . how can I put it? Grief, I s'pose.' He paused, looking very un-Stan-Laurel-like. 'I never fathomed out all the details. But I know he'd lost his wife and one of his sons – because of the war. Another son was still missing.'

For a shocked moment Morley thought that May was laughing. But she was softly weeping. 'You – mad – barmy – beggar – Albert. You're – so – *different*,' she managed between quiet sobs.

# 37

Of course his dad wouldn't talk about his more dangerous wartime exploits in front of women and children, reasoned Morley for the umpteenth time. He'd deliberately pick out light-hearted episodes to . . . reassure
people, make them laugh; he was that sort of man. Now,
down at the pub with his mates it would be a different
matter. Still, it did seem a waste that his dad's only war
wound had been caused in such a daft way when it could
have been a sniper's bullet. And the sore shoulder – from
his kitbag!

He told himself to forget about it: the war was over; his
dad was no longer a soldier. And he shouldn't forget that
he was very nearly a professional footballer. There was, he'd
just learned, a cutting from the *Sports Argus* that proved
it. His dad had put it away somewhere but had promised
to look it out. He should be satisfied. It was Friday night.
He smiled. He looked out of the tram window; two more
stops and he would be in town. He wondered a little anxiously how he would get on at the drysalter's.

Mr Sitwell had explained that morning that poster paint
was too expensive to use for such large-scale work as a
Nativity stable and backcloth – even supposing the shop
would let you have that much. Powdered pigment mixed
with size would be just as effective and only a fraction of
the cost. That was the paint the third-year boys were using

for the Herod's Palace backdrop. After school he made Morley a list of colours. 'And I mushn't forget the size,' he said, writing it down, 'to bind the coloursh, otherwishe they'll jusht fall off. Go to George Trent the Dryshalter's in Essex Shtreet; they'll probably have most of these in shtock. They sell the colours looshe; get half a pound of each colour. And a pound of white. It might be more than you'll need, but it will alwaysh come in usheful.' He'd drawn a map to help Morley find Essex Street.

He had to wait in George Trent's. One assistant was busy with an obviously big order. The other assistant, a plump, middle-aged man with black hair parted in the middle and a pencil behind his ear, was busy listening to his elderly customer.

'Oh ar, he come back, all right. Arter about twelve month, just afore the war, it was,' the elderly, white-overalled customer was saying. 'Couldn't abide it no more.'

'Wasn't you always going on about how he was always dead keen on going?'

'Oh ar, he was keen enough in the *fust* place all right afore he went, like, burrit was the filth he come across when he got there, is why he come back.'

'Filth?'

'Ar, filth.'

'Get out.'

'Strue as I'm standing here.'

'Whereabouts do you mean?'

'Everywhere: houses, gardings, horse roads, shops, picture houses, you just name it. Everythink was acovered in filth.'

'But not out in the country?'

'*Worse* out in the country. Oh ar, it's a well-known fact, it's been *proved*, it's one of the filthiest countries in the world.'

'Mind you, *you're* going on about before the war.'

'Oh ar, before the war, all right. Might be different now.'

Morley was intrigued by this mysterious country and for a moment almost forgot where he was.

The white-overalled customer filled an old respirator bag with brushes and packets and slung it over his shoulder.

'Tell whatsit I was asking about him,' the assistant called after him.

He wasn't quite ready for Morley. He pulled his pencil from behind his ear, licked it and made entries in a book. Morley opened his mac so that his blazer badge with its palette and brushes would identify him as an art student who was perfectly at home in a drysalter's.

The assistant looked up and grinned. 'What can we do you for, then, nipper?'

To make it clear that he was Dutch and not German, Morley clapped his hand to his temple and said, 'Ah, sorry, I haf just forgotten de English name. In Dutch it is – Ah, now I remember in English: burnt sienna! Give me one half pound, if you please.' Not apparently having forgotten the English for the rest of his purchases, Morley reeled them off: 'Brilliant red, brilliant blue, brilliant yellow, yellow ochre and vhite, one pound.'

'No brill yellow, have to make do with lemon: but it's near enough,' said the assistant, bent over some tubs.

Behind the counter were rows of labelled drawers and shelves thinly stocked with packets, tins and jars. There were showcards advertising stuff you probably couldn't get. Morley asked for size.

The assistant soon had seven brown paper packets on the counter, the contents pencilled on the front. 'You're lucky: red and yellow only come in this morning; been waiting weeks. So you're Dutch then?'

Morley smiled and nodded, perfectly at his ease.

'What's it like?' The assistant leaned back, folded his arms and looked really interested.

'Please?'

'What's it like, like, being Dutch, then?'

'It is . . . very gratifying,' said Morley, amused at his answer. 'Better now dat de var is over.'

'Ay, Mr Brazier,' called Morley's assistant to his colleague, 'guess what, he's Dutch, this nipper.'

'Very clean, the Dutch,' said Mr Brazier, continuing to pile up purchases for his customer.

Morley glanced down at his none too clean boots and flicked a grey speck of something from the lapel of his blazer.

'In Holland,' said Mr Brazier, 'the streets is that clean, you can eat your dinner orf the footpath.'

'He don't look all that Dutch to me,' said Mr Brazier's customer.

'Course he don't. They're nearly the same as us. Like our cousins, so to speak. Mind you, they're probably cleverer. They all talk English, for a start off. I bet this lad talks English better than what you do. We used to have a Dutch traveller in before the war. Spoke beautiful. Looked more English than what you or me do. Very clean in his personal habits. Could talk about everything under the sun. Used to give out these Dutch cigars. Very nice.'

'And cheese,' said Mr Brazier's customer, 'they used to do some nice cheeses. And beer, they say, that lager beer –'

'Tulips,' said Morley's assistant, 'they do nice tulips, all right. Our dad used to swear by Dutch tulips. And wireless sets. Our Edna's Tom bought this Dutch wireless set years before the war. Philips. Never ever had no trouble with it, still going strong.'

Morley's confidence grew. Why couldn't he feel like this all the time? He had an urge to talk. 'Vhat, if you please, vas de country of filth to which your friend emigrated to and returned from before de var?'

The assistant had started to help Morley pack his satchel with the bags of paint. 'Oh, that was just old Ben going on about somebody or other. He's told it us all before. I just tek no notice, humour him. I don't really know where his mate went to, or care, to be truthful.' He looked up and winked. 'But I bet you it wasn't Holland, ay?' He seemed so pleased with his answer that he said it again and laughed loudly. He leaned forward. 'Did *you* ever eat *your* dinner off the footpath?' He winked again.

'No,' Morley said, entering into the spirit of the thing, 'I had no need of it, but I am sure it is possible.'

'Diamonds!' said the other customer, triumphantly. 'They do very nice diamonds. Best in the world: Dutch diamonds.'

'They was great explorers and all,' said Mr Brazier. 'The Dutch discovered America a long time before we did. And Australia.'

Morley asked for a receipt. He made his exit, smiling and nodding to each. All responded.

'What about Dutch canals, then? You can drink the water out Dutch canals, I'm telling you,' Morley heard the customer say before the door closed behind him.

He was jubilant. Everything had been so . . . effortless. And fun. Far from feeling awkward and out of his depth in a strange new situation, he'd been the centre of attention. And the respect they had for his country. He glowed with national pride for a moment – before remembering he wasn't Dutch.

# 38

Although Morley had already confessed to using somewhat questionable means in producing his entry for the Wrighton Landscape Competition and been absolved, he had since then won a prize with it. He wasn't sure whether this constituted a further sin. He decided to play safe and confess.

He left it till last. 'And I won a prize by, er, slightly unfair means, Father. Once.'

'Did you have an accomplice?'

'N-No, Father, I –'

'So how did you arrange matters so that it was your ticket that was drawn?'

'Oh, no, it wasn't that kind of comp-petition, Father: it was a painting competition. I c-copied this –'

'Was it not also you who copied the algebra the last time?'

'No, Father, I hadn't but you *thought* I had –'

'But surely, child, you must have told me you had.'

'It was a . . . misunders-standing, Father.'

Canon Reilly sighed heavily. 'You're not making yourself clear, my son.'

Morley thought it best to leave the algebra where it was. 'It was this art competition. I did a picture of this manor house. But I copied it from this photo I took of it. I didn't draw . . . d-directly from the house itself.'

'Frankly, I fail to see the distinction. But you won a prize. Was it a monetary prize?'

'As good as, Father: savings s-stamps.'

'Well, if you feel in any way uneasy in your conscience, then you might consider making a generous donation to the Holy Souls.'

Morley was relieved: it could have been worse. Perhaps ninepence would do it. The pantograph! He hadn't mentioned it. But, then, would the canon understand? And hadn't he covered that with his admission of 'slightly unfair means'? A shilling.

Formalities over, Morley told the canon he'd bought the paint and that he had already started the repainting of the crib that morning. Hesitantly, he added, 'Shall I post the receipt through the presb-bytery door, Father?'

'What, what? Oh, yes,' the canon answered in a voice which seemed to suggest he would immediately forget about it.

The church hall had once been the church before a much bigger replacement, complete with tower, was built in the 1930s to serve the parish's rapidly growing Catholic population. The crib was set up in the former sacristy. Morley worked happily, repainting the battered areas of a plywood low 'stone' wall that comprised the front of the stable. He was so confident that his rendering of stonework was superior to the original that he decided to redo the lot.

He had deliberately left open the door to the hall proper so that his working would not go unnoticed by occasional parishioners going about their various parish businesses. It paid off: every so often someone or a couple would pause, praise his work, remark on his youth and admit that they themselves couldn't draw straight lines to save their lives.

More footsteps were approaching. Morley affected the frown of the dedicated artist oblivious to all but his art.

'Caught you at it, then,' said a deep, authoritative voice, its owner out of sight.

Morley blushed guiltily.

'Hello, son,' said his dad, appearing in the doorway. 'Come to see what you was up to. Your mom was going to come as well but Big Gwen's dad had one of his turns and she went to help out. Anyroad, she thought you'd be starving so she's done you a couple of pieces: Marmite and cheese and there's a bit of cake – in there.' He put down Morley's old leatherette gas-mask case that May had bought him years ago.

Morley was overjoyed at his dad's unexpected arrival; particularly here in what had become his domain, where he was the accepted expert. 'Actually, there's no more I can do at the moment,' he said. 'I've done the roof and the walls. That backcloth's by far the biggest part of the job but the canvas has got to be turned over and stretched before I can do any painting on it. Mr Fisher, he's a sort of handyman, is going to do it for me. All I've got to do now is tidy up a bit.'

His dad examined Morley's work, murmuring and nodding approval.

Another visitor swept through the door. It was the canon. He frowned at Morley's dad. 'I don't believe you are a parishioner,' he said pompously.

'Well, no, I'm not, that's true,' answered his dad.

'Then who, may I ask, are you? And what are you doing wandering into private premises like this? The church is available to all, but this is quite obviously not the church.'

Morley, collecting containers and brushes to take to the sink, clenched his eyes tight shut and held his breath. He became as one with his father, suffering his shame, at a loss to know what to say. A day that looked like being near perfect, completely wrecked. Bloody shitting priest. He stole a sidelong glance in his dad's direction.

His father was calmly standing his ground, hands in pockets, looking the canon straight in the eye. He looked smart in his demob sports jacket and flannels – flannels shortened by Big Gwen only last night. '*I* am the manager of the shop who supplied the paint for painting this crib,' he said in a voice close to the one he'd used earlier, '*that's* who I am. And I'm here delivering material. And who, *may I ask*, are you? Old Mother Riley?' he said, eyeing the canon's cassock and biretta.

'There's no call to be offensive.'

'I never am, unless somebody's offensive to me first.'

The canon adopted a slightly more conciliatory tone. 'All I'm trying to convey is you should have delivered whatever it was to the presbytery; that's where all deliveries should be made. There's a sign. I have to be on my guard with strangers; we have problems with ne'er-do-wells and beggars.'

'I'm not your ruddy postman or your delivery boy. And do I look like a beggar, missus? I get an order for paint to be delivered to the church hall and to the church hall I deliver it. Good heavens, it's my day off and I spend it getting paint from our other branch to do *you* a favour, missus, and this is all the thanks I get.'

'But the boy told me earlier that he'd got all the necessary paint.' The canon looked at Morley accusingly.

'Did have, except not enough white. You need lots of white, missus.'

'And will you kindly stop calling me . . . that. Let me tell you that I am the parish priest here, a canon, moreover, and I'm accustomed to a little more respect. Now that your business is finished, I must ask you to, er' – he cleared his throat – 'kindly leave, please.'

'All right, all right, Bertha, keep your frock on,' said

Morley's dad very gently. 'I'll be off in just a minute or two, soon as I've given your artist some instructions about mixing our paint. I've definitely got much better things to do than hang about round here nattering to an ignorant duck egg.'

# 39

They walked down the drive, Morley's dad quite unaffected by the encounter; Morley enormously impressed, appalled and every so often overcome with uncontrollable nervous laughter. They had watched the canon walk across the church hall with as much dignity as he could muster, heard the tear and his curse as he caught his cassock on the corner of the ping-pong table.

'Don't tell your mom, will you, son, she'd have a fit,' said his dad, laughing. He took a ball from his pocket and threw it high into the air. Then, turning halfway round on the spot, caught it in a crooked hand held behind him. 'Wondered for a minute whether he'd recognize me.'

'But you never ever went to church,' said Morley.

'No, not my cup of tea, but he saw me at your christening; then there was some sort of Christmas fair and a social. Still, they was all well before the war. Catch!' He threw the ball high into the air again.

Morley missed it. He looked towards his dad, fearing derision or disappointment. There was neither.

'Where did you get the ball from, Dad?' he asked, suddenly suspicious.

'Out the church hall; I reckoned they owed it me. Catch!'

Morley missed it again; chased after it and threw it back. 'Pinched it?'

'Borrowed it. You can take it back. Move away a bit.

Just relax and keep your eye and mind on the ball, don't trouble about what your hands are doing.'

Morley caught it. Laughter bubbled up at his achievement. He thought of the canon. He felt fearless. The drive was deserted. He moved even further away from his dad. 'Catch, Dad.'

He threw it high to impress. But his aim was poor. There was a crash of glass as the ball hit a lamp suspended on a bracket over the church doorway. With one accord, they sprinted to the end of the drive and turned left where a high hedge hid them from both church and presbytery, and continued running. Morley felt he had become a real boy: he'd never broken a lamp – or a window before. His dad felt like his brother.

'This wasn't called Beechwood Road when you was christened,' said his dad when they were about a couple of hundred yards from the church.

'What was it then?'

'Cock Lane. Still is the other end where the Cock Inn is. But your old priest didn't like the sound of it; you know, St Peter and Paul, *Cock* Lane. He got the council to change it.'

Morley laughed; shocked a little at the mild vulgarity coming from his dad, but pleased that he was being treated as an equal.

'If we get a move on we might get a drink in at the Cock,' said his dad.

The route was a pleasant one, mainly over field paths. Morley sat outside the pub at a weather-beaten wooden table, warm from his brisk walk. While his dad was inside getting the drinks he ate his sandwiches and cake, idly dug bits out of the rotten surface of the table and played a game.

In imagination, he went back six months and recreated his feelings on learning of his father's reported death. He felt lonely, deprived, punished; a boy with a mother already full of dark moods caused by her husband's absence, now broken by his death. His misery increased as he thought of long-ago activities shared with his dad: sledging, making models, building bonfires, country walks – never, never to be repeated. He forced back the tears. He looked up hopelessly every time someone emerged from one of the pub's doors, knowing that it could never be his dad . . .

Then suddenly, unbelievably, there he was! In his neat, new clothes, one-handedly bearing aloft a tray with three glasses. A miracle!

Morley's joy was overwhelming; tears flowed. He hastily staunched them with his school tie.

'What's up, son?' said his dad, setting down the glasses. 'Not worried about busting an old lamp? Was broke already.'

'Oh, no, I got this paint in my eye, earlier on, must have rubbed it in; it's gone now.'

'I got a couple of pints in; you never know, they might run out. Warm enough for you?'

There was frost in the deepest shadows but the sun shone from an almost cloudless sky. At a nearby table sat a hiker, his rucksack beside him, consulting a map. A small boy and girl chased each other round the pub garden and car park.

'Get some of that down you,' said his dad of the lemonade he'd brought out, 'then I'll top it up with a drop of wallop – so long as the gaffer don't see it.'

They laughed again as they went over his dad's confrontation with the canon. A young woman came out with a generous measure of whisky with the compliments of Harry the landlord. Later she appeared with a pint from a Mr Arnold whose arthritis prevented him from coming outside but who was looking forward to having a drink with Morley's dad another time. Morley was proud of his dad's popularity. He drank his shandy and experienced a rare feeling of satisfaction. His world was confined to his dad, the pub and the landscape of small fields, cottages and farms around them; he wanted for nothing more.

'I'm just going in to have a quick word with the chap who bought me that pint,' said his dad.

A man came out of the bar door, buttoning up his black coat, and went over to the boy and girl who were throwing gravel at each other in the car park. Morley watched them with the same rapt attention as he would a film. The boy wore a grey balaclava. The girl had a navy blue siren suit on under her coat. The man looked too old to be their father. Grandad, decided Morley the sleuth. In the lane the boy turned and put his tongue out. Morley calmly put out his own and swivelled his finger against his temple. He felt more like a normal boy than ever.

His dad was back. 'We're going to get a rabbit,' he said. 'Your mom'll be pleased: she used to love rabbit stew. We got to go and pick it up at a pal of old Mr Arnold's up by Gannow Green. I used to do a bit of rabbiting myself, before the war. Remember? Over there near Bell End. You come the once. And Walter and a chap we used to work with. You were about five or six.'

'Yeh, that's right, Walter carried me on his shoulders for a bit; then pretended I'd broken his neck. Didn't we come to this pub afterwards?'

'No, another one, the Bell, a couple of miles away.'

'Were you a good shot, Dad?' He knew where his question was likely to lead.

'Reckoned to be. One time on this shooting gallery at the Onion Fair, I won everybody a prize: your mom, your gran, May and her friend. The chap gave me ten bob if I promised not to come back.'

'Did you ever go back?'

'Didn't want to put him out of business.'

'Did you ever shoot a *man*?' He'd meant to be less abrupt.

'Well, not at the Onion Fair or rabbiting – far as I know. But what you mean is, did I ever shoot a Jerry? It's all right,' he said, as if Morley was about to deny it, 'I was just the same after the last war. That's all any kid ever wanted to know. But not a word to your mom. Well, for a start off, if it's tanks we're on about, I wasn't always the gunner, sometimes I was the driver. Mind, I reckon it comes to the same thing: between us we killed Jerries, all right.' He looked a little drunk. 'Sometimes in tank formations you can't always fathom what you've done, or who's done what, like. Things get all . . . chaotic.'

He polished off the remaining third of his last glass in one go. 'One time, at the end of 1944, by the German border in this place called Enschede, I did shoot a Jerry face to face. The Germans were s'posed to have gone but they said there'd been some firing earlier on, from these buildings. It was getting dark. This chap was in the corner of this garage, his rifle was leaning on these oil drums and pointing straight at me. I shot him – had to. Not a word to your mom, now.'

Morley was enthralled; his dad was a real hero after all. How could he have ever doubted it? He could already hear himself bragging to Dawkins, Micky and the scruffs – without resort to imagination.

'Were you scared?'

'Didn't have time to be. Was after, mind.'

'That black wallet you gave me: was it his?'

'Naw, swapped some fags for that, much later on.'

'You didn't get any souvenirs? Helmet, badges? Just walked away?'

'Had a look. Didn't look much like one of the finest specimens of the master race.' His dad was gazing into the distance towards Frankley Beeches. He still had his customary grin but Morley wondered if its quality hadn't subtly changed. 'One of the glasses in his specs was broke – and one of the side pieces was gone; he'd got them tied round his head with a bootlace. He'd taken his false teeth out: they were on the floor. He'd been sick all down the front of him. To tell the truth, he might have been asleep for all I know.' He turned and looked at Morley, hesitated. 'I nearly did go for his wallet. Sounds daft, but I wanted to find out who he was, write to his wife and sort of explain –' he laughed loudly '– as how I'd shot her old man. Fat lot of good it'd a done. Come on, son, let's get that rabbit.'

They walked to a whitewashed cottage on the road to Gannow Green, along the route Morley had walked with Dawkins.

'There won't be anybody in,' said his dad as they went along a cinder path to the back garden.

In a corrugated-iron shed five rabbits hung from a stretched wire. His dad cast an expert eye over them and took the one in the middle. He put some cash in an Oxo tin that already had some coins in it.

It should have been a pleasant excursion but Morley was haunted by the image of the German soldier. It was something he would find difficult to forget. His dad had certainly given him what he wanted, but he wished he hadn't thrown in the sordid details. His buoyant mood left him. He thought morosely of how he would have to confess to breaking the church light – and not owning up to it at the time.

# 40

It was towards the end of Monday morning's English lesson. Morley had finished the exercises on *Bevis* and was again reliving the stirring events of Saturday.

He recalled how pleased he'd been at the unexpected appearance of his dad and how impressed his dad had been with his work on the crib. Then his horror and delight as his dad gave fearsome Canon Reilly what for. Old Mother Riley! Morley felt almost sorry for him. He thought of the broken church lamp with a touch of guilty pride and only the slightest churning of his stomach – he'd sort out some sort of explanation before his next confession. He experienced again the closeness he'd felt with his dad at the pub, the rare feeling of calm. Later, the elation when he'd learned that his dad was a hero after all.

The dead German was now shorn of all disturbing details. He was probably a Nazi who had committed all sorts of atrocities. He deserved all he got. And he probably hadn't been asleep either.

Morley sighed contentedly. He started checking his work for mistakes; it was important not to let himself down in Miss Swealter's eyes.

A few minutes later he heard her saying, 'Not *really* unkindly, Rita. Bevis was behaving just as everybody else of his class did at the time: he regarded the carter's lad as beneath him socially and treated him as such.'

'Beneath him socially' sounded particularly interesting – although practically everything the adorable Miss Swealter said held Morley's interest. He leaned back in his seat.

'Of course things have changed considerably since then, not least because of two world wars; distinctions are no longer quite so clearly defined. But, even so, we still, each of us, fall more or less into one of about five social classes.'

'Which one are you in, miss?' asked Hodge.

'Well, I don't want to get too personal. But for a number of reasons, I suppose I'm regarded as middle to upper-middle class.'

'What are we, then, miss?' asked Rita Fellowes.

'It's not really for me to say, Rita. It's about your family background, history, education, your family's established place in society. The sum of a number of things.'

'Posh people are always well off, aren't they, miss?' continued Rita.

'If by posh you mean middle class or upper class then I would say usually but not invariably.'

'Miss,' said Hodge, 'say our dad won a load of money on the pools, then bought a big house and a big car and got maids and that, would he be middle class, or upper class?'

'Neither, Hodge,' said Miss Swealter. 'Even if your father became so rich that he no longer needed to work, he would remain whatever he was before.' She said to the class, 'You can't move into a higher social class by simply becoming rich. If you started behaving as if you had, changing your accent, for example, it would be considered an affectation. Literature is full of people trying to put on airs. And you can always tell. Such people become figures of fun to those both above and below them socially.'

'What about famous people, miss? Gracie Fields, for instance: what's she?' asked Rita.

'Talented and charming as I'm sure Miss Fields is, she's still essentially of the class she was born into: working class.'

'But does it really matter nowadays?' asked Monica.

But, thought Morley, she could afford to say that, she *was* middle class.

'Such people become figures of fun.' Miss Swealter's words insisted on repeating themselves to Morley on the home-ward-bound tram that evening. Would Miss Swealter think that *he* was a figure of fun if she knew what he was trying to do? He rubbed his forehead and found deep frown lines. He eased them out with his fingers. He was confused. What did he want? To improve himself in every way. And this had included acquiring a BBC accent. It seemed essential if you wanted to increase your confidence and get yourself more respect. The Stammerer Who Became a Wireless Announcer. The imagined headline had flashed before his eyes more than once. And the refining of his accent, although gradual, was already well under way, including the particularly tricky business of switching to the long a's that Miss Swealter and Monica and the people on the BBC used. Away from home and school he had experimented with a fully developed version.

But after what Miss Swealter had said – and he didn't doubt that she knew what she was talking about – perhaps he ought to leave his accent where it was. He didn't want to be a laughing stock. His present accent – the version he used at school – wasn't too bad; and he spoke reasonably gram-matically. But to be deprived of such a vital part of the person you wanted to become . . . Could you still sound educated and successful without a middle-class accent? He thought uncer-tainly of the headmaster and Wilfred Pickles. He looked up; he'd reached the Bell at Upfield with no memory of the journey since he'd boarded the tram. Life seemed a bit flat and directionless. But not, as it turned out, for very long.

\*

After dinner the following Wednesday, Morley was in Balsley Library searching for a storybook. There was little in the children's section that appealed that he hadn't already read. He took down *The Dutch Twins*. He'd read others in the series; they were okay but far too juvenile. A librarian carrying a pile of books strode towards him, her flat shoes squishing heavily on the shiny parquet. She was big with a slightly hooked and reddened nose. In spite of these slight shortcomings, Morley had used her, stripped to her underwear, in at least a couple of his nightly fantasies.

He regarded her out of the corner of his eye, admiring the practised efficiency with which she shelved the books. She strode away leaving a nice trace of scent. Morley examined the books she'd replaced. And there magically was an E. W. Frazer. But his joy was short-lived. It was *Conspiracy at Saltersea Bay*, which he had read twice already. He looked at the other replacements. Nothing. Resigned, he took down *Conspiracy at Saltersea Bay*. The familiar frontispiece showed Nigel talking to the newly met Roger Thwaite on the quay at Saltersea Bay. Thwaite was good looking with longish hair. He wore a seaman's pea jacket; a striped scarf was tucked into his open-necked shirt. His feet were bare. The caption read:

> '*Your grandfather was a smuggler? I say, how frightfully thrilling!' exclaimed Nigel.*
> '*And all his brothers,' smiled Thwaite.*

Roger Thwaite was seventeen, Morley remembered, a writer of poems that Nigel and Dick could make neither head nor tail of, an unorthodox thinker, amused at Nigel's preoccupation with games, good-naturedly contemptuous of convention in general. And – Morley turned the pages and quickly found what he was looking for – 'had a deep, drawling voice with a strong Devon burr.' A Devon burr: not a middle-class accent. Yet people took notice of Roger

Thwaite; he was liked and respected and had single-handedly caught a couple of German spies. Nigel and Dick called him a bohemian.

Yes, a bohemian. *That's* what he should have been aiming to be. It was something outside class. It should have occurred to him earlier. That was almost what he already *was*. His background fitted: Ron, his handsome, black-marketeer uncle with his posh – affected – accent that Morley could now be amused by; May, his glamorous aunt with her broad Birmingham accent he would delight in; and, best of all, an eccentric, near-Villa-playing, war-hero dad from a fascist family. The value of having fascist connections soared dramatically. Perhaps he should let it out cautiously to a few selected people quite soon – with the condition that it would go no further. Although it probably would. Before long he'd have built a colourful reputation: mysterious, swashbuckling, even slightly dangerous – like Thwaite.

He went to the reference section, took out a dictionary and looked up bohemian. It confirmed what he knew already: 'A person, esp. an artist or writer, who lives an unconventional or irregular life. Or, unconventional in appearance, behaviour, etc.'

Enthusiasm bubbled. Plans started forming. He could start being unconventional straight away. He'd let his hair grow just a bit longer; sometimes wear his mac draped over his shoulders like a cloak. Speak with a drawl. Dare he substitute a silk scarf for a tie sometimes? Next year, when he'd finished with his brace, he would. Then, well established as a bohemian, he would get a girlfriend. Once more his future was clear.

He told Dawkins about his fascist family on their twenty-minute walk to the playing fields that afternoon. Micky was a safe twenty yards away behind them talking to somebody about bikes – a new interest of his.

'I've got this photo of them all in their fascist uniforms – at least, the negative,' he said. 'Dad destroyed the photo, must have overlooked the negative. I'll show you. Naturally, Dad cut off all connections with them. Walked out. I wasn't sure whether to tell you before: there's still a lot of resentment against fascism. But now I know you better.' He introduced a slight drawl. 'But the military authorities knew all about his fascist family. That's why Dad never got promoted, or got any medals, apparently. I've only just found out.' Douglas listened with interest. Morley was really in his stride. He added the recently learned and genuine wartime exploits of his dad.

'It's funny, Dad was far more heroic than I even told you before. He killed masses of Germans in Germany and Holland. Course, sometimes he was actually driving the tank and didn't always fire himself. They did it in turns. But he killed Jerries, you know, face to face.' He told of the shooting in the garage.

'Dad said he might have been SS but he didn't stop to find out because he was on the lookout for any other Jerries that might have been lurking around.' Morley saw the Jerry as big, blond and blue-eyed, his skin smooth except for fine stubble and blood from an earlier head wound trickling down his cheek. Morley decided to say nothing about the invented story of his dad's destruction of the Jerry machine-gun post. But just in case Dawkins ever said anything to his dad, added, 'It's extremely awkward asking soldiers ab-bout the war, Douglas. We *never ever* ask Dad about anything to do with the war. The bits I do know about he just . . . volunteered himself.' His drawl seemed to encourage the use of longer words. 'And naturally not a word to him about his relations for . . . obvious reasons.'

'Naturally,' Douglas said. 'You know, I'm really looking forward to meeting your dad, Morley.'

God, thought Morley, you don't sound properly

middle-class at all, now I really listen to you, Dawkins. Neither one thing or the other: just soft – the scruffs would say pansy. He was even more pleased with the path he'd just chosen for himself.

They had reached the park on the other side of which were the playing fields. They walked along a path flanked on one side by garden fences, on the other by railings bounding a large area given over to vegetable plots. Some distance ahead Mr Griffiths was talking to a group of grey-clad figures on the other side of the railings and offering them cigarettes. Two or three of the men had spades. One turned to display POW in white stencilled letters on the back of his tunic. Jerries! The first Morley had seen outside photos and the newsreels. He felt excited and extraordinarily moved. As they got closer, he took in every detail of their faces, their *German* faces, and their uniforms faded to assorted shades of field grey. God, his dad had actually shot men like these! Mr Griffiths was talking to them – in German.

The lads walking in front variously stared, pointedly looked the other way or made furtive, sniggering comments. One lad put a finger to his upper lip and raised his arm.

Morley made up his mind. He drew a deep breath and, as he passed the Germans, said with a wide smile and without faltering, '*Guten Tag*.' He held his breath.

'*Guten Tag*,' two or three of them responded, greatly to his relief. One, a very young-looking man, said, 'Good day.'

Mr Griffiths turned and raised an eyebrow. Douglas looked mildly astonished.

'They don't have to be Nazis,' Morley felt it necessary to explain when they had gone past. He was jubilant, though curiously near to tears. He hoped his behaviour was appropriate to his new role.

# 41

Dawkins was clearly fascinated with Morley's connection with the Blackshirts. He questioned him at length walking back from the fields. 'Course, yes, I remember you going on about fascists in that lesson with old Griffiths; it made me wonder a bit at the time. Were they interned? Your relations?'

Morley wanted neither to lie nor to feel at a loss for an answer. 'I don't think . . . all of them.'

'Did you ever meet them?'

Morley saw the blurred images of the people who might have been his relations in the hall with the fluttering blue curtains. The old woman who stared, the younger woman who'd given him an éclair, the man who had given him sixpence.

'Some of them, a long time ago – before the war.'

'And they were *all* Blackshirts?'

'I don't think my grandmother was perhaps quite so . . . committed – she's not on the negative I told you about – but pretty well all the rest w-were.'

If Douglas didn't say, I say, how frightfully thrilling, like Nigel the boy 'tec, he was clearly just as impressed. 'Gosh, Morley! But why didn't you print it, the negative? You know how to do it – you said.'

Morley remembered to drawl slightly, 'Yes, I've printed several, but I've completely run out of gaslight paper.'

'Why don't you take it to the chemist – you could even get an enlargement?'

It hadn't occurred to him. 'Yes, I-I thought of that, but, well, a f-fascist photo – the chemist might get in touch with the police.' He shrugged. 'Might cause trouble at home. Still, you can make everything out p-pretty clearly on the negative. I'll bring it in tomorrow.'

Morley also brought a paint-smudged magnifying glass he'd borrowed from the Pinders. 'It's for looking at these seashells and rocks we're drawing at school,' he explained to Big Gwen.

It was break before Morley got a chance to get Dawkins on his own. They stood in front of a window in the corridor outside the boys' drawing room. Morley took out the negative, quickly looked around to check who was about and held it up against the only area of sky visible between the dark, yellowing lime trees outside. He gave it a quick glance through the magnifier before handing both to Douglas.

'Golly,' exclaimed Douglas, 'sharp as a needle; no camera shake there.'

'The one in the middle,' said Morley, 'is Wilfred, one of Dad's brothers, who went to Germany for the Olympics. The other brother's on the right; he looks a bit like Dad. That's Dad's dad, my grandad, sitting on the left. The w-woman's my Aunt Joyce. I'm not quite sure whether the other chap's a relation or a friend.'

Douglas said, 'Is that old Adolf in the picture on the wall?'

'Who else?' said Morley delightedly. 'I couldn't work it out until I got hold of the magnifier, because there's a reflection on it. Now, if you hold the negative at just the right angle so the light falls on it and view it against something dark –' he shoved his cap, black lining side up on the windowsill '– the blacks and whites kind of reverse th-themselves and you can see it like a p-positive.'

'Yes, I know,' said Douglas, putting the negative down. 'Doesn't work so well with all negatives. I think it's got something to do with what d'you call it, when the silver nitrate –'

'Yeh,' said Morley impatiently. 'But look, can you see the lightning flash on Wilfred's cap in the middle?'

Douglas fiddled a bit with the angle and adjusted the distance of the magnifying glass. He said, 'Ye-ehh – clearly. Gee, Morley, he looks a bit like you.'

Morley looked through the magnifying glass. Douglas could be right. He was pleased.

'Well, nobody could accuse you of coming from a typical everyday family, Morley,' said Douglas, turning towards him. 'Skeletons in cupboards; dark secrets. Mm, a man of mystery, my mate, Morley.'

It was the stuff of which Morley craved.

Morley felt he walked a lot taller after Douglas's enthusiastic response. He was on the point of telling Micky Plant on several occasions but held back, unsure of how he would react. It would perhaps depend on the way he told it. He would think about it. He did, however, without quite meaning to, tell Perky Beswick some days later.

Morley was on the top deck of his homeward-bound tram when Beswick joined him at the Motor Works.

'Warrow, Morle. You're late. Kept you in. For playing up.'

'No, er, Perky, just popp-pped into town, you know.'

There was a familiar, not unpleasant smell of the Motor Works about Perky. He lit a third of a Woodbine with an aluminium lighter that looked as if it had been made at the Works. Morley was impressed at his bravado: he hadn't long turned fourteen. He smoked holding the cigarette with a concealing cupped hand in case the conductor saw him.

'How's the drawing going, then?' asked Perky. But before Morley could answer he said, 'Seen your dad. The other day. We was playing footer. Up the road. He tackled us. Can't half dribble. Run circles round us. Can't half move.'

'Nearly played for Villa once,' said Morley, proudly. 'Before the war.'

'Liar,' said Perky mildly.

'He did!' said Morley indignantly.

'You never said nothing. Before.'

'You wun't have believed us. Only I just found out it was in the paper. Was in the *Argus*. *Sports Argus*. P-Printed.'

'Get out.'

'Oh ar. True all right. Come round. Ask our dad. He'll show you.' He found he was talking like Perky. He slowed down and said with a very slight drawl, 'Yes, I never said noth– anything ab-bout it before, because, well, he didn't play for them – in the end.'

'Wow. Villa.' Perky took a last deep drag on his Woodbine, extinguished it between his fingers and put the end into a tobacco tin he took from his pocket. 'That's your uncle. I seen. Got a green Hillman. Looks like whatsit. Ray Milland.' Perky's questions often sounded like statements.

Morley nodded, pleased.

'Seen him going in your house. The other week. With that blonde tart. That's your auntie. Seen her. Before.'

Seldom had one of the scruffs shown so much interest. Morley preened.

'Wouldn't mind having an auntie like that. Myself. Whoer.' Perky's face remained expressionless. 'You seen her. You know. Without no clothes. On.'

Morley didn't like the way the conversation was going. The tram was approaching Woods Park Road. 'Y-Your stop, Ec. I got to go the terminus to get . . . something from Young's.'

'Come with you. See if they got any fags. Villa,' he said again, sounding almost impressed.

'Course, our dad walked out on his own family,' Morley said impulsively, anxious to hold Perky's interest.

Perky said nothing.

''Cause they was Blackshirts,' Morley added.

His words had no effect.

'You know, old Mosley's lot,' coaxed Morley.

Perky barely nodded.

'They was put in prison in the war.'

Perky blinked.

'They wore these black uniforms,' said Morley forcefully. 'Like the Gestapo. And had these badges with sort of sw-swastikas on them.'

Perky said, 'Our uncle's got this Jerry vest. It's got this Jerry eagle. Holding this Jerry swastika. On the front. Neat. He's going to give it us.'

Young's sold cigarettes singly. All they had were Turf. Perky bought two. Morley bought an unnecessary rubber to corroborate his supposed reason for going to the shop.

'It's funny,' said Perky, almost frowning, when they were walking up Eachley Lane. 'Funny.'

'What is?' asked Morley.

'You. With a dad what nearly played for Villa. And that. And an uncle like him. What's got a car. And a neat auntie like her.'

'D-Don't get you.'

'Well. You. You're just ordinary.'

Morley flinched: this was the ultimate insult to a would-be bohemian. 'Ordinary?'

'Okay. Not ordinary. Different.'

'How?' demanded Morley.

'I dunno,' said Perky exasperatingly. 'Just different.

Different to other kids. You don't do nothing. Much. You got that funny iron thing. On your teeth. You in't much good at footer. And cricket. And that.'

Morley tried to laugh contemptuously at this preoccupation with games. He had the mad idea of telling Perky he worked for a secret department of the government and his ordinariness was a cover. Instead he said, 'I'm good at diff-fferent things. I'm doing this special Christmas scenery in this church. Getting paid for it. And, and I can speak D-Dutch and French . . . and Jerry,' he added wildly.

'Say something. In Jerry, then.'

'*Guten Tag, auf Wiedersehen, danke schön. Wie geht es?*'

'You never said farter,' said Perky. 'That what Jerry kids. Call their dads. Farter. Dirty buggers. If a kid called his dad that. In England. He'd get his ear'ole clouted.'

'*Bitte,*' said Morley doggedly, '*Reichssender Hamb-burg, achtung, eins, zwei, drei –*'

'Hang on. I got a good one. Vee have vays. For making you talk. Tommy.' Perky's German accent was terrible.

'That in't real Jerry,' accused Morley.

''Tis,' said Perky. 'Seen it in this Jerry picture. Up the Rex.'

'No it's English, l-like, with a Jerry accent.'

Perky almost shrugged. 'Ay, heard this one, Morle? There was this Jerry kid. Called Fritz Jaggedknackers. And these two Jerry tarts . . .'

# 42

Oh, and I accidentally broke a lamp, Father.

That wouldn't that be the lamp above the church door, would it, now?

Yes, Father.

But that's been broken this last fortnight. Why did you not own up to it at the time?

And what if the canon told him he had to pay for the damage? Claiming that it was a perfectly good lamp – not already broken as his dad had said. Of course, the canon might not even know that it was broken. And did accidentally breaking an already broken lamp have to be confessed? It was a bit complicated. He had given it some thought, but was still undecided on what exactly he was going to say. Although he found he didn't feel terribly worried: his fear of Canon Reilly had diminished considerably since the canon's brush with his dad. Was there time, anyway?

He glanced out at the clock in the church hall. Nearly twenty past twelve! Confessions were practically over. He'd leave it till next week – just this once. He certainly had plenty to get on with. He painted another cypress tree in front of Bethlehem's town wall. He stood back to assess the general effect. Not bad, but he needed to strengthen the effect of strong starlight by lightening the tops of some of the buildings.

This was his third Saturday working on the crib; he'd also done four evenings. When he'd finished the backcloth there was only the king's crown to repair and paint, and some minor touching up on the drapery of two other figures.

If the canon – Old Mother Riley – came in today to see how the painting was going he'd be seeing a lad far more sure of himself than a fortnight ago. A bohemian! He applied dabs of very pale bluish grey to the tops of the towers guarding Bethlehem's gate with a flourish. Last Saturday after her confession his mother had proudly watched him painting the Bethlehem sky, absorbed in his every movement – a novel experience. This afternoon Dawkins was coming round for the first time – perhaps Micky too.

He thought gleefully of the homeward tram journey with Micky Plant a few days ago. Micky had asked with a grin, 'Hey, Morle, what's all this about your fascist relations, then?'

Nothing could have pleased him more than to be *asked* by Micky. Drawling so slightly that Micky would be unlikely to comment, he said, 'I can't really say, Micky, I've been more or less sworn to secrecy. How did you find out?' He'd cautioned Dawkins not to say anything but happily he must have let something slip.

'I just heard somebody saying something about it at break. But I didn't know what he was going on about.'

'Who was it, and what did he say exactly?'

'Egliss and that lot were going on about Lord Haw-Haw and the trial and that, and somebody said, better ask that kid Charles, they say he's got fascists in the family. Come on, Morle, what's it all about?'

Raymond Egliss! Wow! Part of him wanted to blurt out everything, but the satisfaction of holding back was stronger. Being mysterious was an important part of what he had become. He frowned as if he were in an agony of indecision. 'Look, Micky, it's a question of security.'

'Pooph!' said Micky, sneering. 'Come off it, Morle!'

Morley shrugged amiably as Roger Thwaite his bohemian model might have done. 'I'll tell you as much as I dare, Micky, but not a word to anybody, else Dad'll slaughter me.'

Micky straightened his face a bit at the mention of Morley's dad.

'Dad's not quite what he seems: he's from quite a powerful . . . influential family, but some of them, well, had dangerous political ideas.' He couldn't resist giving his dad a bit of a social leg-up. 'They were very well off, but because he . . . opp-pposed their ideas, he broke away from them and lost what was rightfully his. That's why we're reduced to a municipal house. And he never got promoted in the army or got decor-rated either. And yet he was a hero.'

'I don't see how his family could stop him from getting medals and that.'

'National security, Micky. Dad, through no fault of his own, happens to be related to enemies of the state.' These lines, developed through a dozen imaginary conversations over the week, sprang easily to Morley's lips. He elaborated on what Mr Griffiths had said in history. 'Remember Griffiths talking about Oswald Mosley and all his relations and associates being spied on and f-followed and prevented from getting certain jobs and that?'

Micky nodded vaguely.

'Just the same with Dad. In wartime the government has to be extra cautious.'

Micky had to cajole and even flatter to persuade Morley to disclose more. By the end of the tram journey, Morley had told him more or less everything he'd told Dawkins, while giving the impression there was still more. Morley felt he had become part of a dazzling adult world of momentous affairs far removed from the drab, trivial one of Micky Plant.

Micky was obviously impressed, but nearing Morley's house – Micky had gone to the terminus with Morley – he said peevishly, 'Hey, Morle, you must have gone around telling other people, else how did Egliss and them find out? *And* I bet you told old Dawkins. Why didn't you tell us, then, your mate?'

He had it all worked out. 'Yeh, okay, I did tell Dawkins. But only because *he* overheard somebody talking about it like you did. I don't know who it was or how they found out. The last thing I want is to have it spread around.' He added something further he'd been working on. 'I know I have some pretty sinis-ster relations, Micky, I'm not proud of the fact but then you don't choose your own relations, do you?'

They were at Morley's gate. Micky said, 'You don't really expect me to believe all this tripe, do you, Morley?' But his sneer looked feeble.

'To be perfectly honest, Micky, no. I'd prefer it if you *didn't* believe me and just thought I was making it all up – f-for a bit of a laugh – and then forg-got all about it.'

He chuckled and thought proudly of those last, un-rehearsed lines as he highlighted the dome of the temple rising above the houses of Bethlehem. Bethlehem reminded him of heaven. Heaven didn't have much appeal at the moment in spite of what Sister was always saying. He liked life with its ups and downs. And now it was up. He scanned the backdrop. Perhaps just a couple more big rocks in the foreground.

# 43

Morley stood panting at the tram stop after running all the way from church. It was drizzling and he'd just missed a tram. A Redwell excursion tram packed full of optimistic trippers rattled past, its chain up. It was twenty minutes before a Redhill tram arrived.

The top of his road was empty of scruffs and clear of pig bin rubbish. He gave a silent whoop. He hurried up the path to the back gate and heard Dawkins saying, 'Rolls Royce 600 horsepower engine *and* thicker armour – much faster. Far superior to the Jerry Panther, I reckon. Just a pity it wasn't produced sooner.'

Not the war, or at least, his dad's war, Morley hoped, as he went through the gate.

The shed door was open. Dawkins, in mac, school cap and scarf, and his dad, in shirtsleeves, were sorting through an assortment of nails, screws and other bits of iron-mongery laid on a sheet of newspaper and putting them into jam jars and tins.

'Well, I'm getting to know all about the tanks I didn't get a chance to drive,' said his dad. 'And your friend's just told me of a very good way for sorting out all this stuff. It'll save me hours. Mind you, we've nearly finished now.'

Dawkins said modestly, 'No, no, it was just a rough idea, a series of interchangeable slotted metal plates that you would fit into a kind of small riddle. I got here much earlier than I expected: Dad brought me in the Berkeley. Took less than twenty minutes.'

They had egg and chips with bread and butter followed by tea, and chocolate fingers left over from one of his dad's demob gatherings. Morley's mother had set the table with the best cloth and they ate and drank from the best plates and cups. Morley suddenly felt proud of his mother. She'd had her hair newly set and was wearing lipstick and a smart green frock that had once been May's. He was also pretty proud of his dad – now that having an eccentric father was appropriate to his new role. He was proud of showing off his new friend too, although he wished Dawkins' shoulders were a bit squarer and that his face was less pink and immature.

Morley's dad had gone to Nechells to see some old friends. His mother looked out of the window and said, 'Well, it's cleared up nicely for your walk. Are you going anywhere in particular?'

'Oh, only Redwell Village along the bridle path, and maybe have a bit of a climb up the Beacon.' Morley liked saying bridle path and Beacon: it made him seem like a country-dweller. Countryside, of a sort, was near: in a couple of minutes you were in Eachley Lane, which was almost rural, and a little further on rose the Lickey Hills. It was Morley's territory and, in spite of some reservations, he was eager to show it off. 'Ooh, lovely!' people said when you told them you lived by the Lickey Hills. Though Redwell Village was not a proper village, in Morley's view, with its amusement arcades, shacks selling teas, souvenirs and other things for the trippers, and dominated by – instead of a church – huge public lavatories, which Perky said were the biggest in England.

They were ready. Morley grabbed his camera and rushed quietly upstairs to look out of his parents' bedroom window to see if the coast was clear. It wasn't: the scruffs were there in force. The Reggies, Neil Gunn and the Betts twins aimlessly hanging around the pig bin. Just in the mood for yelling insults at Morley and his new friend.

He looked round his room desperate to find something that might interest Douglas and delay them until the scruffs had either gone, or were so absorbed in playing football that they would pay little attention to him and his friend slipping past. But Douglas had already examined practically everything of any interest that Morley owned. He riffled without much hope through his pile of magazines and boys' papers. Almost at the bottom was his stamp album. A blue, thin, limp affair with few stamps but lots of drawings and doodles, which Morley had scarcely looked at since his brief passion for collecting had died a couple of years ago. It would have to do.

His mother looked surprised as he sat down at the table with the album. 'I just remembered, Douglas, been meaning to ask you before. Thought I might start collecting again but, you know, haven't got a clue. I mean, I thought of specializing – like you do. Have a quick dekko through this a minute. I know it's p-pathetic but if you could just give us a bit of advice.'

Dawkins was only too willing. 'French Colonies,' he said after a minute or two. 'You've got a few more of them than anything else. And these, for instance, Cameroun and French Equatorial Africa, have got nice modern designs – just right for an artist.'

Morley gave Douglas half an ear while wondering if, as a bohemian, he should just stride out confidently with Dawkins, smiling at any taunts the scruffs might fling. Fling a few back – in the accent he usually used with them. I always talk to them like that: they wouldn't understand otherwise, he'd explain later to Dawkins. But say Dawkins recognized the Reggies, the supposed loonies, let out of the asylum for the morning to help the delivery man, as he'd explained to Dawkins on their walk to Clent. How was he supposed to explain their presence here now, almost opposite his house and looking as if they belonged there? Best to wait till they had gone.

Dawkins was still talking about French Colonies nearly ten minutes later. 'Wainwright's in Broad Street – not too far from us – they'll have masses and they're helpful. I'll come with you. Then there's Fyffe and Gray's in Corporation Street.'

Morley stood up. 'All that tea! Scuse us a sec.' The lavatory was downstairs. He loudly opened and closed the lavatory door and shot upstairs on tiptoe.

The scruffs were gone. Yippee! He leapt downstairs silently, opened and closed the lavatory door.

Dawkins was happily saying to his mother, 'On the other hand, perhaps he might go in for stamps with a theme. Railways for instance, or animals. And *definitely* a loose-leaf album. What do you think, Mrs Charles?'

'Oh, anything that's for the best,' said his mother a little helplessly.

He looked up at Morley. 'I'll just jot down a few ideas in case you forget. Have you got some paper or a notebook?'

'Yeh, but leave it for now, we ought to get going. I've got my sketchbook with me, you can write in that, in a café or somewhere.'

They went to the hall. As Morley opened the outside door he heard loud metallic bangs from the road. 'Ah, think I'll get my notebook instead: seems a waste using a sketchbook for writing in. Won't be a mo.'

He tore upstairs, got his notebook from his room, crept to the front bedroom and looked out. They were back: Reggie Kelp banging on the top of the pig bin with half a house brick, Reggie Nolan sitting on the arms of the lamp post, Neil Gunn and the Betts twins pushing one another into the Kelps' overgrown hedge. They were showing off like mad. He went as close to the window as he dared. Just within sight round the corner were Maureen from next door and Sheila from down the road. They were talking and laughing together as if the scruffs didn't exist. The situation couldn't be worse. He'd be *really* asking for trouble if he went out now.

Douglas was already outside the house. Morley all but dragged him back inside. 'Just remembered, the café'll probably be closed. Better do your notes here, n-now.' He ushered Dawkins to the table. His mother gave him the sort of sour look he was familiar with from the past.

Douglas was as placid as ever. He made careful notes in a small neat hand in Morley's notebook. 'I've got masses of stamps I haven't sorted yet and lots of duplicates. We can do some swaps. You've got a few British Post Offices Abroad which I could make use of. I'll bring some in.'

The metallic bangs from outside continued. Morley gave himself a serious talking to. Nigel and Dick the boy sleuths and their chum Roger Thwaite the bohemian were listening. You're a funk, scared of a few ignorant kids who are nobodies. Tell Dawkins your mother's found the Reggies . . . a foster home across the road, that she works at the hospital they were in. Remember who you are, where you come from. You've just painted a brilliant backdrop. One day you're going to be famous. Get out there!

'Wow, that's going to be really useful,' said Morley of Dawkins' notes. 'Ah! Just remembered, there's another caff that's almost sure to be open, if we go over Bilb-berry Hill instead of the Beacon. We can carry on there. Lord, I, er didn't realize it was so late.' He pocketed his notebook, and then quickly – before his courage deserted him – led the way outside. But the banging had stopped. Morley held his breath and cocked his ear. All was quiet. At the front gate he saw that the road was empty.

He hurried Dawkins round the bend. It was still possible that the scruffs would be in the Betts twins' front garden. But that too was deserted. They passed the library and the dairy in Eachley Lane, Morley in his relief babbling about stamps with an enthusiasm that he didn't feel. 'Yes, you're right, Douglas, those, erm, Equ-quatorial and . . . that aren't like normal, you know, traditional stamps at all, they're m-more . . . What was Sitwell saying the other day? Forms reduced to their essential something or other.'

They were at the gulley that led to the Lickey Hills. Opposite the gulley was Hiller's shop. Outside, standing near a large tree, were the scruffs.

# 44

For a moment Morley considered hurrying past the scruffs, apparently lost in such close conversation with Dawkins that it would seem that he hadn't noticed them. Then all too clearly he imagined the stream of insults that would be flung at them, following them all the way up the gulley. Oi, stuck-up, in't we good enough for you, then? Look at them pansies from that daft school – or, probably, far worse. They might come after them. He tried to think himself into a confident mood by remembering who he was and what he was going to be, but there wasn't enough time. If only Dawkins didn't look so soft and could look more like big, assured Raymond Egliss. He slid his camera surreptitiously into his mac pocket. He wanted no demands from the scruffs to take another picture of them.

He did his best to look confident. He cleared his throat, preparing to say, Warrow, lads. But it wouldn't quite come.

Nolan said, 'Where you going, then?'

'Only R-Redwell and that,' said Morley, aiming for an accent midway between his scruff and school accents, 'just to –'

'Perky said your dad played for Villa,' said Kelp.

'*Nearly* played for Villa,' corrected Nolan.

'That's what I said,' mumbled Kelp.

'You din't, you lying twat. Mind you, you gorra be pretty good to *nearly* play for Villa. It was in the paper, weren't it, Morle?'

'Oh, yeh,' Morley said, feeling a little happier, 'was in the paper, all right. *Sports Argus*. You can come round to ours and ask our dad if you like.' A huge puddle from the morning's rain lay directly in front of the step to Hiller's shop. Distractedly, Morley watched as a tall spindly man made hesitant approaches to jump across.

Kelp said, 'And he was in the Gestapo and all.'

'Who was?' asked Nolan.

'His dad.'

'Course he weren't, you dumb cluck, he was in our army, the English army, in the tanks. It was Morle's uncles and that what was in the Gestapo. They joined the Jerries, didn't they, Morle?'

He was flattered, pleased that Perky had thought his affairs interesting enough to spread around. But alarmed at the scruffs' distorted grasp of things – and so near home. He tried to dampen things down. 'No, n-no, not really, they only just wore these black shirts and that, to, well . . .'

Kelp picked up a sharp stone and started chipping the enamel off a Lyons' Tea sign screwed to the tree. 'Why?' he asked. 'Why they got black shirts on for?'

'They bight have beed gagsters. Or refs. Refs wear black shirts,' said the adenoidal Betts twins, little fingers dislodging gum from their back teeth. 'Was they refs, then, Borle?'

Refs lacked the glamour of the Blackshirts but were a lot better than nothing. He temporized. 'Yeh, they were a footballing family. Refs and players, you know.'

'Our grandad says that we should have had a Gestapo over here,' said Nolan. 'They knew how to sort things out all right. Somebody bashes you up, pinches your bike, you tell the Gestapo and' – miming the aiming of a rifle – 'bang! Bang!'

Two shabbily clad lads of about eight or nine splashing their way into the shop looked up, startled.

'Was *they* in the paper, an' all?' asked Kelp, still hammering.

'Well, there was this photograph of them, in their black . . . ref shirts.'

Things were turning out much better than he'd dared hope. It was time to go while the going was good.

But Kelp, who had suddenly dropped his stone, was staring challengingly at Dawkins. Why the devil couldn't Dawkins straighten his shoulders and push his cap to one side and stop shivering? thought Morley. 'Do *you* draw bare tarts at your school like him?'

Morley held his breath and gritted his teeth in dismay.

But he'd underestimated his friend. Dawkins roughened his accent a shade. 'Oh, yeh, every Tuesday afternoon. This tart comes in for us to draw; about eighteen.'

'Thought you said you din't start drawing bare tarts till *next* year, when you was fourteen,' said Nolan, looking at Morley suspiciously.

'Yeh, you said it was the law, Borley,' said the Betts twins.

'It is,' said Morley, 'we shouldn't *really* be d-doing it till we're fourteen.' A suitable explanation failed him. 'But we –'

'One of our teachers left,' said Dawkins. 'So we have to go into this other classroom with the second years who are doing . . . bare-tart drawing.'

Neil Gunn had wandered off and was stamping his boots into the puddle to splash the urchins coming out of the shop; drenching himself in the process.

'Don't go t-telling anybody,' said Morley to add a touch of conviction.

'Mmm, dunno about that,' said Nolan leering. 'What's it worth, then? I know, draw one, to show us.'

'What?' Morley asked.

'A bare tart.'

'Now?'

'Yeh.'

'I haven't got any, no, any paper.' Conscious of his sketchbook and notebook in his blazer pocket.

Dawkins had his book out. They gathered round. He drew a narrow-waisted, big-breasted nude woman with her hands behind her head. It was like one of the figures the Yanks painted on the front of their planes.

'Whoer!' said Nolan. 'That's real neat. Can I have it?'

Dawkins tore out the page.

'Do us one,' demanded Kelp.

Dawkins obliged with a similar drawing.

'Cad *you* draw bare tarts as deat as that, Borley?' asked the Betts twins, champing their gum noisily.

'Ab-bout the same,' said Morley cautiously. Dawkins handed him his sketchbook and pencil. It wasn't a proper drawing book: the paper was thin, grey and speckled. Morley began a drawing he'd done dozens of times before. A nude woman based on a pre-war snapshot of May reclining on the beach at Weston – on those previous occasions, though, he'd always superimposed heavily shaded frocks or fur coats on the figure in case prying eyes discovered them.

He thought of his crib painting. Holy pictures in the morning, dirty pictures in the afternoon. He felt a tremor of guilt, then the fear of a passing policeman. But dominant were feelings of relief and recklessness. He'd had no desire to outdo Dawkins but once started and with such a dedicated audience he couldn't resist the temptation to go one better. He shamelessly exaggerated May's curves and the size of her breasts over his faint preliminary outline and moved her legs further apart. He added stockings and a suspender belt.

The scruffs were so loud in their praise and lustful exclamations that a young soldier who had just leapt out of the shop with his ATS girlfriend detached himself from her and came over to see what the fuss was about. Another youth followed. They watched for a few moments, eyes wide. The first one winked; the other said, 'It's a gift.' An elderly man in a splashed mackintosh, sopping wet shoes and trousers and very thick glasses peered over shoulders, muttering to himself.

'Well, I never! Whatever next!' Morley heard the ATS girl say as she and her boyfriend disappeared up the lane. For just a moment he became concerned about witnesses who might tell tales. But, he reminded himself, all the people he'd seen so far were strangers: trippers, most probably, who had caught the wrong tram and were on their way to Redwell. He breathed easily. His chest expanded. He was becoming somebody to be reckoned with, all right. Talented, different and from a very . . . unique family. There were no limits to what he might become. He gave May a cigarette.

Morley did a drawing for each of the Reggies. Dawkins did one for the Betts. Neil Gunn wanted nothing and seemed completely mystified by the proceedings. He said he was going home to dry out.

They hung around with the scruffs for another twenty minutes. Morley's fear of them left him. The drawings seemed to have a civilizing effect. They showed interest in their school uniforms. They asked about the motto on their blazers: '*Plus Est en Vous*'. Morley interpreted it as: 'You're cleverer than what you think you are.' He added that he'd always thought Kelp was a lot cleverer than he seemed. Kelp warmed to him and said he wouldn't mind going to their school; perhaps he would next year. Morley began to feel more like Roger Thwaite. He undid the top button of his shirt and loosened his tie. He tried a very subtle version of his drawl and spoke in an accent that increasingly approached the one he used with Dawkins.

The scruffs didn't comment. He felt that he had been re-evaluated and found okay.

'It's cause they're more whatsit – educated than what you are, you dope,' he heard Reggie Nolan saying to some unheard question, presumably from Reggie Kelp, as he and Dawkins entered the gulley.

His spirits soared. He was grateful for Dawkins' support in dealing with the scruffs. He said, 'You're a useful chap to have around, Douglas. Those kids can be a bit funny sometimes; and are always getting things mixed up.'

'So I gathered,' said Dawkins. 'Mind, there were some pretty queer types at my last school. Those two were the loonies, weren't they?'

Morley decided to let things be. 'Mmm, but they're gradually being allowed more time out now – practically all day Saturday.'

Towards late afternoon, the weather brightened. They climbed the steep slope of Bilberry Hill. Morley became quite warm. He took off his mac and draped it cloak-style around his shoulders. Dawkins was too cold to follow suit. They stopped to gaze around at the impressive darkening landscape.

In spite of Dawkins' doubts, Morley took a photograph of the sprawl of Birmingham twinkling with peacetime lights. He held the camera against a tree and counted a three-second exposure. He looked with charitable condescension at his fellow climbers with their dull lives, their dull clothes, their dull relations, their lack of ambition.

His cheerful mood continued and released his mind and tongue. He found that he could talk about anything on earth, impersonate the headmaster and Mr Sitwell and nip in the bud Dawkins' tendency to hog the conversation. He did, however, in the tearoom at Cofton, feel that he owed it to Dawkins to allow him his lengthy monologue on French Colonies and stamp collections with themes.

266

'You've got hidden depths, Morley, a bit like a chap I read about somewhere,' said Dawkins as he was about to board his tram next to the giant lavatories at Redwell. 'Now where on earth was it?'

But before he could expand or Morley say something complimentary in return, the queue bore Dawkins swiftly forward onto the tram.

Morley walked home along a dark Eachley Lane going through the events of the day. Another golden Saturday. Surely heaven could offer no more. Yet this time, unlike the other Saturday, nothing terribly special had happened. It had just been . . . satisfying. Another day to remember whenever he felt low. But at the moment, he couldn't imagine himself ever again feeling low.

He shrugged as he thought of the possibility of tales of his bare-tart drawing getting back to his mother. He'd laugh and shake his head, and say, Gosh, the things those kids dream up! He wondered, not too seriously, what exactly he'd say about his naked-woman drawings in confession. He'd confessed to doing rude drawings before, of course. But not drawing in public to an audience. The corruption of others; Neil Gunn not yet twelve.

I did a drawing of a naked woman, Father, and there were some boys watching. One was a bit younger than me. I was showing off. That should do it.

Ah, yes, my son, a naked woman. Was she showing her jaxie?

Yes, Father.

And her tits?

Yes, Father.

Her arse?

No, Father, I didn't think it was possible – in the same picture.

Anything is possible, my son. Our Blessed Lord said, Ask anything in My name.

He'd have to confess that as well – he giggled – to Old Mother Riley. Just a little bit more.

There was this artist in Rathkeale, said the canon, who did a worm's eye view, and got jaxie, tits and arse all in the one picture.

Ah, but weren't you always the little artistic one with your little pictures, said Sister, looking at Morley's sketchbook. And this one so real you could imagine yourself having a little feel of her little twinkie.

He was shocked at what he had done but couldn't stop laughing. He tried to silence the voices but they seemed to have a life of their own.

He tried a diversion, something he'd indulged in several times since wearing long trousers. Beneath his mac/cloak he hitched up his trousers to his knees, enduring the cold, damp air on his lower legs for several seconds before releasing them to luxuriate in the sudden rush of warmth. The lane was deserted. He repeated the operation several times between still insistent snatches of jaxie, tits, arse, jaxie . . .

He walked into an area of light from a newly functioning street lamp. He heard youthful voices, it seemed, from an upstairs window. Then a boy's voice said quite distinctly, 'Look, Lucy, that boy's wearing magic trousers.'

Morley blushed. He didn't look up. He stopped playing with his trousers. The canon and Sister were silent.

# 45

Morley's father was blowing out dust from the back of the wireless with a bicycle pump. 'Lord, there's got to be five or six years of dust in here. The last time I did this must have been before the war.'

Morley was sitting at the table doing his maths homework. 'And it's dust that causes the crackling?'

'Could be.' His dad moistened a matchstick with oil and cleaned out the dust that clung in the corners of the cabinet. 'But there's lots of other reasons – bad connections and that. I'll see to them in a minute.'

'It doesn't do it all the time,' said Morley's mother as she came through from the kitchen, 'but it was quite bad this morning – on all the stations. At about eleven. I'd just come back from the shops.' She went back into the kitchen, then reappeared. 'Oh, I meant to say, something peculiar happened outside the butcher's. Mrs Kelp came up to me and asked me if I could I get her some nylons. Me! Nylons! As if! I said what was she asking *me* for. She said she just thought perhaps I could. Then she had the cheek to say she wouldn't tell anybody else if I could get her some *and* she'd pay over the odds.'

'It's Ron,' said his father, 'it's got to be. They've heard about what he gets up to.'

'But I never say anything to anybody about Ron's affairs – even to Big Gwen; it's not something you boast about.

And even if Big Gwen did get wind of something, she knows I wouldn't *dream* of doing anything that wasn't straight.' She was getting quite upset. 'I mean, Ron did used to offer to get me things you couldn't get easily, but there are far more important things in life than just getting what you want.' There was a hint of the old sour expression.

Morley's dad put down his matchstick. 'You worry too much, duck. I bet Mrs Kelp goes around asking everybody, so before long she comes across somebody who's got what she's after. It's what I'd do. I'd take no notice if I was you.'

'I dare say you're right,' said Morley's mother. She sniffed, then smiled. 'I think I'll just pop down to Big Gwen's. Her Beryl's had that scarf of mine for over a fortnight. I know it's a bit worn but it is pre-war. And I could do with my knitting pins back.'

'Nothing changes, then,' said Morley's dad. 'I'll bet the scarf'll be covered in paint, and Perce'll have used the pins to mend his clock or something. I should let them keep them, duck, and I'll get you half a dozen *new* scarves – and a whole barrow load of knitting pins.'

'What are you going on about? Where on earth would you get the coupons from for a start off?'

'Well, I know this chap, can get you anything . . .'

'Piecan!' she said, catching on, and hitting him on the head with the *John Bull* she was taking to Big Gwen's.

'Talking about people who go round asking funny questions,' said Morley's dad as they heard the outside door close, 'that mate of yours, Douglas, a nice, polite lad but he does go on a bit, doesn't he?'

'He didn't ask you about the war, did he, Dad, I mean what you did and that?' Morley asked anxiously. 'You know, a lot of soldiers don't like . . . strangers –'

'Oh, no, not really. He was going on about Blackshirts

to start off with.' He frowned as he opened up the pins of a valve with a table knife.

Morley swallowed hard. 'Oh, Blackshirts,' he said airily, appalled at what Dawkins might have said in spite of his warning. He thought guiltily of his secret knowledge, the photos he'd taken of his dad's old house, and the Black-shirt negative. His dad didn't *deserve* to be deceived. 'Oh, yeh, I suppose he would: he's always on about it. We've been learning about Blackshirts in history at school.'

His father replaced the valve in the back of the wireless. 'That's better: much tighter.' He took out another. 'What was it he was asking about? Oh ar, did they always wear proper black shirts? Or jerkins like Mosley. And did they all have a whole uniform, or just the shirt? And did they have to buy their black shirts or were they issued free? Seemed to think I was an expert. Then he suddenly stopped, seemed a bit embarrassed. Asked me about guns. Then started *telling* me about *tanks*.'

Morley sighed with relief. Innocent questions. And, after all, he had told Dawkins about his dad's skirmishes with the Blackshirts in town *without* swearing him to silence. Never-theless, Dawkins had been sailing pretty close to the wind.

'Mind you, I *do* know a thing or two, as it happens, about the Blackshirts,' continued his father, 'though I don't think as I should really be telling you . . . Still.'

God, was he going to tell him about his family? Would it make him terribly angry?

But his dad continued to look his usual cheerful self. 'It's just that I went to a few meetings up town before the war; saw Mosley. I've been as close to him as I am to you now. Got into one or two scrapes, had a few laughs.' He replaced the second valve, unscrewed the plug and ex-amined the connections. 'But your mate couldn't have known about that. Even your mom don't know. *You* didn't know about it, did you, son?'

'Well, a bit, sort of. Walter said something –'

'I used to tell Walter to keep his mouth shut cause of your mother: she's sensitive about some things. You haven't said anything – to your mom?'

'Oh, no. I gathered . . . how things were. Not a word. Anyway, it wasn't so much Walter, it was his m-mate. Les, I think his name was. He was a bit drunk at the time. It was in Nechells. I went to see Gran.'

'Les Hallows. He's a wild one if ever there was one. Had a drink with him when I was in Nechells the other week. Still as mad as ever.' He shoved the plug into the socket. 'Let's see what it's doing now.' He tried the Home Service then the Light Programme. 'That's all right. Let's see if it stays like that. See, your dad isn't just a pretty face. Still, I'll check the earth outside as well, tomorrow when it's light.' He sat back, lit a cigarette and drew deeply. 'Yes, Les Hallows, Walter and me, this one time – but not a word to your mom, now.'

His father was a better storyteller than either Walter or Les, and Morley was once again borne to the streets of pre-war town, witnessing with the clarity of a film his dad's adventures with the Blackshirts and Reds at one of Oswald Mosley's meetings. He had lost his fear of hearing something ridiculous and laughed uproariously at his dad's account of escaping from the public lavatories outside New Street Station disguised as a lavatory attendant.

'It was easy, really, I just roughed my hair up, took my shirt off and shoved it down the back of my trousers, got hold of this mop in the corner. Then just come out in my vest and went straight past these three Reds waiting outside. Like this.' He put down his cigarette, picked up the broom from the kitchen and demonstrated. Keeping one arm rigid at his side, he closed an eye, contorted his face, let his jaw drop and limped with a fast, bottom-swinging gait up and down the room.

'They never even looked at me. They were just stood there looking down the steps. I carried on into the station, ditched the mop and met up with the others in the Shakespeare.' He put the broom back in the kitchen and said ruefully, 'I know I should have really took the mop back.'

He sat down, sighed heavily and frowned. But almost immediately his usual cheerful expression was back. 'Just your old man doing his bit for freedom. It takes a lot to get me riled, but there was something nasty and frightening about old Mosley and his lot. Yet there were them who thought the sunshine shone out his you-know-what. Intelligent people you'd think could see through him – and grasp what was happening in Germany. Chap called Newton that had an ironmonger's in Nechells Park Road, a teacher at the Catholic school your mom went to and others.' There was the click of the back gate. 'Remember.' He put his finger to his lips.

Morley again felt very close to his dad. He was relieved that he hadn't got onto the subject of his family. He would have felt awkward seeing him looking pained and angry.

Morley's jubilant mother came into the living room bearing a paint-free silk scarf which, although not the one she had lent Beryl, was, she claimed, very much better; her knitting pins, with only one head missing; a squashed packet of Chesterfield; and a nearly full bottle of paint-daubed Ribena.

Big Gwen had told her not to bother her head about Mrs Kelp and the nylons: the woman was crackers. Had she forgotten the time when Mrs Kelp asked if she could borrow her, Big Gwen's, coal-house door for a couple of hours because the rent man was coming round to inspect the house? She'd lost hers: Ernie and Reggie had used it to make a sledge the winter before last and left it smashed up at the bottom of the Beacon. 'You can hardly credit it, can you?' said Morley's mother happily.

# 46

B ut Morley's mother seemed rather less happy three evenings later. Something of her old distracted air had returned. For some time, Morley had half feared that her joy on his dad's safe return would sooner or later wear thinner. It was a shame: everything was set for a pleasant evening.

There was a roaring fire that seemed all the cosier because of a sudden very cold squall outside; the weekend was only one day away; there was a *Champion Annual* to read that he'd borrowed from Micky; the wireless was functioning perfectly; and his dad was looking admiringly through his sketchbook and exercise books.

'This looks as if it's been printed,' said his dad of a recent pen and ink drawing of an Elan Valley dam in Morley's history book. 'Me, I wouldn't even know where to start. Where do you get it from, I wonder? There's nobody . . .' He looked serious for a moment. Perhaps he was checking for artistic talent among the members of his family.

Morley quickly put in, 'It's f-funny, kids at school are always saying the same. There's nobody in Douglas Dawkins' family either. Nor Micky Plant's, so it doesn't necess-ssarily have to follow.'

His mother was in the kitchen doorway wiping her hands on her pinafore. 'Duck, I know you always tell me the truth, don't you?' Her eyebrows were raised in appeal.

Morley had the insane impulse to say, No, not very often, but I will now – if I can. Like his dad, this new version of his mother deserved the truth.

'Have you been saying anything to anybody, about Ron, duck, perhaps without *meaning* to? You know, about how he gets coupons and things?' She was wringing her hands.

He felt virtuous in spite of the discomfort that he always felt on being questioned by his mother. 'No, never, ever. Why what's happened?'

She twisted her face. 'People asking for . . . certain things. *Again.*'

'I told you to take no notice,' said his dad, looking up from the drawing of Morley's hybrid house: their own house with the grafted-on front door of the doctor's house in Eachley Lane. 'She's touched.'

'It wasn't her, it was Mrs Gunn.'

'Neil's mom,' said Morley.

'Never heard of her,' said Morley's dad.

'Well, I hardly really know her myself. They only moved here a few years ago. Always rushing back from the shops, when I'm on my way there. Pretends she hasn't seen you. Wouldn't say boo to a goose. Yet, this afternoon, she came over here and asked me if I've got any spare clothing coupons. I ask you! I said to her, "Do we *look* like the sort of family to have any left over?" The cheek of it! And that gormless, scruffy lad of hers with the seat out of his trousers half the time who hangs around our pig bin. You'd think it was *her* who'd have coupons left over.' Something was boiling over; she rushed into the kitchen. 'Bugger it,' she said.

It was the first time Morley had heard her swear since his dad got back.

She came back into the room. 'Then the Gunn woman changed her tune. She said, "Oh, no, I didn't really mean *your* coupons, I mean, do you know somewhere you can *buy* them from? We'll pay, all right." She said she wouldn't be asking if it was just for her, but it was for her daughter's wedding dress and going-away costume. Can you believe it? I nearly slammed the door in her face. She didn't ask next door – both sides, nor Big Gwen: I asked. So why me? And why now all of a sudden?'

Morley had been in bed for almost twenty minutes. The pillow was warm from its proximity to the airing cupboard but the bottom of the bed was still icy. He had his feet drawn up but was beginning to feel cramped. He daringly shoved them down the bed but quickly pulled them back.

His thoughts kept returning to Ron. He was sure he'd never let anything slip about his black-market activities. He still regarded his film star-like uncle as an asset – in spite of what he personally thought and knew about him. He cut a dash. It was in his own interest to keep quiet about his crooked side. He'd defended him: told Micky Plant, who had once sneeringly asked why Ron wasn't in the forces, that he had a high up job with the Ministry of Supply.

He cautiously inched his feet a little further down the bed. His mother had kept returning to the subject of the clothing coupons all evening in spite of his dad's reassurances. They were probably still talking about it now. The wireless had been off for some time but they hadn't come to bed. Every so often he could just catch the murmur of conversation. He couldn't sleep or even indulge in pleasant thoughts while this was going on. In his agitation, he suddenly straightened his legs, getting a perverse pleasure from the discomfort.

He got out of bed, debating whether to listen to his parents' conversation downstairs through the hole in the floor, but decided that it was too cold. What he feared was the loss of his mother's new cheerfulness. He turned on the light to find something to read. He picked up the *Champion Annual*. But back in bed he couldn't find a comfortable position that didn't let in the cold.

He slept fitfully. He dreamt of Ron in a black shirt marching at the head of a column of similarly dressed men. His right hand was raised in a Nazi salute. The crowds on either side of the street cheered and saluted in return.

'Told you he was in the army,' Morley said to Micky Plant.

'No, he's id the gagsters,' said the Betts twins. 'Like Jabes Cagdey.'

In the park, his father in a black shirt was jointly refereeing a football match of Jerry POWs with black-shirted Canon Reilly. Everybody was wearing black shirts: Percy Pinder, Raymond Egliss, Mr Sitwell, Mr Griffiths . . . Morley was dyeing his school shirts black.

'That's better, duck,' said his mother, 'they won't show up the dirt.'

There was a knock at the door. A crowd of neighbours was outside clamouring for black shirts.

'Where the devil can *I* get black shirts from?' asked his mother helplessly.

'You don't need coupons for black shirts,' said Big Gwen.

He woke up, his mind befuddled with Blackshirts and with a vague idea of why his mother was being pestered by the neighbours.

# 47

It was just after six on Friday night. Morley had just come from church, where he'd completed the restoration of the king's crown. He was about to call on Neil Gunn but found him sitting shivering on the gutter outside his house, struggling to eat a piece of toast spread with condensed milk that was dripping onto his hand.

'Our mom says I gotta eat it over the drain so's I wun't mek a mess in the house and path and everything,' he said. 'Our Iris's boyfriend's coming. He's in the sailors.'

'Gunny,' said Morley very carefully, 'your mom come round ours to get some coupons, you know, cloth-thing coupons, to get clothes with. Why did she come to ours?'

'Our Iris's getting married and everything and wants this white frock. And we got no coupons.'

'Yeh, but why did she come to *ours*?'

'Cause you might get her some for our Iris's frock and everything and –'

'Yeh, yeh, I know that. But why did she think *we* would have any? Why did she come to *our* mom? Not anybody else?'

'We hadn't got no coupons, and our Iris said her boy-friend said, get some on the black whatsit.' He shrugged.

'Yeh, and what did you say, Gunny?'

Neil screwed up his face. 'I said Morle's dad's in the black whatsits, and all his uncles and everything. They get these shirts and everything.' He licked condensed milk off his fingers and wiped his hands up and down his trousers.

Morley explained slowly that Neil had got mixed up about everything. That he did have an uncle who did wear a black shirt but that was because he was a football referee. That his dad didn't come into it. That they definitely couldn't get coupons. That he was to tell his mom, and she to tell Mrs Kelp.

Neil Gunn nodded absently, put his thumb in his mouth, sniffed and kicked some stones into the drain.

Morley dawdled towards home, thinking. He wasn't surprised that Neil Gunn was the culprit. He was disturbed, though, that he, Morley, was the cause of his mother's distress. Still, he'd done what he could to straighten things out. Things would blow over.

His mother was out.

'She's gone off to the whadyoucallit, the Union of Catholic Mothers,' said his dad.

There was a baked potato, tinned peas and a half rasher of streaky bacon for his tea. A programme of popular songs from Radio Luxembourg was playing softly. The white cloth covered half the table; the other half was spread with newspaper, on which stood his dad's old enlarger and the wooden box containing his negatives and other photographic paraphernalia from the closet in the bedroom.

Morley thought of the Blackshirt negative in its old brown envelope under the lino in his own bedroom: it seemed to be yelling its presence. He would look for a better hiding place.

'Never had chance to use it,' said his dad of the enlarger. 'Ron give it me just before I was called up; said it might need doing up. But apart from some little holes in the bellows, there don't seem much wrong with it. I was thinking we could do some enlargements of one or two of the things in this lot.' He indicated the box. 'And some of the ones you've took yourself. But they say you can't get hold of the bromide paper.'

His mother not there to restrain him, Morley was bolting his tea. 'No, you can't,' he said, 'nor chemicals or films – nothing. Russ can get Yankee films from his PX okay but I don't know about anything else. Mind, Ron might –'

'So long as your mother don't find out.' He looked thoughtful. 'She's still mithering about people thinking she can get hold of things.'

'Has anybody else been asking?' asked Morley anxiously, trying to slow down and savour the bacon, which he'd left until last.

'No, not really, it's more she imagines they might do. She said she come up the road with – who was it? – Mrs Nolan, and she said Mrs Nolan *seemed* as if she was going to ask her for something. I bet it *is* Big Gwen who's said something about Ron.' He was examining a condenser. 'Is there any meths anywhere?'

'Yeh, in the shed in a sauce bottle on the window ledge. It's faded, looks like water, but it's m-meths all right.' He licked his finger and picked up minute bits of brittle potato skin from his plate and chewed them slowly.

He was strongly tempted to confess that it was his fault that people thought his mother could get stuff on the black market. But how could he do this without giving the full explanation – Blackshirts and all? The subject of his dad's family was dynamite: he quailed at the prospect of upsetting his dad. Not to mention making his mother feel even worse than she did already. No, it was kinder to leave things as they were. He hadn't really done anything wrong: had just been thoughtless.

He took his plate into the kitchen to wash it. The shed was only a yard away from the kitchen window. His dad had recently fixed up a light over the workbench in there. Morley could hear him banging around: he had probably found something else to interest him. He wondered how he was going to spend the evening. But first, another hiding place for the negative.

He retrieved the envelope from under the lino in the corner of his bedroom. It contained the Blackshirt negative, his two photos of Clarence Street and their negatives and the birthday postcard. He looked around. Nowhere in the structure of the room, Nigel the boy sleuth would warn; your pater's likely to be doing odd jobs around the house before long. Nor slipped into a school book that might get lost. Do it properly. Morley remembered how in *Dick Stands Alone* Nigel's chum had secreted the key to a code in the cover of a book. *Monroe's Universal Reference Book* was on the window ledge. It was suitably battered. He took a razor blade from his pencil box in his satchel and sliced carefully into the lower edge of the back board. He increased the depth of the cut with his penknife. Perfect! He tried putting everything in but their combined thickness was too much. Still, the negative was the main thing. He slid it in. It was as if he were also banishing his dad's family. At the moment, he had little curiosity about them as individuals. It was enough that they existed: shadowy, sinister but still the most valuable part of his unconventional background.

He would enjoy the challenge of finding an equally ingenious hiding place for the other things – later. His wellbeing was returning fast. He was a bohemian, a person of affairs going about his mysterious business. He would buy his mother some flowers or paint her a holy picture: that would cheer her up. The slit gaped a little. Seccotine: a couple of dabs.

Downstairs, his dad was cleaning the enlarger's lens with meths and cotton wool. 'Might be a bit old-fashioned but this lens alone'd cost the earth, nowadays – if you could get hold of one. Old Ron didn't know how generous he was being.'

There was a bottle of Family Ale and a half-full glass next to the baseboard of the enlarger; smoke spiralled from a Chesterfield in the ashtray.

Morley nodded in agreement. 'Just doing a bit of school work upstairs.' He rummaged in the dresser drawer. What remained of the Seccotine had dried up. He found some balsa wood cement. Just as good.

In his room again, he applied three blobs, then closed and held the slit tightly together between his fingers, standing close to the hot-water tank in the airing cupboard: the rest of the room, though not icy, was still cold.

> '. . . *by the way if you hate to go to school,*
> *You may grow up to be a mule,*'

Bing Crosby crooned from the speaker. Morley joined in quietly.

> '*Or would you like to swing on a star?*
> *Carry moonbeams home in a jar?*
> *And be better off than you are . . .*'

The glue was dry. There was a box of matches near his nightlight on the window ledge. He used the glasspaper edge of the box to render all the edges of the book's covers to a similar slightly knocked-about state.

You're a genius, he told himself. A bloody genius. I defy you to find it, he said to Nigel and Dick the boy 'tecs and Roger Thwaite their bohemian chum.

He put the book back on the window ledge and gazed at it for some moments, then took it up to admire his handiwork at close quarters again.

A voice was singing:

> '*A-B-C-D-E-F-G-H-I got a gal in Kalamazoo,*
> *Don't wanna boast,*
> *But I know she's the toast . . .*'

Morley joined in happily, though not so loud that his dad might hear. It was now Perky Beswick's favourite song because his girl worked at the Kalamazoo Works near Upfield. He laughed. Poor dreary old Perky with his dreary old jokes, his dreary old girlfriend, working in his dreary old factory.

But thoughts of Perky were suddenly vaguely troubling. It didn't take long to work out why.

Perky worked at the Motor Works, as did Morley's dad. Sooner or later they'd find themselves sitting next to each other on the tram or walking to or from the tram stop together. Perky would ask about Villa. His dad would be pleased. But then Perky would ask about his Blackshirt relations – might even say *Gestapo* relations – who'd been in prison. Even though Perky hadn't seemed interested when Morley had told him on the tram, he hadn't wasted much time in telling the scruffs.

His dad, who was so angry and ashamed of his family that he had kept them secret from his own son, would be horrified.

How did you find out? Who told you all this?

Your kid. Morle. He told us.

Perhaps he was worrying unduly. Perky might forget. Nothing had got back to his parents about his bare-tart drawing and there'd been *five* witnesses to that.

But they're as guilty as you, said Nigel; *they* were the ones who asked you to *do* the drawings; they have little reason to tell their parents.

Anyway, drawled Roger Thwaite, even if they did, you've got a fertile imagination: you've wangled yourself out of worse scrapes.

But the business between your pater and Perky is serious, continued Nigel. It's a time bomb. You'll have no rest until you've defused it.

Giving himself no time to reconsider, Morley quickly

recovered the negative from the book, inhaled deeply, pulled back his shoulders and went downstairs.

The room was in darkness. Illuminated cigarette smoke wreathed in the beam of light from the enlarger.

'Look at this,' said his dad, pointing to the negative image, 'your mom and May at Weston. Sharp as a needle – even at this size.'

'Wow, yeh!' exclaimed Morley dutifully. He cleared his throat. 'Dad, I, erm, came across this . . . other neg-gative.'

# 48

Heart thumping, Morley handed the negative over carefully by the edges. Now his dad would be forced to explain everything about his fascist family, while he, Morley, would have to admit that he had already worked out most of it for himself.

His dad inserted the negative into the carrier. 'Fetch yourself a glass, son,' he said, indicating the bottle of Family Ale.

The enlarged image was sharply defined. Morley quickly ran his eyes along the uniformed figures, took a big gulp of beer and anxiously watched his dad's face, curiously lit from the white baseboard's reflected light, for an abrupt change of expression.

It came. His dad grinned broadly and gently shook his head. Morley was bewildered: how could he find his despised family funny?

'Good lord, that takes me back, all right. Let's see, this must have been about 1937 or '38. Fred, Les . . . old Tommy from the Co-op, Doris Loxley, Walter . . . and your old man.'

'You!' exclaimed Morley, even more bewildered. 'And Walter!'

'Ar, it's Walter wearing the cap. But you can tell it's me easy enough, can't you? Even from the negative?'

'It looks . . . more like a relation. You look too serious and your hair's different.'

'I was very serious, that day,' said his dad, pulling a comic long face, 'and I'd stuck my hair down with corporation hair oil. Seemed more . . . appropriate, like. See, I know a few long words and all.'

'But *you* were in the Blackshirts? And *Walter*? A-And whatsisname, Les?'

'Well, not quite: more your Navyblueshirts. I think we'd only got a couple of black shirts between the lot of us.'

Morley's head was bursting with questions but he said nothing, drank some beer and waited.

'What time is it?' asked his dad. 'I don't want your mom suddenly coming in on us.'

'She doesn't usually get back till after nine after the Catholic Mothers,' said Morley. He peered through the gloom at the mantelpiece clock. 'It's only just gone eight.'

'Get us another one of these, son,' said his dad, pouring what remained of the Family Ale into Morley's glass.

Morley fetched the beer from the pantry and filled his dad's glass.

'Cheerio,' said his dad, a little absently, his head still bent towards the projected image.

'What were you doing, then, in the picture, Dad?' prompted Morley.

His dad turned towards him. 'Playing a trick to put the wind up the gaffer of the Villa Tavern.'

'The gaffer of the Villa Tavern?' Morley echoed, feeling let down, trying not to show it.

'Ar, Jack. Not a bad bloke really but a bighead with a heavy-handed sense of humour. And a bit of a bully; mostly to Willie this barman.'

'What did he do to him?'

'Found fault with him all the time. Yelled at him in front of everybody. Used to cross his eyes, like Willie. Willie got wounded in the head in the last war and it made him bunk-eyed. He couldn't always get his words out properly neither – shell shock. So Jack had to go and mock the way he talked and all. But Willie was all right. You could buy a round of, let's say, half a dozen drinks, all different, and Willie would remember everything – you never had to say it again.'

Morley was curious in spite of himself. 'Didn't you or the others ever say anyth-thing to the gaffer?'

'Oh ar, but I don't reckon it did much good. He'd just say Willie was idle, cag-handed, drunk too much and needed firm handling. Anyroad, there was a lot of talk about war at that time and what would happen if England become a Nazi state like Germany. So we started to try and scare old Jack by talking out loud in front of him about some landlord in Munich who'd been strung up for shoving beer slops back in the barrel, as well as knocking a waiter about who'd served with honour in the last war. We said that old Hitler had a soft spot for ordinary sol- diers, because he'd been one himself. "There'll be National Socialism here as well soon," we told him, "you'll see. Better mind what you get up to, Jack."'

'And did he,' asked Morley, 'Jack, put the slops back?'

'I dare say he did, and give you short measures on whisky and water down the ale a bit. A lot of gaffers do. Mind you, having a go at your landlord about his booze was nothing out the ordinary, just a bit of a joke. To be fair to him, he kept quite a decent pint.'

Morley had never seen the inside of the Villa Tavern, but pictured dark polished wood, decorated mirrors, leaded lights, a crackling fire, and heard the lively banter between the landlord and his dad and mates. Somehow, it seemed part of a more colourful and vibrant world than the one he inhabited. He picked up the Chesterfields and looked questioningly at his dad. His dad nodded.

'Sometimes we'd point to a picture in the paper and say, for instance: "God, look at him, Jack, free fortnight's holiday on the Isle of Capri, all found. Ordinary sort of chap. Runs a bar in Berlin. What's it say: 'Reward from the Reich to a loyal Party Member for excellent service to customers and staff.' Good idea. Better start practising, Jack, won't be long before it's the same here." He'd never come over to have a look: it'd have only shown him up cause he wasn't too strong on reading.

'"You're talking tripe again, it'll never happen here," he'd say.

'"Jack, it's already started," we'd tell him. "What about all these Blackshirt marches and meetings? And Nazi sympathizers all over the place – even here in Nechells. And all these groups working in secret, paid for by the German Reich. There's informers everywhere and all, Jack, making lists, who'll go and drop certain folk in it when the new regime comes in."

'"Are my eyes green?" he'd go. "It's all show and wind; nobody really takes no notice, no more."

'Then I said, "I wouldn't be too sure about that. Look, Jack, you're an intelligent bloke, you read the papers, listen to the wireless. How many court cases of ill-treatment or underpayment of workers have you come across in the last year or two? Or landlords watering down the wallop? None, I'll bet, cause everybody's playing safe. They all know that putting an end to oppression of the workers and stopping tradesmen exploiting customers are two of the main aims of National Socialism." Oh ar, I knew the right language all right.'

Morley had almost forgotten his disappointment as he became immersed in his dad's tale. 'Did it work?' he asked. 'Did he change; st-stop bullying Willie?'

'Well, to some extent when we was around, but there's no telling what happened when we wasn't. I mean I was only going to Nechells once or twice of a week. And Walter and Les didn't go to the Villa Tavern all the time. And

Fred and old Tommy never drunk there at all. Still, when any of us three was there we carried on putting down the poison. "We're only warning you for your own good, Jack," we'd say.

'Then Walter said, was there anything we could do with a Blackshirt uniform cause he could get hold of one. He had this girlfriend, Doris Loxley, who was in dramatics and they'd got this proper uniform they'd used in a play. I think it was me that got the idea of taking a photo and getting half a dozen of us on it. Anyway, Walter was the one that wore the uniform cause it fitted him best. Smart; an Action Press uniform they called it. A bit like what the old Gestapo used to wear. The rest of us had to put up with any old shirt dark enough to come out like black on the photo; black ties were easy to come by. If Jack ever showed the photo to somebody in the know, he'd have thought the rest of us was just probationers.'

'Probationers?' asked Morley.

'Ar, people that had only just joined. They was allowed to wear just an ordinary black shirt and tie – nothing else. In the uniform line, I mean. Mind you, all Blackshirt uniforms had been banned by then – well, in public. So it made us seem more like a – an underground movement, more scary. Our mate Fred got us the picture of Adolf you can see in the negative; he'd been a genuine sympathizer once upon a time. I took the photo in the function room of the Beehive. Used a tripod and the delayed action.'

Morley tried to blow smoke through his nose, failed and spluttered.

'Watch it: they stunt your growth,' said his dad.

'But you didn't just show Jack the photo, did you?' asked Morley, wondering how he himself or Nigel the boy sleuth would go about it.

'Oh, no, we was a lot cuter than that. We got this old wallet, stuck our photo in it with a fake name on the back and the Blackshirt branch and unit, and a couple of other photos Walter found at the paper mill. Then this list that Doris typed up. It said, "For Further Investigation". All the names on it we made up except for Jack's. What else? Ar, this piece of paper with stuff about a fascist meeting that Doris typed out and all. We got this mate, Arthur, who wasn't on the photo, to hand it in to Jack and say he'd found it in the yard by the gents. We kept out the way: we was down the Beehive. Arthur come and told us all about it.

'It took old Jack a long time to fathom things out, Arthur said. Nobody seen him for close on an hour. And when he come back in the bar he looked as white as a sheet and his hands shook.'

'Did he say anything to Arthur?' asked Morley.

'Oh ar, he said, "That wallet what you found, Arthur: did you look inside it?"

'Arthur knew just what to say cause we'd gone through everything with him. "Ar," says Arthur, "these photos and papers. But I couldn't make nothing out cause I in't got my glasses with me. Whose is it?"

'"Nobody I know," says the gaffer. "I better take it to the police. Notice any strangers around, Arthur?"

'"Only this tall chap in the lounge. Trilby, long coat; seemed educated; was writing stuff down in a notebook," says Arthur. "Didn't stay long." He said Jack looked scared stiff.'

'And, course, none of you ever mentioned a lost wallet?' asked Morley.

'Not a word; the idea was just to keep old Jack guessing.'

'He didn't seem susp-picious that the wallet had been p-planted?'

'Doubt it. Oh ar, I forgot, we put this postal order in. Only a half-dollar one, but it would never have struck an old miser like Jack that anybody would have chucked money away just playing a trick. There was a made-up name on that and all – different to the one on the back of the photo.'

'And he never asked any of you if you knew anybody who'd lost a wallet, either?'

'No, he didn't. For all I know he might have really give it in to the copper station to show he was an honest man if anything ever come out later. But I reckon he didn't really know which way to turn, so he kept quiet. But he changed. He paid Willie more; treated him better; bought us the odd drink every now and again. Never called me Titch no more. Nor made no other cracks about my height.' He grinned widely. 'Used to miss it, to tell you the truth.'

Morley stubbed out his cigarette. 'And did he k-keep it up, Jack?'

'We made sure he did. Every so often me or Walter or somebody would pretend to write things down in a notebook. It was only a Woolworth's one but I glued a bit of three-ply on the front, painted it black and drilled a hole to fit in a Blackshirt badge – one of them we pinched from the Mosleyites up town. Looked a treat.

'Then a bit later on Jack come and asked Walter if he knew anybody who knew how you went about joining the Blackshirts because he'd got this mate who was keen. Walter said he'd make enquiries for him. "Mind you," says Walter, "I've heard you got to wait several months while these officials check up on you, to see if you're the right sort of chap. They've got very particular just lately . . . You better tell your mate."'

# 49

Morley had lost himself completely in his dad's story: it was a stunt after his own heart. It left a warm glow. But all too quickly he was aware that his unusual background had been snatched away. What was he going to say to Dawkins and Micky Plant?

A more important thought struck him: if his dad's family weren't Blackshirts what were they, or what had they done? There couldn't be anything else half as exciting. But please, God, not people to be ashamed of.

It was just after half past eight. He had to confess before his mother got back. The darkness was helpful.

His dad was applying bits of passepartout to the tiny holes in the bellows of the enlarger. 'Dunno how long this'll last but it'll do for the moment. Saw some spare blackout material somewhere; might try gluing some of that on later.'

Morley reached for the Chesterfields without asking. He flicked the base of the soft packet as he'd seen the Yanks do, expecting the smart emergence of an inch of cigarette, which he would nonchalantly extract with his lips. Instead, half a dozen shot out – three or four onto the floor. Feeling foolish, he got down to pick them up.

'I know I'm important but you don't have to go down on your knees,' said his dad.

Morley grinned obediently. 'Dad,' he said, getting up, 'I

thought that that negative was real: I didn't realize it was a trick. I thought it was your brother not you on the negative, that all the other p-people in the photo were your family, that they were all fascists – real f-fascists. And that was why Mom and you never talked about them and why Mom got m-mad at me when I asked her about your family when we were doing our family trees at school and I needed to put in *all* the fam-mily to get good marks and that . . .' He was out of breath. Laugh at that, Dad! he mentally challenged, lighting his cigarette with fingers that trembled a little, waiting for an unknown fearful side of his father to emerge.

His dad sat back on his chair, saying nothing for a few moments. He rubbed his eyes. 'Well, nobody could say you haven't got a good imagination, son. Goes with the art, I imagine. Thought they were fascists? That's a good one. Mind you, come to think of it, there wasn't all that much difference. We should have told you really, now you're older. But, then, I wasn't around. You shouldn't blame your mom too much: she's had a rough time of it and there were other things on her mind. And I'd always said to her never to say anything. Anyroad, to cut a long story short, there was this terrible bust-up at home and our dad kicked me out.'

'But why?'

'I committed a crime. A very *serious* crime.'

'What?'

'I was courting a Catholic. There was nothing worse I could have done, according to our dad. See, he was a maniac. A religious maniac. They say he run wild in his youth, got up to all sorts of things, serious some of them – bit like me – then for some reason he got scared and tried to make up for things. Two of our brothers died in childbirth and a sister when she was one through meningitis. He thought he was being punished for not trying hard enough, so he got worse. Really harsh. Chapel all the time, prayers that went on for ever every night – as well as in the morning. No wireless set. I never went to the pictures till I was seventeen and even that was in secret. Used to have to meet my mates in the old stable at the bottom of the garden – in secret and all. Never had a drink until I was in my twenties – mind you, I've made up for it since, all right. He didn't think much of the idea of me playing professional football either. Treated your mom like dirt when he found out she was a Catholic. And the rest of them weren't any better. He had the bloody cheek to tell me I got to finish with her – or else.

'So I told him a thing or two. Swore at him. Told him that I didn't believe in his stupid god. That really done it.' He polished off the last of his ale in one go and lit another cigarette from the one he had nearly finished. He grinned. 'Listen, name any book in the Bible – first that comes into your head.'

'I dunno, I, well, erm, Matthew,' said Morley, utterly confused.

'"Then shall he say also unto them on the left hand, Depart from me, ye cursed, into everlasting fire, prepared for the devil and his angels." Another.'

'All right, Luke, then.'

'"Father Abraham, have mercy on me, and send Lazarus, that he may dip the tip of his finger in water, and cool my tongue; For I am tormented in this flame."'

Morley named two more books. His father unfalteringly reeled off a hell-fire verse from each. 'Not as rusty as I thought I'd be. I reckon I could carry on all night, except I don't reckon you'd want me to. Eternal damnation for the wicked was what we had to particularly concentrate on. And it was shoved down our throats every day. Anyroad, enough of that. I'll tell you a bit more about how it was another time – but not now.'

Morley was relieved. He felt chilled by his dad's disclosures and he still had to hurry up and finish confessing. He admitted to carelessly letting slip a few of his mistaken ideas to one or two friends; that some of them might have misunderstood, which might lead to all sorts of queer things happening. People like Perky Beswick asking funny questions about the Blackshirts; other people thinking that his mother was connected with the black market. It was *his* fault that she was upset – and after being so happy lately. He felt the onset of tears; his lower lip was playing up. He couldn't bear the idea of crying in front of his dad – although it would certainly show that he was sincerely sorry. He compromised with a sniff.

'Well, we all make mistakes,' said his dad soothingly. 'I just made a big one: I didn't get enough booze in and I've finished off the last bottle and there's nothing else about.'

'Hang on,' said Morley, dashing into the kitchen. He reached under the wash boiler with the washing stick and returned to the living room triumphantly holding up a Virol jar a third full of American whiskey.

'A lad who can pull off a trick like that can't be altogether bad,' said his dad. 'Now to show you're the *perfect* son, see if you can find a drop of pop or something to make it go a bit farther. Oh, and don't worry about your mom: I'll square things up with her.'

# 50

Morley sat in the sweat- and wet clothes-smelling sports pavilion listening to the rain pounding the roof and hoping that it wouldn't stop. About half an hour ago, he had for the first time at Balsley School of Art been chosen to play football for a Team. Admittedly, one of two lowly teams that had to make do with the hockey pitch and were sometimes constrained to complete their numbers with lads chosen from the ranks of the Untouchables, but nonetheless a Team. With pride mixed with anxiety, he had walked with the others to the pitch. As Mr Plume blew the whistle, however, panic had almost paralysed him. Then followed ten minutes of ferocious and wasteful dashing around – his dad's advice entirely forgotten. Exhausted, he was relieved when a sudden downpour almost tropical in its intensity forced everyone to rush back to the pavilion.

'Okay, you can all skedaddle,' said Mr Griffiths, coming into their midst, rotating his shoulders forwards and backwards and yawning. 'Soon as you're ready to make a dash.'

When the rain had dwindled to sporadic drizzle, Morley decided to risk it.

Micky hadn't brought his mac. 'You shove off, Morley,' he said not unkindly, taking a *Champion* out of his blazer. 'I want to finish this off.' He had been much more friendly since meeting Morley's dad.

On his way out of the park, Morley had to skirt the steep uneven piece of ground that the dozen or so Untouchables had to make do with. Until today, he had been one of them. He felt a glow of satisfaction. Though the prospect of again being chosen for a team next week was slightly daunting. Wouldn't he be happier, less anxious, playing with the Untouchables? After all, wasn't he supposed to despise games in his new role? If he still had a role. Mind, to be chosen was a pleasant experience and he'd done nothing to disgrace himself – though there had hardly been time. And if he were chosen again, he would remember to forget himself, keep calm and keep his eyes on the ball, just as his dad had told him.

Dawkins wasn't there to witness his friend's success: he had brought a note from his mother asking that he might be excused from games because of a cold. He was back at school doing odd jobs under the supervision of the caretaker. Weed, thought Morley, amused.

Weed! Still, that was what the scruffs had called him more than once. He even called himself one in gloomier moments. An unsettling thought struck him: did people think he was like Dawkins? He automatically squared his shoulders, drew himself up to his full height and walked a bit more briskly. He did his best to look alert and purposeful. Dawkins was his mate but he definitely didn't want to be *like* him. But similarities insisted on popping up: the lengths both had gone to to pretend to be somebody else, that neither ever joined in the rougher games in the yard or were interested in football when everybody else seemed barmy about it – it went on. He started to make a list of their differences. He'd got to: Dawkins is nuts about cars and engines and stamps and I'm not, when he suddenly wondered why he was bothering; it didn't matter. He laughed aloud. 'So what?' he shouted to a wet, deserted world. He turned his attention to other matters.

He wondered again what he would do with the money from his cashed National Savings stamps. He would have nine shillings left after he'd put a shilling in the Holy Souls' box. He decided he was being a bit mean: far more pleasant than unpleasant things had happened to him recently. Perhaps he might part with another threepence. The familiar pale, unfocused image of God was just perceptibly nodding. Eight and ninepence left. New brushes were tempting. Sable. Red sable. Mr Sitwell had been going on about them. Pricey, but for real Quality there was nothing to touch them. He would have enough cash to buy two or three – depending on size – if you could get them, of course. If you couldn't, there were dozens of other exciting possibilities. Perhaps he'd go to town tomorrow night after school. Again he laughed aloud.

The rain had increased its ferocity. Water sliced through the hand-holes and gaps at the edges of the windows of the number 71 tram. It was draughty as well on top but Morley had gone upstairs to check if the bedridden old man was back. He wiped the misty window as far as he could reach in every direction with his sleeve and gave the rain-sodden view outside his full attention. Number 144 was approaching. He was back! Morley waved vigorously at the watery blur of the bedridden man's face and fancied rather than saw a smile. He headed towards the comparative comfort of downstairs. The conductress was on the platform singing 'Don't Fence Me In'. She said, 'Mek your mind up, Eustace,' and continued singing. Morley coloured only slightly and grinned; she was like this with everybody.

He sat on one of the fixed seats near the rear platform. The rain streaking the windows made him think of the rain in far-off Holland and his ever-clowning dad doing jobs for another old man, going to great lengths to make him laugh. God would have approved of his dad all right.

His non-Catholic, unbelieving dad. The image of the dead German soldier came into his head. He pushed it away and thought of his dad's parents – it was difficult to think of them as his grandparents. Next week he and his dad would be going to see them.

Although Morley's dad had had two letters from his mother during the war he had chosen not to respond. Then the day after his disclosures to Morley he had relented. He got a very lengthy reply by return, full of regrets, begging him, Morley's mother and the little lad to pay them a visit. 'I'll go if you'll go,' his dad said, laughing. Morley's mother said she wasn't yet ready.

They lived quite near, in Selly Park. Their previous house had been one of the bombed row in the street Morley had visited with his camera. Although robbed of their fascist connection, Morley was quietly looking forward to the event. His grandad had been nothing to be ashamed of: a foreman at Alfred Bird and Sons in Digbeth. You didn't *have* to add that it was a custard factory if Mr Griffiths ever asked about grandparents' occupations. You could say confectionery or dessert manufacturer. But did it matter? Custard factory would raise a laugh and he could laugh with the rest.

There was also the prospect of visiting George, the eldest of his dad's brothers, in the near future. Injured and demobilized from the army two years ago, Morley's dad had learned, he ran a smallholding near Redditch with a friend. Wilfred the younger brother had not been heard of since he joined the army in 1940. Morley's dad suspected that he was probably alive but keeping out of the way. Joyce, his dad's sister, had emigrated to Australia just before the war and had a son of fifteen and a daughter of twelve. Cousins! The daughter might be attractive. A pen pal, thought Morley – if differences could be straightened out.

He became aware that his cap was soaking wet. He took it off and thought of the blazer badge sewn on it on his first day at Balsley School of Art. The humiliation, which had made more urgent his strivings to be perfect, famous and admired. At the moment, though, he noticed with interest, he felt quite comfortable with the way he was. The idea that you could never be really happy until you had become somebody very different from what you already were suddenly seemed a bit daft. You'd be going on for ever. And did you really need an outlandish background to make people take you more seriously and make you feel better? Okay, so without his dreams and an unusual background what was left? What was he? How would others describe him?

He gazed at the diagonal pattern of rivulets on the window opposite and the answer popped into his head. Capable. That was it: capable. Of making a friend; of repainting the crib – everybody who'd seen it had been impressed, even the canon, who'd congratulated him in confession on Saturday. He'd even caught the chalk and been chosen for a Team. Not to mention his prize. Even though he had used a photo instead of a sketch, he was sure that he was perfectly capable of producing the same standard of work without the photo. Perhaps he might find that he could now deal successfully with awkward situations without being Dutch – although he could still be Dutch on the odd occasion for the fun of it. He imagined a gathering of everybody he knew, Miss Swealter, Canon Reilly, Russ Hartmann, Big Gwen, Dawkins, the scruffs . . . They were murmuring, *Very* capable lad; capable of *most* things he turns his mind to; not a lot *he* isn't capable of; okay, not brilliant at everything in the world but capable of loads of *unusual* things. Capable. The word had a re-asssuring ring. It repeated itself rhythmically in his head. He mouthed it, ca-pa-ble, ca-pa-ble, I-am-ca-pa-ble. He accompanied each syllable with a gentle tap on each knee in turn.

He sensed someone was looking at him and turned his head. It was the man from the asylum with the caved-in mouth and pyjama bottoms showing below his trousers. He was leaning forward, closely watching Morley's performance. The man winked. Much to his delight and surprise, Morley found himself winking back. Properly! It was the first time he'd ever managed it. He did it again. Then, afraid he was appearing too friendly and the man might start a conversation, he rubbed his eyes, coughed and turned away. He felt all of a piece. At ease: nothing was worrying him. He thought of his shortcomings and shrugged. Mind, he reminded himself, he could still become perfect or famous or anything else that might take his fancy – if he later decided he wanted to. He was capable.

# ABOUT THE AUTHOR

Photo: Emma Richardson

MICHAEL RICHARDSON spent his teaching career as head of art in three Birmingham secondary schools. His first novel, *The Pig Bin*, was awarded the Sagittarius Prize 2001. His short stories, poems and articles have appeared in the *Sunday Times*, *Mayfair*, *Private Eye* and *London Magazine*, and his paintings have been widely exhibited. He enjoys walking in rural areas supplied with old-fashioned pubs not too far from each other, inventing things and, like Morley Charles, masquerading as a foreigner when the occasion demands.

# ACKNOWLEDGEMENTS

Everyone at Tindal Street Press – Alan, Emma, Luke and Penny – for all their invaluable work. Kate Packwood, and Sara Maitland of the Literary Consultancy for their suggestions early on in the book's history. For information on things Dutch and the pre-Vatican II Church: Roma de Roeper. For other Catholic input: Ina Murphy. Arthur Pritty for his often hilarious accounts of his adventures in wartime Holland. Roger Smith for his startlingly clear recollections of Art School days. My daughter Emma who helped me be more efficient. My wife Anny for imposing a strict working regime, and for her perceptive observations while listening to many different versions of the manuscript.

To all these my heartfelt thanks.

# THE PIG BIN

## Michael Richardson

### WINNER OF THE SAGITTARIUS PRIZE 2001

'Your mind's full of rubbish, Morley,
just like that pig bin!'

It is the spring of 1945 in Birmingham. Morley Charles
is just into long trousers. He has a backwards-sounding
name, a stammer that miraculously vanishes when he
pretends to be French and he's just discovered the pleasures
of his own body. But Morley is Catholic and now he needs
the appropriate word so he can confess to Canon Reilly . . .

'Morley Charles, the hero of Michael Richardson's first
novel, is a charming, comic creation. We meet him during
the closing months of World War Two, a stuttering working-
class lad in Birmingham with his Dad still at war, and his
Mum at her wits' end with him . . . Wartime atmosphere is
spot on, and there's at least a smile on every page'
*Time Out*

'This accurately observed first novel looks at the angst of
a young Catholic boy growing up in the Midlands at the
close of the Second World War'          *The Express*

'Intensely readable, authentically reminiscent . . . Morley
Charles has a stammer and a predilection for girlier school
activities like reading and art  . . . he seems to have missed
the class on coolness everyone else attended'     *What's On*

ISBN: 9780953589524

*Are you a keen reader of contemporary fiction?*

*Want to discover some more excellent writing
from the English regions?*

# Become a Friend of Tindal Street Press

Ten of a total of 33 Tindal Street titles in eight years
have achieved national prize listings.

By becoming a Friend of Tindal Street Press for a year,
you can choose FOUR from a selection of titles that includes:

### DISTINCTIVE LITERARY FICTION

| | |
|---|---|
| Clare Morrall | *Astonishing Splashes of Colour* |
| Anthony Cartwright | *The Afterglow* |
| Austin Clarke | *The Polished Hoe* |
| Grace Jolliffe | *Piggy Monk Square* |
| Ed Trewavas | *Shawnie* |
| Jackie Gay | *Scapegrace* |
| | *Wist* |
| E. A. Markham | *Meet Me in Mozambique* |
| | *At Home with Miss Vanesa* |
| Catherine O'Flynn | *What Was Lost* |
| Will Buckingham | *Cargo Fever* |
| Daphne Glazer | *Goodbye, Hessle Road* |
| | *By the Tide of Humber* |

### SHORT STORY ANTHOLOGIES

*Her Majesty*
*Mango Shake*
*Loffing Matters*
*Are You She?*

### NOIR CRIME FICTION

| | |
|---|---|
| Mick Scully | *Little Moscow* |
| Alan Brayne | *Jakarta Shadows* |
| David Fine | *The Executioner's Art* |
| Nicholas Royle (ed) | *Dreams Never End* |
| John Dalton | *The City Trap* |
| | *The Concrete Sea* |

As a Friend of Tindal Street Press, you will be supporting a unique publishing operation focused on literary fiction with a regional and contemporary edge. And you will enjoy special discounts on our varied fiction list.

**For £25 you can enjoy a fine selection of original regional fiction.** Send your cheque to Tindal Street Press, with a list of your preferences and interests, to 217 The Custard Factory, Gibb Street, Digbeth, Birmingham B9 4AA. We will then dispatch your choice of four titles (subject to availability).

By supporting Tindal Street in this way you will also join our **Friends of Tindal Street Press** mailing list, where we will keep you up to date with launch invitations, events, readings, forthcoming publications, prize listings and author information.

See our website **www.tindalstreet.co.uk** for our full range of titles

*'If you want originality these days, look to the independent presses. Tindal Street Press is one of the best (and certainly has the best address – The Custard Factory, Birmingham)* The Times

## PRIZEWINNING FICTION

**Hard Shoulder** (eds Jackie Gay and Julia Bell) *Raymond Williams Community Publishing Prize 2000*; **The Pig Bin** (Michael Richardson) *Sagittarius Prize 2001*; **A Lone Walk** (Gul Y. Davis) *J. B. Priestley Fiction Award 2001*; **Whispers in the Walls** (eds Leone Ross and Yvonne Brissett) *World Book Day Top 10 2003*; **Astonishing Splashes of Colour** (Clare Morrall) *Shortlisted for Man Booker Prize 2003, British Book Awards Newcomer of the Year 2003*; **The Polished Hoe** (Austin Clarke) *Overall winner of Commonwealth Writers Prize 2003*; **The Afterglow** (Anthony Cartwright) *Betty Trask Award 2004; shortlisted for James Tait Black Memorial Prize 2004, John Llewellyn Rhys Prize 2004, Commonwealth Writers Prize (Eurasia) 2005*; **Piggy Monk Square** (Grace Jolliffe) *Shortlisted for Commonwealth Writers Prize (first novel) 2005*; **Meet Me in Mozambique** (E. A. Markham) *Longlisted for the Frank O'Connor International Short Stort Award 2007*; **What Was Lost** (Catherine O'Flynn) *Longlisted for the Orange Broadband Prize, Man Booker Prize and Guardian First Book Award 2007.*